A WEB OF
SECRETS

Jews, the Third Reich, and a Web of Secrets

Book Three

USA TODAY BESTSELLING AUTHOR
ROBERTA KAGAN

DISCLAIMER

ISBN (Paperback): 979-8487217929

BOOK ONE

CHAPTER ONE

HIS GIVEN name was Walter Lerch, but everyone called him Lucky, a nickname he earned by cheating death more times than he could count. For a boy who worked in the coal mines, this was a gift which his mother gave thanks for in the small Lutheran church she attended every Sunday. In a mining town such as this one, it was not uncommon for women to pray daily as their husbands and sons left their homes and walked down the dirt path to enter into the dark belly of the mines.

Walter's father had not been as lucky as his son. He had worked in the mines for years and had been hurt several times. But he came to a terrible end when he was trapped with five other miners by an explosion. The mine bosses came, and they made a slow effort to dig the men out. By the time they were unearthed, they were all dead. Although his mother despised the mines, she and her son had to eat, and in this small village, there was little else for a man to do to earn a living. So Walter was forced to begin his career as a miner at twelve. He was a happy-go-lucky sort of boy, who tried to make the best of things, always putting on a good front for his mother. He told her he wasn't scared and reminded her, with a smile, that his nickname was Lucky. But that night before his first day at the mine, when he was alone in his room, he wept.

The following day he got up and ate the breakfast his mother had prepared for him. He could see her face was red from crying. "I'll be all right, Mutti," he promised her. "I just know it."

She nodded. "I packed you a lunch," she said, handing him one of his father's old lunch pails.

"Thanks, and don't you worry," he said, forcing a smile until she closed the door behind him.

Then he joined the other miners walking toward the beast of a mine that morning.

When he arrived, there was an old man standing in line outside waiting to enter the mine.

"You're a young one. Not the youngest I've seen though," the old man said. "What's your name?"

"Lucky," Walter said.

The old man let out a loud burst of laughter. Then he said, "Well, Lucky. You'd better hope that your name holds out for you. Because I been around a long time, and I'm going to tell you right now that the mine is a cruel mistress. She will take you one way or another. You mark my words, son," the old miner said, then he patted Walter on the back as he walked into the dark cavern, his lunch pail in his hand. Before Walter could get away from him, the old man added, "Either it'll get you by turning your lungs black, so you suffocate and can't take a breath, or it'll snuff the life out of you in an explosion. There's just no way around it. Can't say when it'll happen, but it will. I'm sick. I got lung disease. But I would say I'm one of the lucky ones. You see, I lived a long time. Fellas I know died much younger."

Walter turned to look at the old man, who coughed blood into a dirty, white handkerchief. But he didn't say anything. Instead, he forced himself to walk on into the darkness.

That night when Walter returned home, he hid his fears from his mother. She adored and doted on him. His dinner was always ready when he returned from the mine, and his clothes were always washed.

The years passed, and his mother began to relax. It seemed that Walter was truly lucky. He was never injured in the mine, and so far, there had not been any serious accidents. To his mother's disappointment, he was growing into a man. If it had been her choice, he would have stayed a young boy and hers forever. But he was growing, and his mother knew that the time was coming when he would want a woman. When the other boys his age began to court local girls, his mother had something bad to say about every one of the girls in town. She needn't have bothered because none of them piqued Walter's interest. He'd known them since they were children, and he couldn't see them as anything but friends.

Then when Walter was seventeen, a pretty blonde with sparkling blue eyes moved in with his neighbors. Listening to his mother talk to her friends, he learned that the girl's name was Hedy. She'd come to live with her uncle and aunt when her parents and two siblings were killed in a fire. She was a petite, pretty little bit of girl. And he found himself thinking about her a lot and wondering what she was like. Then he took to watching her from his window when she walked by. He loved the way her hair bounced and her hips swayed. Walter decided he had to get to know her better, and so he must find a way to speak to her.

That Sunday, although he was exhausted, he got up and went to church with his mother, who was elated to have him. Most Sundays he complained that he was too tired and refused to get out of bed in time to go with her. But that particular day, he rose early and worked vigorously to ensure he'd removed any trace of the coal from his face and hands. He diligently scrubbed under his nails to remove as much of the black soot as possible. Then he put on his only suit. It had been his father's and was still too big for him, but when he looked in the mirror, he nodded his head. *I guess I do look pretty good.*

When his mother saw him, she let out a sigh. "Don't you look handsome?" she said.

He smiled, quite sure that he was a handsome young man, and he would find a way to speak to Hedy. His confidence was strong, and he was very sure of himself until he saw Hedy sitting beside her aunt. She was by far one of the prettiest girls he'd ever seen. *Far too good for me*, he thought. As he eyed her from across the room, Walter began to lose his confidence and feel that his attraction was nothing more than a hopeless fantasy. Even so, he couldn't take his eyes off her.

After the church service ended, Walter accompanied his mother home; he watched Hedy walking just a little way in front of them. She held her four-year-old cousin's hand as she followed her aunt and uncle quietly. Her full hips swayed in the flirtatious way that made his heart beat fast and heat shoot through his body. *Hedy looks like she is sad*, he thought as she kept her head down. *I'm sure she must still be heartbroken at the loss of her parents*, he thought, feeling a wave of sympathy come over him, and with it came a strong desire to comfort and protect her.

When Hedy and her family turned the corner to head down a street to their house, Walter watched. *I don't know how I am going to do it, but I have to find a way to talk to her.*

Each week Walter gave his mother his pay envelope and then took out a few coins to spend as he pleased. It wasn't much, but it was enough to purchase a pretty hair comb when he went into town that afternoon. He sighed as he handed the Jewish store owner his coins. *Jews*, he thought, *they have all the money.* The store owner wrapped the hair clip for him, then he stopped and looked into Walter's eyes. "A gift for your girlfriend or your mother?"

Walter nodded. "Yes," he said, but he didn't say whether it was for his mother or his girl.

The shop owner nodded too and didn't ask any more questions. Smiling, he took a pretty white hair ribbon from the shelf. "My gift to you," the shop owner said. "If you give the comb to your girl-friend, give the ribbon to your mother. They are both very important people in your life, no?"

Walter nodded. He suddenly felt ashamed for having had those bad thoughts about the Jewish shop owner. "Thank you," he said.

The shop owner smiled. "Zie gezunt, be well," he said.

CHAPTER TWO

WALTER RAN ALL the way to the house where Hedy was staying with her aunt and uncle, the Brenners. His heart thundered as he knocked on the door. The door opened, and Mrs. Brenner peeked out. "Walter Lerch? What do you want?" she asked.

"I was . . . I was . . . I mean . . . I found..."

"Spit it out. I don't have all day." Mrs. Brenner was a heavyset woman with thick arms and legs.

"I was wondering if I could speak to Hedy," he managed.

"Hedy?" she said, then she added, "Hmmm," as if she hadn't realized until this moment that Hedy was a young woman, and boys would be dropping by to court her. Mrs. Brenner studied Walter as though she were seeing him for the first time even though she'd known him his entire life. "Yes." She nodded as if she'd come to some sort of secret realization. "Yes, of course you may see Hedy. Come in."

Walter walked inside. He looked around. The house appeared very similar to the house he shared with his mother, very clean but sparsely furnished.

Hedy walked into the room. She cocked her head and stared at him skeptically.

"I'm Walter Lerch," he said, feeling stupid. Then he extended his sweaty hand with the hair comb curled inside. "I found this when I was walking home from church this morning. And since you were walking right in front of my mother and I…" He cleared his throat. "Well . . ." He hesitated and sucked in a loud breath. "I thought it might have fallen out of your hair. I thought you might have lost it."

She took the hair comb and looked at it. He saw the admiration in her eyes. It was, after all, a very pretty comb and one that very few of the girls who lived in his little village would be able to afford. It had cost him his entire week's allowance.

After a few moments, she said in a regretful tone, "It's not mine."

Hedy handed Walter the comb.

"It's yours now," he said.

"Oh no. I couldn't do that," she said, "I'm sure whoever lost it is probably searching desperately for it. Why don't you take it to the church and leave it there? I'm sure the girl who lost it will look there for it."

"I lied to you," he said in a burst of bold admission. "I bought it for you. No one lost it. It's yours. You see, I didn't know how to talk to you. So, I thought up this plan."

A smile broke from her face. *She's even prettier when she smiles*, he thought. Then he said, "Will you please accept it?"

Walter saw that Hedy's hand was trembling as she took the comb from him. "Thank you," she said. Her voice was soft like the purring of a kitten.

He turned to leave, but then he stopped in his tracks and whirled back around. "Perhaps you might consider taking a walk with me next Sunday after church?"

She smiled at him, still holding the comb in her trembling hand. "Yes, I would like that."

"You would?"

She nodded. "Yes, I would."

He smiled, wanting to jump in the air and scream, *Yes!! Yes!!!*

Yes!!! But he contained his excitement and said, "I'll see you next week, then?"

"All right," she said.

Walter almost tripped over the old rug by the door as he left. He turned to see if she was watching. She wasn't. She'd already gone to the back of the house. He was relieved. He didn't want her to see him looking foolish or clumsy. Once he got outside, the sun caressed his shoulders. A big smile came over his face, and he felt like he'd just grown wings. His feet were so light as he ran home that he wondered if he was actually flying.

CHAPTER THREE

THE FOLLOWING Sunday was exceptionally hot, and the small church seemed airless as Walter sat perspiring beside his mother in his wool suit. He would have worn something else, but his mother said she thought it made him look handsome, and she insisted that he wear it when he went to church. Sweat beaded on his forehead and trickled down from his armpits. If it had not been for his wanting to see the girl, he would never have come to church on such a hot day.

Some of the men in the congregation had already removed their jackets and were sitting in their shirtsleeves. But he knew his mother would never approve of this, would think it was disrespectful. She would give him that look, and he would know she was disappointed in him. So he sat quietly, his head beginning to throb from the heat, hoping that the sermon would be short.

It seemed that the pastor knew it was too hot for an extensive service, and he didn't keep them long. Everyone was hot and tired as they piled out of the church. Walter's eyes searched the area until he found Hedy. She was standing quietly beside her aunt, holding her little cousin's hand. Walter looked at the little girl, who was clinging to Hedy. *She would make a good mother*, he thought. The road was dusty as Walter and his mother walked home quietly. He hadn't told her yet about his upcoming date with Hedy. But he knew that she wasn't keen on him finding a wife. She'd made small comments in the past when his friends had gotten married. Comments like, "That boy is leaving his poor, old mother to fend for herself," or "You put everything you have into raising a child, and for what? So he can go off and leave you for some girl? How can a son go off and take care of stranger while he leaves his old mother to struggle at the end of her days?"

Walter was the only child of a loveless marriage, and so his mother had doted on him and pampered him since the day he was born. "I've devoted my life to you," she had told him as often as she could.

And although he sometimes found he resented her, he loved her as well. But lately, he found that love for his mother wasn't enough to keep him happy. There was yearning inside him that made him hungry for the touch of a woman. Sometimes that yearning was so powerful it caused him to do things like touch himself at night while imagining Hedy naked. Then when morning came, he was so ashamed of what he'd done that he couldn't look his mother in the eye. But if she knew, she acted as if she didn't notice. And he was glad she never mentioned it.

"Mother," he said as they walked toward their home.

"You should take off that suit coat. It's too hot out here for that," she said, stopping and helping him to remove the coat. Then he reached for it. But she ignored him and carried it. "There that's better, isn't it?"

He nodded.

"Loosen your tie."

He did as she asked, then he said, "Mother . . ."

"Is there something you wanted to say?"

"Yes, actually there is. I wanted to tell you that I am going out for a little while after we get home."

"Where are you going? You have to eat first. I am going to cook a chicken today. With fresh carrots and potatoes. Yes?"

"Yes." He nodded. Then he stammered, "I-I have somewhere to go."

She stopped walking and looked at him sideways, her eyes filled with skepticism. "You should eat first. I am going to work hard to prepare a nice meal."

"I'll eat when I get back," he said, wishing she were different, wishing he could ask her if he could bring Hedy home with him to eat. But he didn't dare.

"So, you won't be long, then?"

"Not too long."

She nodded. "You should come back quickly. The food shouldn't get cold. It would be such a shame to ruin such a good meal. We don't have chicken every day, Walter."

"Yes, I know. And I will come home quickly."

They walked for a minute or so in silence. Then she turned to him. "You're not going to tell me where you're going?"

He knew this was coming. No matter what he said, it would be the wrong thing. But he sucked in a deep breath and decided to tell the truth. "I am going for a walk with Hedy."

"Hedy? Who is Hedy?"

She knows who Hedy is. Why is she is asking me? he thought. But instead of arguing, he just said, "Hedy is the Brenners' niece. She came to live with them a few weeks ago when her family died in a fire."

His mother clucked her tongue. "A bad omen. Her family died in a fire. Maybe there is a curse on her," his mother said. She'd always been very superstitious. "Oh, I know her kind. That kind of a woman carries a darkness inside of her that spreads like a fire so fast, you won't know what hit you. I don't think you should get involved."

Even though Walter knew before he told her that she would react that way, he felt his heart sink. *Of course, she's going to make this difficult for me.* "The death of her family was not her fault, Mother. You can't blame her for that."

"They are all dead, yet she is alive? What does that tell you? It tells you that there is evil inside of her, and the evil kept her alive so

14

she could kill again." His mother shook her head "You're not a fool. You should know this."

"I don't believe it. And I am going to see her this afternoon," he said insistently.

"This is what happens to boys," she said to no one. Then shaking her head, she added, "A woman has a son. She devotes her life to him. And then what happens? He turns from being the loving little boy she gave her life for into a man who is driven by one thing and one thing only. You know what that is? It's that snake that lives in his pants and takes away his ability to think straight." Then she turned to him. "You mark my words, son. You are making a mistake."

Walter didn't want to discuss the snake that lived in his pants, especially not with his mother. She'd never talked about sex with him before. His face was red with embarrassment, and he couldn't look at her.

They didn't speak anymore. As soon as they arrived at home, Walter's mother went into the kitchen. She brought in a bucket of water from the well and began fiercely scrubbing a handful of potatoes. There were so many things he wished he could say, but he didn't. Instead, he just went out to the well, washed the sweat off his face and then left the house.

On his way to see Hedy, Walter picked a bouquet of wildflowers. Holding them in his trembling hand, he knocked on the door. Hedy opened it. She looked radiant. Her face was flushed, and her skin was slightly dewy from the heat. She stepped outside. When he handed her the bouquet, she began laughing.

He looked at her not understanding. "What is it? What's so funny?"

She took the flowers from his hand and dropped them on the ground. He felt his face fall. "They're weeds. They're not flowers; they're weeds," she said, still laughing.

Walter was hurt. He turned and would have walked away had Hedy not slipped her hand through his arm. "Come on," she said. "You are rather adorable."

He wasn't sure what was happening. He thought perhaps she

liked him. Or maybe she was just making fun of him. Either way, he didn't know what to do, so he just walked along beside her.

They didn't speak. Mostly because he didn't know what to say. Then once they were alone, she sat down under a tree and pulled him down beside her. Taking his face in her hands, she kissed him long and slow. He'd never felt anything like that. His body began tingling. Then when she put her hand on his thigh and moved it up to his penis, he felt like he might ejaculate. He was already hard. Still, she said nothing. Then she lifted her dress. When he saw that she was naked underneath, he had to look away or he knew he would ejaculate. She pulled him down, and within seconds he was inside of her. They moved together to the ancient rhythm of life.

Once it was over, he lay down beside her, spent. She sat up on one elbow and touched his face. "Your first time?" she asked.

He nodded, embarrassed. "You could tell?"

She giggled. "Yes."

"I'm sorry."

"It's all right. It was fine."

"Was it your first time?" he asked. "I hope I didn't hurt you."

She shook her head. "You didn't hurt me," she said.

They lay side by side for a while. She unbuttoned his shirt and stroked his chest. He thought that if he went to heaven when he died, he would feel like he felt at this very moment, looking up at the bright blue sky with its powder-puff clouds and lying beside the most beautiful girl in the world.

He turned toward her and kissed her softly. She smiled and his heart lit up. Then she turned him on his back and mounted him. This time she controlled the movement, moving very slow so as to slow him down.

Once it was over, she got off him and lay down beside him. He glanced over at her shyly. He'd heard about sex from the other boys, but before today, he hadn't so much as kissed a girl. She moved her body up on her elbow and smiled at him. "Better the second time?" she asked.

He swallowed hard. "Wonderful," he said, his voice still breathy from the exertion.

"I guess this means you like me?" she asked, cocking her head.

He nodded. "Oh yes, I like you very much."

CHAPTER FOUR

WALTER NEVER FELT like this before. He was giddy with joy as they walked back to Hedy's home. Neither of them spoke for several minutes. Then in a soft voice, she asked, "Have you ever wanted to get married and start a family of your own?"

"Yes, I have. But I live with my mother, and she needs me. I couldn't just abandon her."

"What if your mother could live with you and your wife. Would that make it easier, better for you?"

He stopped and looked at Hedy. "Would you? I mean, would you ever consider marrying me?" he stammered.

"I was wondering how long it would take you to ask." She let out a short giggle.

He didn't realize he'd just proposed. But now that she'd said it, he was glad he did. Clearing his throat, he asked, "My mother? Would it be all right with you if she lived with us?"

"I suggested it, didn't I?"

He nodded. "You did."

"Then, of course it would be fine. All right, then, let's get married in church next week. I don't know anyone here in town, so I don't care if we don't have a wedding."

"I don't need to have a wedding. It's just my mother and me. We don't have anyone else."

He was surprised and delighted that she had taken control of everything. Now, however, he still had the task of talking to his mother, and he knew she was not going to be as pleased as he was.

CHAPTER FIVE

"You go for a walk and come home engaged? You hardly know this girl," his mother growled. "Don't you think that's a little fast?"

"Yes, but I know I like her."

"So, you like her; she likes you. What's the hurry? You walk this Sunday, next Sunday you get married? Something isn't right with that girl, Walter. Can't you see that? Why does she want to get married so fast? She doesn't know you either."

He couldn't think of anything but the way he felt. And he felt gloriously attached to that girl who had enveloped him with her velvet body. "She likes me, Mother, and I like her. In fact, she likes me enough to ask me if you would want to come and live with us. She's a good girl. You should give her a chance."

His mother shook her head. "I don't know about her, Walter."

"You wouldn't be happy no matter who it was that I was marrying. You don't want me to get married," he said.

"I don't like the way you're talking to me either. It's like she's bewitched you. You wait and see: if you marry her, you're going to find out that she's no good."

Walter wanted to holler at his mother, but instead he walked out of the house and into the yard where he sat down under a tree. As the warm sun filtered through the branches caressing him, he was transported back to the afternoon. And suddenly he wasn't thinking. Instead, his senses were consumed with memories of Hedy. Her hair smelled of strong soap as it fell on his face. The soft feel of her skin. The taste of her kiss, and that secret place of warm, wet velvet, where he lost himself entirely.

CHAPTER SIX

SUNDAY COULD NOT COME FAST ENOUGH. All week Walter wanted to visit Hedy, but he couldn't. It was late when he returned from the mine, and his mother always seemed to have something she needed him to do. But finally, Sunday came, and after the church service, Walter and Hedy were married. Even as they were speaking their wedding vows, Walter could see his mother shaking her head. But he ignored her. He didn't care. All he knew was that tonight when he and Hedy were alone, he would find his way back to heaven in her arms.

Until now, Walter had listened to his mother's skepticism and superstitious fears. He told her that they were nonsense, but in the back of his mind he'd always been fearful. However, when she said anything bad about Hedy, he refused to listen. In his eyes, Hedy could do no wrong. She was beautiful; she told him that she cared for him, and for the first time in his life, she made him feel things he'd never thought possible. So, when they went to their room at night and he turned to close the door, he ignored his mother's head-shaking and finger-pointing. But once he fell asleep, in his dreams, his mother's superstitious words still haunted him.

Walter knew his mother hated his wife, but he'd never been

happier. Although she was a quiet girl much of the time, when they were alone, she laughed at his jokes and made him feel loved. They made love every chance they got, and when she told him she was pregnant, he rejoiced.

When Hedy went into labor seven months after she married Walter, his mother stood at the bedroom door shaking her head at Walter. He knew what she was trying to tell him, but he didn't want to hear it. He was in love with his wife, and if she'd had another man before they met, he would rather not know about it.

But as Hedy lay panting in pain with the midwife at her side, Walter stood in the living room wringing his hands. "Do you think she married you because she loved you after a fifteen-minute walk, or do you think it was because she was pregnant with another man's child?" his mother asked.

Walter glared at her, but he couldn't help but wonder if his mother was right. Did Hedy really love him, or had she just married him to give her child a name? His mother knew her son. She knew he was questioning his choice, and she smiled at him—it was a wicked smile. Walter felt the skin on his neck prickle.

Hedy did not labor long; it was only a few hours before the baby began to crown. Walter's mother said, "That's very strange for a first birth. I wonder if this is her first. Perhaps there are others you know nothing about."

Walter tried to ignore her.

But when the baby was born, and he heard the lustful cry, he forgot his mother and ran into the room to see the child he would call his own.

"It's a boy," the midwife said as the baby let out a soft mewl. She was an older woman, experienced with childbirth. Her gray hair was stuck to her forehead with sweat. "You have a son."

Walter looked at the tiny infant. He gazed at his wrinkled red skin, the bald head, the small hands and feet, and his heart swelled. But then Hedy let out a cry of pain, and all attention turned from the baby, back to her.

The midwife looked to see. "It must be the afterbirth," she said.

But then she gazed up at Walter, and with surprise she said, "There's another one. It's coming right now."

Walter's mother heard this from the doorway.

He glanced at his mother. Her face was colorless. She made the sign of the cross. Then she held up two fingers and shook her head. Her eyes were dark with fear. "There's a demon in her womb," she said in a whisper, but it was loud enough for Walter to hear. "I knew it all along."

He felt his body tremble because he'd heard that superstition too. Not only from her but from others. He shook it off; he didn't want to believe it as the child came forth. This one was a boy as well, and although he looked just like his brother, he was stronger somehow. Even as an infant, his cry was loud and lusty, where the first child's cry had been so much weaker.

"You have a second son," the midwife said. There was a slight tone of fear in her voice, and Walter knew that she, like his mother, believed in all the old wives' tales. He refused to believe. Instead, he lifted the boy into his arms.

"He's a strong one," Walter said admiringly. Then he smiled at Hedy, who lay on the bed sweating and spent. "We have two sons."

She nodded.

"What shall we call them?"

She shrugged. "I don't know," she said weakly as if all her life force had gone into the second birth.

"Let's call them Erich and Oskar," he said. "Would that be all right?"

"Yes. Whatever you want."

Then he gently handed the strong baby to his wife. She took him into her arms. "This one will be Oskar," Walter said of the strong one. Then he lifted the other boy and said, "And this one will be Erich."

She nodded. "I'm so tired. I need to rest."

"Is she all right?" Walter asked the midwife, who took the baby from Hedy's trembling arms.

"She'll be fine."

CHAPTER SEVEN

EVEN BEFORE THE twins could speak, they had a language of grunts by which they communicated with each other that only they understood. They were beautiful babies, both of them blond, blue eyed, and chubby cheeked. Although they were twins and looked exactly alike, their personalities were totally different. Oskar was a demanding baby who screamed when he was hungry or wet. While Erich was a quiet child who waited patiently for his needs to be met. Erich was the weaker baby, yet he was also the smarter child. Sometimes Hedy thought he seemed like an old soul. Of the two boys, Oskar was the first to crawl and then walk, but Erich was the first to smile.

As the boys grew, they were inseparable. They didn't need other friends; they had each other. And because Oskar was so much stronger, everyone seemed to mistake Oskar for the older brother. Erich didn't mind. The boys adored each other; no one and nothing came between them. Sometimes Walter thought they seemed to be like one person in two bodies. As they got older, it became even more apparent that Erich was smaller and weaker, but once they started school, Erich began to shine. Although Oskar excelled in sports, Erich was a better student than Oskar. And while his brother was out running track, Erich was in the library reading. But even though they were not babies anymore, their secret language continued.

Their grandmother favored Erich, because he was so easy and congenial, and she always told Erich, "You are so much like your father, who is my son. Now that other one, your brother . . ." she would say, meaning Oskar, "he is not a Lerch. I can see in his face that he is not my son's child." He's always getting into trouble. But even though Oskar was a handful, Hedy favored him. Oskar didn't care what his grandmother thought of him. He didn't like her anyway. He thought of her as a strange and superstitious old woman, who he was ashamed of. But he longed desperately for his father's approval, and his love. However, no matter what he did, his father would not bend toward him. Oskar felt like a stranger in his father's house.

CHAPTER EIGHT

1914

As the boys were reaching their teens, war broke out. Most of the boys in town were eager to enlist. They had no idea what it meant to fight in a war, but they wanted to be heroes.

THE DEEP FRIENDSHIP that Oskar and his brother shared only strengthened as they found themselves on the brink of manhood. Even the wall Walter tried to put between them didn't separate them. Their grandmother was getting older, and she had slowed down considerably. Many days she did not feel well enough to get out of bed. This saddened Erich because he loved her, but Oskar was glad. His grandmother had always looked at him with that accusing gaze of hers, whispering under her breath that he was a child of the devil. The old woman had never made a secret of the fact that she hated Hedy, and that made Oskar dislike her even more.

Most of the other boys their age had already started to work in the mines like their fathers and their grandfathers. Money was tight for the Lerches, and it would have helped financially if both of the boys had been bringing home a salary. But because their mother was insistent that they finish school, and their father was always willing to bend to her will, neither of the Lerch boys were working in the mine.

The other boys in the neighborhood resented the Lerches for not having to work, and they often made nasty comments when they saw Erich. But never when Oskar was around. He was protective of Erich, who was smaller and weaker, and anyone who tried to mess with Erich Lerch soon learned they would have his brother to contend with.

Neither of the boys had ever tried to make friends, although Oskar often played soccer in the park with groups of boys who were acquaintances from school. Erich and Oskar had each other and that was still all they needed. Walking to and from school together each day, they often fell back into speaking their own language so no one else ever knew what they were saying. Oskar had trouble in school. He couldn't concentrate for long periods of time without needing to get up and run around or find something physical to do. Erich knew his brother had trouble sitting still, so he helped Oskar with his homework, mostly doing it for him. And on the weekends when the boys went fishing, and Erich was not strong enough to reel in the fish, Oskar never teased Erich about being weak. Instead, he just reeled them in for his brother.

Then one warm and clammy afternoon, as Oskar felt his eyes closing as he fought sleep during a mathematics class, there was a loud boom. Oskar's eyes flew open. In a mining town, this dreaded sound sent a wave of panic through the classroom. The teacher was trying to maintain control, but the students were frightened. Oskar ignored the teacher's demands that the students stay at their tables. He jumped up and ran out of the woodworking classroom to find his brother. Once he saw Erich through the window in the door of another classroom, Oskar ran inside.

"Excuse me, what are you doing here, Herr Lerch? Go back to your classroom and listen to the instructions your teacher gives you," said the teacher, who was a skinny old man with a strong voice.

Oskar ignored him. He grabbed his brother by the arm. "Come on. We have to get to the mine. We have to find Vater," Oskar said.

The air was filled with smoke as they ran toward the explosion. Erich had to stop several times because he was coughing so hard, that he couldn't run. Forced to bend at the waist to catch his breath, Oskar held his brother while Erich seemed to be choking. "Are you all right?" Oskar asked with genuine concern.

"Yes," Erich managed, and then he spit a large ball of mucus. "I'm all right. Let's go."

Oskar put his arm around his brother, and they ran together. When they got to the mine, crowds from the town were already gathered, waiting for one of the bosses to come out and tell them what had happened and exactly who was involved. Their fear was as thick as the smoke.

"Do you think our father is alive?" Erich asked.

Oskar shrugged. "I don't know," he said.

From somewhere in the crowd, Hedy appeared. She grabbed both of her sons' shoulders and held them close to her. "Are you boys all right?"

"Yes, Mother," Oskar said, not wanting to worry her.

She put her arms around each of her sons, and all three of them looked toward the mine. Oskar glanced up at his mother, her face was covered in sweat and dirt. His heart ached for her, because at that moment he felt certain his father was dead.

Then the mine boss came out and said that the explosion had trapped twelve miners. Everyone was silent . . . listening, waiting. Hedy Lerch's face was covered in soot from the smoke as were the faces of everyone else in the crowd. She stood rigid with her hand covering her mouth. Her sons huddled by her side as the boss read the names of the miners who had not been accounted for. It came as no surprise to Oskar when the boss read the name . . . Walter Lerch. But he caught his mother as she fainted.

"Get me a wet rag," he yelled. "Someone get me a wet rag."

But no one listened. Hedy finally came to on her own a few minutes later.

They stood there with the other families of the twelve missing men. Time passed, hours that felt like years: night fell, but none of them moved. They waited as crews were sent into the mines to see if they could bring the missing men back alive.

"He might still be alive, Mother," Erich said hopefully.

But Oskar knew better; he felt it in his bones. For no explainable reason, he sometimes felt things. And when he did, those premonitions were almost always true.

The three of them waited without food or water until they received the news.

Two days later, when Walter Lerch was declared officially dead, Oskar walked with his mother and brother home from the mine.

Their grandmother was wild eyed, sitting in the kitchen, when they walked into the house covered in soot and broken with exhaustion and grief. She glared at Oskar. Then she turned to Hedy and asked, "So?"

Hedy shook her head.

The boys' grandmother let out a cry. "You!" she said, pointing a trembling arthritic finger at Hedy and then at Oskar. "You brought the devil into this house. I knew from the first time I saw you that you were no good for my son. Until you came here, he was safe. But before that, your parents died because you brought the devil to them. You are a bad seed, Hedy, and you and I both know that you were already pregnant before you met my Walter. You used him to give your bastard son a name." She shook her head, and there was a wild madness in her eyes as she continued. "Yes, Hedy, you were pregnant from the devil. Erich is the son of my Walter. But that other one, that Oskar, that boy came from another man. An evil man, maybe a demon."

"You're nothing but a crazy old woman," Oskar said. "Shut up. Nobody needs to listen to your nonsense right now. Everyone is suffering the loss of Vater."

"He's disrespectful too. A good-for-nothing, ingrate of a child. The devil's child, I tell you." Their grandmother shook her head. "You mark my words: that boy will be the death of all of us," she said, pointing at Oskar.

Oskar could see that his mother was exhausted. She was covered in dried sweat and dirt. Tears stained her cheeks. "Please, Mother Lerch. I know you've lost your son and you feel bad. But I feel bad too. I've just lost my husband," Hedy said.

"Oh yes, I lost my son!" the old woman growled. "You act as if you cared for him. I know you didn't. I know you never loved him. I told him as much. I told him, and I told him. But he refused to believe me. You are a witch, and you cast a spell on him."

Oskar hated the old woman. He wanted to strike her. He wanted to choke the life out of her and forever stop her miserable chatter. She glared at Oskar as she limped over to where Erich stood and put her arms around him. "You are all I have left of my only son. You are the only Lerch left to carry on our family name."

Erich stood dumbfounded, staring at his brother. He'd wept all night, and now he was at a loss for words. But he managed to say, "Grandmother, please don't say these things. Oskar is my brother. He is your grandson too. Don't blame him."

"Echh." She shook her head, then pointed her crooked finger in Erich's face, and in a terrifying, warning voice she said, "You mustn't be blinded like your father was, or you'll suffer the same fate he did. I am warning you. Beware of him."

Oskar couldn't bear to listen anymore. He turned and went into the room he shared with Erich and waited for Erich to come. He didn't clean the dirt or sweat off of his face, but he lay down on the bed and closed his eyes.

It wasn't long before Erich entered the room carrying a hunk of bread and some water. "I thought you might be hungry."

Oskar sat up. "I'm not hungry. Just tired."

"Try to eat. It's been two days," Erich said.

Oskar nodded and managed a smile for his brother. He drank the water, then he took the bread and began to eat.

"I am still stunned. I can't believe our father is gone," Erich said.

"I know. It all happened so fast, so unexpectedly."

"I am going to quit school and go to work in the mine," Erich said. "We need the money. There is no other way for us to survive."

Oskar dropped the bread on the bed and stared at his brother. "You can't," he said. "It's too dangerous. You'd never last there."

"I can." Erich nodded his head. "And I will, because I have to."

For several moments, the boys were silent. "if you're going to work in the mine, then so am I."

"One of us should continue to go to school."

"You're the smarter one; you should stay in school. I'll go to work. I'm physically stronger. I can survive," Oskar said.

They looked at each other for several long moments.

"I can't let you do that," Erich said.

"I would rather go than let you go. You and I both know that you couldn't take the mine. You're always getting sick. And the air in there is anything but pure. Let me do it," Oskar said. "Let me do it until I can find some other kind of work. Meanwhile, you stay in school."

Erich turned away. For several moments he didn't answer.

Oskar said, "Erich, you know I'm right."

Erich nodded. "Yes, I know," he said.

"So, you'll do as I ask. You'll stay in school?"

Erich nodded.

CHAPTER NINE

THE FUNERAL SERVICE took place outside the mine because the bodies could not be recovered. Once it was over, Oskar walked over to the mine boss and asked him to give him a job. The boss, one of the richest men in town, wore a grave expression. He knew from past experience that a mine explosion would spook his workers. They would be more nervous and cautious, and it would take them much longer to get the work done. Looking down at Oskar, the son of one of the men who was lost in the explosion, the boss sighed. "You have my sympathy, son. I sure am sorry about your father. He was a fine man and good worker. He'll be missed. I know you and your mama are going to need money, so, if you want to come and work for me, my answer is yes; I would be happy to have you."

He didn't question why a boy would be willing to take his father's place in the mine right after his father died in an explosion. He knew why. These were poor people. There were no other jobs in town. They depended on the mine for their very existence. The boss knew it well because he had risen in the ranks to the job he now occupied. Once, long ago, he'd been a boy like Oskar, needing to provide for a family. He'd walked into that mine with fear in his heart, but knowing all the while that someday, somehow, he would find a way to get out. He just hoped it would be before he was killed in an accident. *Well, he needs a job,* he thought, feeling a little guilty as he always did when he hired a kid. Looking at Oskar's young face, he told himself, *Maybe he'll be lucky, like I was. Who knows?* Then he cleared his throat from the thick smoke in the air and said, "You'll start Monday morning. Be here at five."

"Yes, sir," Oskar said.

The first time Oskar went down into the dark mine, he was terrified. He had heard that the mine had a life and mind of its own. It had eyes that watched from the black coal walls and decided who would live and who would die. And every day as he walked through the dark walkways, his heart beat loudly, and the terror he felt never left him. But each week, he brought his pay envelope home to his mother so that she could buy food for the family. His grandmother still ranted at him like a lunatic saying he was the spawn of a demon, and even though he hated her, he never denied her anything. Each morning as he left for the mine, he watched as Erich woke up and began to get ready to go to school. But because he loved his brother so much, instead of being jealous that Erich was still in school and not working in the mine like he was, Oskar was glad.

The young fellows who worked in the mines belonged to a community group owned by the mine bosses, who often sponsored picnics or dances. Oskar didn't usually attend. But one afternoon, he heard some of the other boys from the mine talking about a dance that was going to take place the following Sunday. He listened as they talked about the local girls who would probably be in atten-dance, and something stirred in him. Until now, he'd been satisfied to spend his time off with his brother, Erich, fishing or hunting. But now he was starting to wonder what it might be like to kiss a girl. And so he decided he would attend the dance.

He thought about asking Erich to come with him. But he wasn't sure if the mine bosses would allow Erich to attend seeing that Erich did not work for them. "I'm going to a dance tonight," he told Erich.

"Without me?"

34

"I can't bring you with me."

"Why do you want to go anyway?" Erich asked.

"I don't know. I just want to see what it's like."

Erich looked disappointed. And Oskar almost changed his mind and didn't go. But he was curious to see what would happen if he did. So, not looking back at his brother's sad face, he walked out the door and headed to the community center.

When he arrived, he was sorry that he'd decided to come. He felt uncomfortable and awkward even though he looked handsome in his father's old suit. As he watched the couples dancing, he thought, *I can't dance. I should probably just go home.* But before he could leave, a pretty young girl walked up to him. "Hello," she said.

"H-hello," he stammered.

"I'm Mary."

"I'm Oskar."

Mary was shifting from foot to foot, and he had a feeling she wanted him to ask her to dance.

"I don't know how to dance," he admitted clumsily.

"That's all right." She smiled. "Let's get some punch and sit down."

Oskar nodded. They sat down at a table. She smiled at him. "Are you the boy who has a brother who looks just like you?"

"Yes, I have a twin."

"But he doesn't work in the mine. Does he?"

"No, he doesn't. He's still in school."

"My mother says your brother is certain to make something of himself."

"Yes, I know he will. He's smart."

"But what about you? Do you want to work in the mine for the rest of your life?" She moved closer to him. He could smell a sweet fragrance on her that smelled like flowers, and he wondered if it was actual perfume.

Oskar shrugged. He didn't know how to answer.

"Well, do you?"

"Of course not. But what else is there for a fella like me?"

"You could try to go back to school too."

"Someone must support our family."

"But must it be you? Maybe your bother should do something too. Why must it be just you. What happens if you get married and have children? Who is going to support your mother and brother, then?"

He was angry. No one could speak ill of his brother, not now or ever. He could tell that Mary liked him by the way she was leaning against him. She wanted to be his girl, but trying to come between him and Erich was the wrong way to get to him.

"I have to go home," he said. Then Oskar stood up and walked out of the hall leaving Mary sitting at the table with her mouth open. If he hadn't turned and walked away from her, he might have hit her.

CHAPTER TEN

1917

Their grandmother was so old, she could hardly walk, yet she still found the energy to hurl insults at Oskar when he arrived home from work each day. As she grew warts on her face, and her gray hair grew thinner, he found her more and more disgusting. But there were bigger problems to contend with in Germany now. The country was in turmoil. The war was escalating and, being that the Lerch boys had just turned seventeen, Erich was constantly talking about how it was his responsibility to enlist. He spoke of honor and courage the way only a protected and sheltered boy could.

"I haven't been working in that mine for two years so that you could go off and get yourself killed in a war," Oskar said to his brother angrily.

"Everyone is signing up. We owe it to our country. We must protect and defend Germany," Erich said, but deep in his heart, he was secretly afraid. And he was secretly glad that his brother was discouraging him from enlisting. He liked to talk about bravery and courage, but the truth was Erich knew he was a coward.

"I owe nothing to Germany," Oskar grunted. "My allegiance is to you and to Mother."

They hooked their fingers together as they had done when they were children and said a few words to each other in their special language. Then they both laughed.

CHAPTER ELEVEN

THERE WAS no one in the world that Erich admired and loved more than his twin brother. In Erich's mind, Oskar was everything he had ever wanted to be. Oskar was strong and brave, and although Erich was smarter, he would have gladly traded his brain for some of Oskar's brawn. When their grandmother warned Erich that Oskar was some sort of demon, he refused to listen. Erich knew the truth; his brother was a saint. Erich was ashamed to admit it, but he was a weak boy, sickly too. And if it hadn't been for his brother, the other boys would have made his life miserable. As it was, they teased him when Oskar was not around. But they knew better than to ever touch him. They were all too afraid of Oskar's wrath.

Finally, after a couple of months, peer pressure got to Oskar. Many of his coworkers had volunteered for the army. And those who didn't were referred to as cowards. Not that anyone ever called Oskar a coward to his face, but he knew what they were saying. One night after a bad day at the mine, where there had almost been a tragic accident, Oskar came home and announced that he planned to join the army.

"But you said you weren't going to enlist?" Erich said.

"I changed my mind," Oskar said.

"Why?"

"Because I'm not a coward. And every day I face danger in that mine without any purpose. At least if I am in the war, I can be a hero."

Erich looked at his brother. In his mind's eye he saw Oskar as a hero returning home to a hero's welcome. There was admiration in everyone's eyes. He wanted that too. And if he was with Oskar, he knew he need not be afraid, Oskar would protect him. "Then I am going with you," Erich said.

"No, you're going to stay in school. I'll send whatever money home that I can."

"But if you're going to do it…"

"Erich, listen to me. You aren't as strong as I am. This is war. People get killed. Weak people stand less of a chance."

"So, you think I am weak? Is that what you think of me, Oskar?"

"I think you would do better staying in school."

"If it's so dangerous, why are you going?"

Oskar put his head in his hands. Then he turned to look at his brother. "Today we almost had an explosion inside the mine. I had this terrible feeling of helplessness. If the mine decided to swallow me up, it could. Inside that dark beast I have no control over my destiny. At least in the army I will have a fighting chance. It will be my skills that will decide if I live or die."

"An explosion," Erich said, turning white. He was terrified of the mine. "You could have died, like Father. I don't know what I would have done without you."

Oskar nodded.

"Let me come with you. Please don't leave me here. Please take me with you. I must be with you," Erich begged.

"I don't know how I will be able to protect you in the army."

"I can't stay behind without you," Erich moaned. "We have never been apart."

Oskar and Erich locked eyes. They were so close that they could often read each other's minds. "Please," Erich said. "Please. Take me with you."

Oskar shook his head. "I can't stop you from enlisting. I wish you wouldn't, but I can't stop you."

Together, the following day, the boys went to the volunteer office to enlist in the army.

CHAPTER TWELVE

THE BATTLES WERE bloodier and more frightening than Erich had ever imagined they could be. He found himself hiding in foxholes with dead bodies and walking for miles never knowing how close the enemy was or if they were about to be attacked. Erich clung to Oskar who was always looking out for him. And then, one afternoon during a long and hard battle, Erich was wounded. He was shot in the leg. When he fell to the ground, he cried out for Oskar, who turned around. When he saw his brother on the ground holding his leg, he ran to him. In order to protect Erich, Oskar dragged him into a foxhole. There he kept his hand on Erich's wound while the bullets flew above them.

"You'll be all right," Oskar repeated several times. Then he took a pocketknife out of his breast pocket and ripped a piece of fabric from his uniform which he tied around his brother's leg. "That should stop the bleeding. I'll be right back. I'm going to try and get help. You need a medic," Oskar said as he climbed out of the foxhole and left Erich. Then turning around, he added, "Don't move, you'll be safe here."

Oskar was only gone a few minutes when a young enemy soldier jumped into the foxhole with Erich. It was almost nightfall and growing dark. But Erich could see that he wore the uniform of the enemy. His heart pounded. He reached for his gun. But then their eyes met, his and this young soldier's, who looked as frightened as he was. Erich swallowed hard. The soldier held his gun fixed on Erich. Erich held his gun fixed on the soldier. Neither of them moved. Then there was a loud blast, and without warning, the soldier fell where he stood; blood splattered in Erich's face as Oskar jumped back into the foxhole. "Why didn't you shoot him?" he asked, his voice firm and filled with panic. "He was an enemy and about to kill you."

Tears filled Erich's eyes. He shook his head. Then he said, "I couldn't. I was afraid. But I am glad you did. You saved my life."

"You'd better get stronger. In this life, you must be strong if you are going to survive. You have to be stronger than your enemy. Killing is part of it. It's only hard the first time. Then it gets easier. Finally, once you master it, it makes you feel like a real man."

The words were planted like a seed in Erich's mind as he fell unconscious.

The rest was a blur. But when Erich awakened in a hospital, he was told that he'd lost a lot of blood. "Is my brother alive?" he asked the pretty young nurse.

"From what I have heard, he's fine," she said.

"Is he here?"

"No, he wasn't wounded."

Erich spent the next three months in the hospital. Although he would never admit it to anyone, he was glad that he was not going back to the front. And if he'd had his way, his brother would be coming home with him. The last time he'd seen Oskar was in that foxhole, and the last thing Oskar said to him was that he must be strong. He must learn to kill if he was ever going to call himself a man. There had been no word from Oskar since.

Often, during his hospital stay, Erich had sat gazing out the window and thinking about his brother. The thought that Oskar might be dead terrified him. Oskar had been his twin soul, the other half of himself. He'd protected him, listened to him, and understood him. Erich closed his eyes and saw his brother's face, and he wished with all his heart that he could be more like him. Shame filled him when he remembered the jealousy that had consumed him when he saw how the other men in their platoon admired his brother or when he noticed how women responded to Oskar. But all in all, Erich loved his brother, and his love was more powerful than the dark green serpent of envy that sometimes poked its head into his heart and mind.

Erich was finally released from the hospital after three months of recovery. When he arrived back home, his grandmother and mother were relieved to see him. He was weak from spending months lying in a bed. But he was alive, and that was a gift.

Each day his mother mentioned that she was terribly worried about Oskar. She hadn't received word from him since Erich had been wounded. Erich had a gnawing feeling that his brother was dead. It came to him when he least expected it, while he was helping his mother to cook or sitting quietly beside his grand- mother. At night his dreams were consumed with battlefields, and in each of his dreams, his brother fell. But his death was never tragic. In every dream, when Oskar died, he died a hero. Some- times in his sleep, Oskar's face would come to him so vividly that he would awaken sweating, calling out Oskar's name. But then as quickly as it appeared, the vision was gone. As time was passing, an emptiness grew inside of Erich. It felt as if he were only half alive. And because he always believed that Oskar was the other half of himself, he grew more and more certain that Oskar was dead.

Every day Erich and his mother waited for word from Oskar. But no letter arrived.

"It would be the best thing that could happen if he was killed," their grandmother whispered to Erich one day as they sat on the porch sipping tea. "That one is the devil, I tell you. That boy isn't my grandson. He came from the other man, and you mark my words, that other man was the devil. You are my son's child. But your brother is not."

Erich stared at his grandmother. He wanted to slap her right out of her chair and watch her fall on to the floor. If he had the nerve, he would have strangled her to forever silence her harsh and hurtful words.

"He's my brother," Erich said weakly, wanting to say so much more. "I love him. Please, don't talk about him like that."

"Yes, but he is not of this world. He's a demon, I tell you. When two babies are born at the same time from the womb of one woman, it means they are from different fathers. You are the child of my Walter, but your brother is not."

Erich got up and left her sitting outside. He went to his room and sat down on Oskar's bed. *Damn you, Oskar. Where are you? I need you. You can't leave me like this. You can't be dead. How will I ever go on? You always knew the right things to do. I need your strength and your wisdom.* Hot tears stung Erich's eyes. He felt a cold breeze come through the room. And at that moment he knew for certain that his brother was dead.

That night after their grandmother fell asleep, and loud snoring was coming from her room, Erich went to his mother and asked, "Grandmother said something to me today. She said that I was Walter's son, but Oskar came from another man. What does she mean by that?"

His mother shrugged, but Erich could see that she was nervous. "I don't know."

"Yes, you do."

"I don't," his mother said angrily.

Erich grabbed his mother's arm a little too tightly. She winced. "I'm sorry," he apologized. "I didn't mean to hurt you. But I have to know the truth. I have to know everything. Please, Mother, tell me."

His mother let out a long sigh. "I suppose you deserve to know," she said, "but you must promise me, you won't tell your brother what I am about to tell you. If he returns. And I pray with my whole heart that he does." Hedy's face looked older and sadder. "You must not say anything to Oskar before I have a chance to talk to him and explain."

Erich nodded. "I promise," he said.

"Well . . ." She hesitated, then she cleared her throat. "As you know, there were two of you inside of my womb at the same time."

Erich nodded.

"There is a superstition, but many people believe it. It goes like this, when two babies are born at the same time from one womb, they are from two different fathers. Do you know what I mean by that?"

"I don't."

"I mean that you are Walter's son. But . . . your brother . . ." She began to cry. "Your brother . . ."

"Go on."

"Well . . ." She took a deep breath. "I was pregnant with your brother when I met your father. I hadn't counted on caring so deeply for him. At the time I just knew I needed a father for my child. So, I guess you could say I tricked him, and we got married."

"My father knew this?"

She shook her head, tears running down her cheeks. "He never knew for sure. And your grandmother only guessed. But I am sure your father assumed because you boys were born seven months after our wedding that perhaps something had happened. And, of course, with all of your grandmother's cruel accusations, he might have been convinced. But he was a good man, and he never asked me anything."

"And you never told him."

"No, I didn't. Why hurt him? I loved him by then, and I was sorry for what I had done. Andrei, who was Oskar's father, was nothing more than a memory to me by then. In fact, when I thought of him, which was rarely, I thought of him as a character from a story, not as a real person. Your father was solid. He was my friend, and my husband.

"Then Andrei was his name?"

She nodded.

"How do you know that Andrei was Oskar's father and not mine? He could have been Walter's son, and I could have been Andrei's."

"I know because although you boys looked alike, you had very different personalities. You are like your father. Oskar is like Andrei."

46

"And Grandmother knows this? How?"

"She knew her son very well. She sees him in you, but not in your brother. And she has no heart or compassion to love the child of another man. Your father had a good heart. He loved both of you boys; even if he knew, he never let on."

Erich hesitated, taking all of this in, then he said, "Tell me more. Who is this Andrei? Who was this man that is my brother's father?"

She shook her head. "I would rather let the past go."

"Tell me, please."

"There's no point in telling you. It doesn't matter now anyway."

"It matters to me. I want to know. I need to know."

"Oh, Erich, please, just let it be."

"I can't. You've said this much. Now, please, just tell me what I need to know."

His mother looked at him and shook her head. "All right," she began, then with a sigh, she continued. "Before I came here to live with my aunt and uncle, I lived in a small village. There wasn't much excitement until one day a band of Gypsies came through with their horses and their covered wagons. They were so different than the townsfolk I grew up with. They were mysterious, with their dark, curly hair and dark eyes. I was mesmerized.

"My best friend, Helga, and I watched them as they rode into town, their horses' manes blowing in the wind, the women in their colorful skirts, and the men brave and wild. As one of the wagons came through, a young, very handsome man followed on horseback. His dark hair was long and fell over his eyes, but he pushed it back when he saw me. He stared at me as if I was the most beautiful woman he'd ever seen. My heart raced; he was so bold and so romantic. Ahhh." She sighed again.

"Anyway, that night Helga and I waited until our families were asleep, then we sneaked out of our homes and went to the Gypsy camp. We wanted to get our fortunes told. At least that's what we agreed on. I secretly wanted to see that man again, who I'd seen on horseback. As we followed the smoke from the fire, which was lit at the Gypsy camp, Helga said she wanted to buy an elixir to make her hair thicker. The Gypsies were known to sell all kinds of things like that. Medicines that could cure any ill. Most of them didn't work. But we didn't know it then. We didn't find that out until later, after they were long gone.

"When we got to the camp, there were beautiful women in the most colorful costumes I'd ever seen, dancing around a campfire. Their faces were illuminated by firelight, and they looked so alluring and mysterious that I wished I were one of them. I turned to my girlfriend and told her how I felt. Helga shook her head and whispered to me that I was out of my mind. "The Gypsies are looked down on wherever they go. You wouldn't want to be one of them. They have to keep traveling because people don't like having them around," she said.

"But I didn't care what other people thought. I was young and caught up in the romance of it all. I wanted to be a part of a world where there were well-cared-for horses with long manes, hauntingly beautiful women, and handsome men. And, well . . . it all seemed very romantic at the time. One of the old Gypsy women came out of a tent and said, "Are you girls here for a tarot reading?"

"Yes," Helga said eagerly.

The Gypsy nodded. "Good. So, who is first?"

"Can I go first?" Helga asked me.

"Yes, of course," I said. "I'll wait here for my turn."

"Tarot cards?" Erich asked. "What are they?"

"They are a form of fortune telling used by the Gypsies. Whenever they came to town, the local girls would escape from their parents to have their fortunes told by the Gypsies' tarot cards. I wanted to know my future too, even though my mother said that reading cards was the devil's work."

"Is it?"

"I don't know. I never had my cards read. Instead, as soon as Helga disappeared into the tent, I began looking around for him." She looked away from Erich, her face red with shame.

"Mother, please go on."

Hedy swallowed hard. "Andrei snuck up behind me and touched my shoulder. His hand seemed to burn into my flesh. When I turned around, I looked into his eyes. I had thought they were black, but they were blue, the darkest blue I'd ever seen. In the light from the fire, it felt as if I saw the depth of the ocean and sky within that man's eyes." Her face was lost in the memory.

Then he said, "I saw you as we rode in today. I was hoping you would come. I've been looking everywhere for you all night." His voice was soft and deep, and at that moment I lost all knowledge of right and wrong. I only knew that my heart and mind responded to him in a way it had never responded to anyone before."

"Maybe he was the devil," Erich said.

Hedy didn't hear him. She was deep in the memory, so she continued her story: "I don't remember how it happened. How it started, I mean. I can't recall the words he said to me after that. All I know is that I was under his spell. I wanted him, and he . . ." She shook her head.

Then she returned to the present moment and stared at her son. "We spent the next week together. I never went home. Not for an entire week. Andrei wanted me to come traveling with him and marry him. I was willing. In fact, I thought that we would be married and live together forever. I said yes. I promised him I would marry him.

"But I felt that I couldn't leave town without ever seeing my family again. I couldn't go without telling my parents where I was going. So, early one morning, I left the Gypsy camp, and I returned to my father's house to tell him and my mother what had happened and that I planned to marry Andrei. My father, who, until that day had been a quiet man, went mad with rage. He had never raised a hand to me before.

"But that morning he beat me. He broke my nose and sprained my wrist. But the worst thing he did was lock me up in my room. I couldn't get out, and so I couldn't get back to Andrei. Three days passed, and then one morning I woke up to my mother's voice telling me, 'The Gypsy camp is gone. They've left. Your father says you can come out of your room now.' She unlocked my door. Neither of my parents said a word about what had happened.

"Each night I waited by my window. I was hoping that Andrei would return for me. But he didn't. And then a week later, my parents arranged for me to come and live with my aunt and uncle here in the Ruhr Valley. I wept, but they didn't care. Instead, they told me that as far as I was concerned, they were dead. They would rather be dead than be shamed the way I had shamed them. My mother didn't even come with us when my father dropped me at the train station. And he didn't speak to me the entire ride. He just talked to his old horse who was pulling our wagon. When we got to the train station, he said, "Get out of my wagon, whore."

I began to cry. "Papa. Please, don't leave me like this." But he drew his whip, and the horse whinnied, then he turned the wagon around and drove away. I wept that entire train ride. When I arrived at my aunt and uncle's home, they, too, had to protect their reputation. They didn't want anyone to know the real reason I'd been sent to live with them. So, they made up a story for their neighbors, telling everyone that they took me in to live with them because my parents died in a fire."

"And then you met Father?" Erich asked.

"Yes, and then I met your father, my Walter."

"And you loved him?"

"Not at first," she admitted. "At first he was nothing but a hard-working man, who I knew I could count on to take care of my unborn child. I was pregnant, you see. But after Walter and I were married, and as time went on, then I came to love him very much."

"And so, you think Walter was my father, and Andrei was my brother's father?"

"Yes, I believe it is so. But I don't believe your brother is evil in any way. Nor do I believe that Andrei was a bad person. He just lived a different way of life. One I don't know if I could have lived, although I was certain I could have at the time." She sighed. "Your brother is a good boy. He has always been a good son and a good brother to you."

Erich had no more questions for his mother. He'd heard enough. His stomach ached when he thought about his mother and the Gypsy man. Everyone knew that the Gypsies were dirty, much like the Jews, not people one should become friendly with, let alone intimate. But he would never look down on Oskar, nor would he ever tell anyone his brother's secret. *Besides,* he thought, *there are rumors that the Gypsies are magical, and that magic runs through the veins of my beloved brother. Haven't I seen it in the way Oskar charms everyone we have ever met?*

Erich tried to offer his mother a reassuring smile, then he said, "Thank you for telling me this, Mother. I know it's late, but I need some air. I'm going out for a walk. I guess it all came as a bit of a shock. "

The doctors who treated Erich's leg when he was in the hospital were certain that he'd walk with a limp, but it was not so. Now that he was completely healed, no one could tell he'd been wounded. Still, he had not gone through the injury without sustaining some problems. When he walked for long distances, pain still shot through his leg, forcing him to stop. But for the most part, he was back to normal. And there was no doubt in his mind that, if he chose to, he could have returned to battle; he was well enough to do so. But now that he'd seen the horror of war up close, he was glad to be home and safe. So he faked a severe limp to keep others from asking why he was at home and not defending his country.

CHAPTER THIRTEEN

When the young, handsome soldier arrived at the Lerches' home, the left arm of his uniform jacket was hanging. That was because his arm was gone. As soon as Erich saw him, he knew why he had come. The young soldier stood in the doorway looking uncomfortable for a few moments, staring at Erich. "You look just like him," the soldier said in awe.

"My brother," Erich said. It was more of a statement than a question.

"Yes, if Oskar is your brother."

"He is my brother."

"My name is Werner Hoffenberg. Oskar was my friend. More than my friend. He saved my life."

Erich stared at him. "Where is he?" Erich asked, fearing what he already knew.

"I'm sorry. Your brother died saving me. But I wasn't the only man he saved. I mean, I was the only one at the time. He and I were separated from our troop. The enemy was close. I got thrown by an explosion; it blew off my arm." He pointed to where it used to be. Erich nodded. "Oskar saw it happen. He could have saved himself.

He could have run away and left me, but he didn't. He carried me to safety in a trench.

"We were huddled in there when an enemy soldier found us. Oskar stood in front of me and shot the fella before he could shoot me. But not before he hit Oskar point-blank in the heart. Your brother was a true hero. He was the kind of man I hope my son, if I ever have one, will be. But I am so sorry for your loss. I know that my coming here and telling you how sorry I am doesn't make it any better, but I truly am sorry."

Werner took a deep breath. "I am sure you know that this was his way. He was a strong and courageous man. Once I saw him put his life on the line rescuing our entire platoon. You should be proud to have had such a brother. Proud to share his face."

"I am," Erich said bitterly. "But I am not happy that he sacrificed himself for you." He wanted to punch Werner. If killing him would have brought his brother back, Erich would have killed him.

Hedy walked into the room. "Why is this man standing in the doorway? Come in, won't you?" she said. But Erich could see that his mother was trembling. She knew why the soldier had come, yet she hoped she was wrong.

Werner walked inside. Then he told Hedy about Oskar. She almost fainted. Erich had to steady her. He helped her to a chair, then sat down beside her. She gripped his hand so tightly that it felt as if it might break. But their grandmother, who was sitting in the kitchen listening, quietly sighed. "It's for the best," she whispered loud enough for Erich to hear. If he hadn't been so broken inside, he might have gone into the kitchen and knocked Grandmother to the floor. But even though he'd suspected for a while that his brother was dead, the confirmation hit him like a kick in the stomach and he couldn't move. He was paralyzed with shock and grief.

Werner handed Erich Oskar's dog tags. "Again, I am so very sorry," he said, then stood up and left.

Erich squeezed the dog tags, the metal felt cold in his hand. He thought about how his brother had worn these dog tags around his neck, and that this inanimate object had once lain on his brother's chest. With trembling fingers, he brought the necklace up to his lips.

Tears formed in his eyes. *How can I go on living without my brother?* Erich stared blankly at the dog tags. He couldn't speak. He couldn't swallow. His throat felt like sandpaper. Although he'd been feeling an emptiness for a while, the reality of Oskar's being gone was so harsh that he almost couldn't bear it. His mother was weeping. His grandmother was sitting on the sofa beside her and whispering, "It's a blessing in disguise."

Alone in his bed at night, he spoke to his brother in their special language, and he waited, somehow believing that Oskar would answer. But he didn't. Erich felt as if a part of himself, like a limb, had been amputated. And he wondered if he would ever feel whole again. Erich began to think about suicide. He didn't want to live in a world without Oskar. The idea terrified him. He was afraid of the pain, and he hated himself for being so weak. But with each passing day, he grew more depressed, and he began to think of ways he might take his own life without suffering. Then one night about two weeks after the soldier had come with the devastating news, Erich had a dream. In his dream, his brother came to him. Oskar was so real that tears streamed down Erich's face as he slept. Erich reached out his hand and felt the warmth of Oskar's shoulder.

"How are you, my brother?" Oskar asked.

"How should I be? I miss you terribly."

"I know you do. I have been watching you. And I've been worried about you. That's why I've come to you. For that reason, and also for another reason."

"What is it?"

"I've been thinking." Oskar winked at Erich the way he always did when he had a plan.

"Yes. Tell me," Erich said.

"The war is almost over. As everyone already knows, Germany will lose. Once Germany surrenders, I want you to leave the valley. Go to live in the city, where there is more opportunity."

"But why?"

"Because I want you to take my name. We look alike. Exactly alike. Tell everyone you are me. No one knows I died that day, only Werner, the man who came to see you, and he is only one small man. He won't live long. There will be a great and horrible flu and he will die from it."

"A flu?"

"Yes, a flu. A bad flu. It will take many people. However, don't worry. You will be fine. Now, this is what is important; those who knew me on the field considered me a war hero. No one will remember that I had a twin. My victories during the war will help you to go far in the new government which is coming sooner than you know."

"I don't understand."

"There will be a new government. You'll see. And pure German war heroes will be highly regarded. You will never have to work in the mines, my dear brother. Never have to sweat in the darkness surrounded by coal, or feel your breath stolen by the dust."

"But . . . I am not a hero. I am a coward. You know that better than anyone."

"I know that you are my brother and that you and I are one person. We always have been. We were born from the same womb. And now you will become me. If I cannot reap the benefits of my hero status, at least I will know that you will. And that will give me as much pleasure as my own success would have."

"I would rather have you here beside me," Erich said. "I don't have your courage; I don't have your strength. I've always depended on you to take care of me. I hate the weakness in myself."

"I'll always be here beside you. If not in body, then in spirit."

"I don't know how to ask you this, but are you magical in some way? I mean Mother told me some odd things."

"Perhaps. Perhaps I am. I know about my father, about Andrei. Maybe I have his Gypsy blood. Maybe you do too. But no one in Berlin must ever know. And . . . you must make sure they never find out. You don't look like a Gypsy. No one will ever suspect that you came from such strange beginnings."

"Can you tell me more about the new government that's coming?"

"It will be a powerful one. And if you assume my identity, you have the opportunity to shine."

55

"I am so confused."

"Don't think about it too much, just do as I say. And one more thing, one more very important thing. Be careful who you give your heart to. A day will come, a day far in the future, when you will love so deeply that it could make you act foolishly. Beware of that day. It could well be your demise if you aren't careful."

"Oskar!" he said. "Foolish in love? Who is it that I fall in love with? I can't imagine because I have never been in love."

But Oskar had begun to fade away. "Oskar! Come back, please, please, I have so much to say to you. So much to ask you." But Oskar was gone. Erich awoke crying out, "I love you, my brother."

Erich's eyes were open. He was trembling in his bed, the sheets wrapped around him, his face dripping tears mingled with sweat. He sat up and looked out the window at the stars. He was trying to sort out the dream and everything it meant. He knew his grandmother believed that dreams were premonitions, and he wished he could go and ask her what all of this meant. But because she hated Oskar, Erich did not feel comfortable sharing his dream and the words Oskar told him, with her.

CHAPTER FOURTEEN

November 1918

That autumn, just as Oskar had told Erich in his dream, Germany surrendered. Following the surrender, the Treaty of Versailles was signed, leaving the German soldiers who had fought feeling broken and defeated. To make matters worse, the terrible pestilence which Oskar had warned of fell upon the land. A disease so epic in proportion that it seemed almost biblical. And as Oskar promised, Erich was unscathed, but his mother and grandmother both perished. Erich didn't care at all about his grandmother, but he wept for his mother. However, losing everyone left him in a position to do as Oskar had commanded in his dream.

Erich had never wanted to venture out of the valley once he'd returned from the war. If he had his way, Oskar would have returned, and the two of them would live in the valley forever. They would have married, had children, and been neighbors. But the fates had other plans. And so, Erich packed his things, and with a heavy heart, he boarded a train for the nearest town. He knew he wasn't quite ready for Berlin. Not just yet.

As the train chugged along the tracks on its way into the future,

Erich knew the time was coming when he would say goodbye to "Erich" and take the name of Oskar Lerch, a name he would carry for the rest of his life. But first he had to make himself worthy of using his brother's name. And so, as he rode the train, he devised a plan.

CHAPTER FIFTEEN

BEFORE ERICH WOULD BEGIN to use his brother's war hero status to make a name for himself and build his future success, Erich decided that he must learn how to impersonate a wealthy gentleman. No one would take a boy who came from a mining town seriously.

Using the alias name of Wilhelm Becker, he applied for work at several places where he knew he would have contact with wealthy, educated men. It had to be a place where Erich would be able to listen to them speak, to watch their mannerisms and then to learn to imitate their ways. A few weeks later, he was hired as part of a crew at a club that served wealthy, educated men.

The guests ignored him as he walked through the club each day. It was almost as if he were invisible while he was collecting the trash or cleaning vomit when someone drank too much. This often happened with the younger men. But Erich never complained; he watched and listened carefully. After his long workdays, he went home to the small room he'd rented in a men's hotel where he practiced the mannerisms he'd learned, in the mirror.

Then one night while he was cleaning up an overturned ashtray, he overheard two young university students talking about a philosopher whose books they were reading for a class they were attending.

Both of the young men were fascinated by the philosopher's books. Erich wanted to know more, so he decided to go to the library and take out a book by the author they were discussing. Although he didn't know it at the time, this book by Friedrich Nietzsche would change his life.

As he read about the power of the superior man, he felt that Nietzsche was speaking directly to him. *I am smarter than anyone I know, and that puts me above everyone else. I am certainly far smarter than those useless fools at the club. They may have been born into money, but I am truly a superior man. And now that I understand this, I know that I can have anything I want because it is my right to take it,* Erich thought as he devoured the book. Then he returned to the local library and took out all the books that Nietzsche had written.

A seed had been planted in his mind. And from that time on, he never again saw himself as a weak man from an impoverished background. He saw himself as the superior man, a man of great intelligence who could use his superior brain to manipulate the world for his own gain.

Over the next two years, he saved every penny he could. Then using his newly formed way of speaking, he found a job at a men's clothing store, still using the name of Wilhelm Becker. His fine way of speaking got him hired immediately. And during the first month of his employment, he convinced the boss that he was a fast learner and a trustworthy employee. And soon the boss was giving him more responsibilities. Wilhelm never disappointed. He was willing to work long hours and never questioned any requests. Soon his boss began to trust him fully.

At first, he only left him alone in the store for a few minutes while he went to buy a sandwich. But then, once he saw that Wilhelm could handle things, he began to leave him for longer periods of time. He began to feel comfortable spending an afternoon with his mistress while Wilhelm manned the store. On one such afternoon, the boss said he was going out. He asked Wilhelm if he would close the shop for him. Wilhelm readily agreed.

After his boss was gone for a half hour, Wilhelm took several suits in his size along with matching shirts, socks, and ties. He put them into a bag and then walked out of the store, locking the door behind him. Now he had the right clothes. He purchased the best shoes he could afford. Then he went back to the seedy hotel where he'd been living, packed his bags, and walked to the train station where he bought a one-way ticket to Berlin. From this day forward, he would use the name of Oskar Lerch. He was ready now.

Once he arrived in Berlin, he joined the Nazi Party. Then under the name of Oskar Lerch, capitalizing on his brother's status as a war hero, he began his career. He lied, telling everyone that he'd met Adolf Hitler in the trenches during the war. He served for a short time in the Wehrmacht, where he made it a point to impress his superiors with his loyalty and devotion. He knew how to make his superiors feel important and consequently, they liked him.

When he was offered a promotion into the Sicherheitsdienst, the secret police, he was elated. Blond, blue eyed, tall, and handsome, he was the perfect example of an Aryan man. And within a year, he was offered a position in the Einsatzgruppen, a special force that followed the soldiers committing mass murders, as they invaded the countries of Europe. At first, when he'd had to shoot hundreds of innocent Jews, it had made him ill. But he knew that if he showed weakness, he would never be chosen to rise in the party. So, although he was sickened by the stench of blood and death, he put on a devil-may-care attitude, picked up his weapon and fired point-blank, killing men, women, and children.

In the beginning, he would leave the scene at the end of each day, trembling. But as time passed, he convinced himself that the Jews, Gypsies, and undesirables he was killing were subhumans. And the killing became easier. His superior officers liked the way he pretended to worship them, and when an opening came up for a position at Auschwitz, it was offered to him. He accepted, glad to be able to settle in one place rather than travel with the death squad. He found the camp to be a filthy and disgusting place full of disease. But he loved the power the job gave him.

The only thing about Auschwitz that really bothered him was Dr. Mengele's obsession with twins. When Oskar met Mengele at a party, and he heard the doctor talking about what he called his work which, in fact, was little more than torture using twins, it had bothered Oskar. Mengele explained that he liked to work with children who were twins, and he often took not only Jewish children, but children from the Gypsy camp.

That night Oskar went home and drank until he could fall asleep. Once he did, he dreamed that his brother was alive and that they were children again. They were arrested and brought to Auschwitz because Mengele had learned somehow that his brother was the son of a Gypsy. In his dream Mengele was torturing his brother. Oskar woke up unable to catch his breath. And from that time on, he was friendly but distant with Dr. Mengele, and he also made an effort to stay far away from him and from the Gypsy camp.

He continued to work at Auschwitz. Keeping the Jews in line came easy to him. He had no sympathy for them at all. He could see them suffer and not feel a thing. His job was easy; in fact, it grew better and better as he flattered his superiors and rose in rank. With every promotion, he received plenty of perks.

BOOK TWO

CHAPTER SIXTEEN

Oskar glanced at the bottle of wine on the seat between himself and Kara as they drove to their room at the Hotel zum Türken. It was only a few minutes from the birthday party they'd been attending at the Berghof, Hitler's home, but they drove instead of walking through the underground bunker which was connected to the hotel. They did this because Kara wanted to see the area at night. Oskar inhaled deeply as he admired the magnificent retreat area of Obersalzberg in the Bavarian Alps. *What an honor*, he thought. *To be invited to the Berghof for the führer's fifty-fourth birthday. And not only invited to the party, but I was given this bottle of wine by our führer with his picture on it. Few have been honored in this way. I have really made my way in the party.*

He glanced around him and admired the exquisite homes of Martin Bormann, Hermann Göring, and Albert Speer. *Albert Speer, I met him a party. A handsome fellow. But I don't like him at all. He was the only one of the SS officers who seemed unconvinced by the lie that I told them all about my being an educated architect. A clever man indeed, but a pain in the neck for me. I would have found a way to kill him had it not been for his closeness to the führer and his work on the autobahn. Instead, I just had to smile and endure his technical questions about architecture. He never outright said I was a liar, but he smiled at me in that infuriating way of his, and I knew that he knew the truth. So far, he has kept his mouth shut, and as long as he does, there is no need for me to take any action. I will just continue to do my best to avoid him.*

Reaching for Kara's hand, he turned to look over at her. She was truly beautiful with her son, Karl, asleep in her lap. Everyone at the party, even the führer, had admired her beauty. She turned to see him looking at her. The diamond earrings he'd stolen for her from Kanada sparkled in the starlight. *It's a good thing she doesn't know where those diamonds came from, right off of the ears of some dead Jew. It would upset her so. She must never find out.*

"You look gorgeous," he said.

She smiled. "Thank you."

When they arrived at the hotel, Kara glanced over at the guard tower, then she turned to Oskar. "What is that? It looks rather frightening."

"It's nothing to be concerned about," he said gently. "The SD and the SS control this hotel because it's so close to the Berghof. That way when Hitler is staying at the Berghof, they can keep a watch over him and keep him safe." Oskar gently took Karl from Kara's arms and carried him up to their room. Kara undressed Karl and put on his nightclothes. He turned over and fell back to sleep. Then Kara went into the bathroom to get ready for bed, and Oskar opened the bottle of wine. He lifted it to his lips and drank. Pleased with himself, he let his mind drift to all that he'd accomplished.

It had been years since Oskar had left his home in that small mining town to come to Berlin, and during that time, he'd risen to an oberstrumführer. People liked him, with his easy laugh and good manners. He had a way of making his superiors believe that he could be trusted. Once they considered him a friend, he learned their secrets and their dreams. Then he would help them achieve their goals, and in turn they would help him. He'd recently been asked by his superior officer to take on a job he really didn't want. The Nazis were in the process of establishing a slave labor camp at a coal mine. Oskar's superior officer asked him to transfer to the mine and help coordinate the Reich's efforts.

The last place he wanted to be was a coal mine. *I worked my entire life to get away from the mines. At first, I was furious, but I am too careful a man to allow anyone to know my true feelings. And I know I am superior. If my brother had not come to me in a dream that night, I would not have understood. But I know that this is just a steppingstone for me. I will rise above all of them. Maybe even above the führer himself.* In his mind he could hear his brother say, *"You are the boss. You are not a miner. You have come too far to quit. Stay with it. You won't be in the mine forever."*

I hate this filthy job of supervising the forced labor at the coal mine. But I really can't complain. My carefully orchestrated life is playing out even better than I ever expected. Over the years, using my brother's name and his success as a war hero, as well as helping my superiors to keep nasty little secrets, I've found my way into a successful career in the Nazi Party. Then once he'd become established, he'd met the girl of his dreams, Kara, a beautiful blonde woman with an adorable young son by the name of Karl, and he knew she was the one for him.

Oskar was sitting at the desk sipping from the bottle of wine when there was a knock at the door. He glanced over at Karl who was sleeping soundly, then quietly cracked the door open. There stood one of the lower-ranking officers with a note in his hand. "This is for you, Oberstrumführer. It's from the residence of the führer."

"Thank you," Oskar said. He took the note and handed the man a reichsmark. Then he sat down and opened it. The light of the moon filtered through the shades just enough for him to read:

"You and your lovely wife are cordially invited to a brunch tomorrow morning at eleven a.m. at the Kehlsteinhaus, the Eagle's Nest. Signed, Eva Braun."

Kara will certainly be excited to see the Eagle's Nest. And the truth is I am quite honored to be invited. He'd heard of the Eagle's Nest. And when they'd first arrived at the party, before it had gotten dark, he'd caught a glimpse of it up on the hill above the hotel. It was supposed to be magnificent with views of the Alps, and if it was a clear day, it was said one could see Salzburg from the resort. He'd heard that it was commissioned by Bormann and given to Hitler as a gift for his fiftieth birthday in 1939.

67

He wondered why Bormann would have chosen to have a retreat built so high on a mountain. *It seems strange to me because I've heard that the führer has a fear of heights and vertigo. I believe there is an elevator up to the retreat somewhere in the mountain. I'm sure we'll receive more directions in the morning. Won't this be a memorable experience. When we are rubbing elbows with the upper echelon, Kara will definitely realize how fortunate she is to have been chosen as my wife.*

Then his mind drifted back to the beginning, when he'd first fallen for Kara. *No matter what I tried to do to woo her, she refused my affections. But I knew that no matter what she said or did, I would have her for my own.* And although it angered him when she rejected his attentions, he refused to give up. *I've always known that I am smart,* and *Nietzsche's superior man never takes no for an answer.* So he thought about what he could do to find a way into her heart, and he came up with a plan. *I was like a spider: I watched and waited for the right time. I wove my web, and then, as I knew it would, my opportunity finally came.*

Oskar began to spin his treacherous plan when Ludwig, Kara's brother-in-law, mentioned that he, his wife, and Kara would be attending a gala in Poland. Oskar had been invited to this gala, too, and had been planning to attend. Then when Oskar heard that Kara would be at the party, he knew that this was his chance. So he'd asked her if he could be her escort. She reluctantly agreed. *I hinted to that half-wit Ludwig that he should tell Anka to have Kara find a local babysitter for Karl, so we could all enjoy the party without worrying about the child. Ludwig fell right into my plan.* He let out a laugh. Then he glanced over at Karl, hoping he hadn't awakened him. After all, he was feeling powerful, and he wanted to make love to Kara tonight. He let out a sigh of relief. Karl slept soundly.

I can still remember how pleased I was to learn that Kara had left her little boy under the supervision of an old Polish woman. Everything was falling into place. I made a few important calls to solidify my plan that night, and then began to get ready for the evening's events.

At the party that evening, Kara looked ravishing. She dined and danced with me. I hate to admit just how smitten I was. But although she treated me respectfully, I could see that she had no real affection for me. Unbeknownst to anyone else at the party, my plan was already in motion, and I knew soon I would have her right where I wanted her. I already knew where the babysitter lived because I had Kara and Anka followed when they dropped Karl off.

Oh, but she was the belle of the ball that night. Everyone wanted to dance with her. But she was too good for any of them. Even me. But inwardly I laughed because I knew that her aloof attitude was about to be smashed. While she was sipping the fine wine the party had provided, I knew her son and the old Polish babysitter were already on their way to the police station.

The following morning, I pretended not to know a thing. After breakfast, I asked Ludwig if he would give me a lift to the train station. He could hear the conversation in his mind even now.

"We have to go the babysitter's flat to pick up Karl. But I suppose I could drop you off first," Ludwig had said.

"Oh, no. I insist that you pick the boy up first," Oskar said.

"Are you sure? Don't you have a train to catch?"

"I do. But please, don't worry. I have time."

They drove to the babysitter's apartment. But when Kara and Anka went upstairs to get Karl, they found the apartment had been ransacked. Karl and the babysitter were gone. Kara screamed. *She was tearing at her hair, beside herself with fright. And that was when I stepped in to act as her hero. I called my superior officer, who owed me many favors, and asked for plenty of time off work, which, of course, I was granted due to the fact that I knew so many of my superior officers' most precious secrets.*

Then Oskar arranged for them to keep their hotel rooms for as long as they needed them. *Kara thought I paid for the rooms, but I used fear and intimidation to force that hotel owner to give us the rooms for as long as required. He was afraid of me, so he did what I told him to do. And he was quite generous from that day on, I must admit. But the best part of all this was that now I had Kara all to myself. I would hold out on bringing Karl back until I won her love.*

Oskar and Kara combed the city of Warsaw together in search of her son. All along he'd known where Karl was. He had arranged for Karl to be housed at the home for the Lebensborn. And just as Oskar had predicted, by the time he'd allowed them to find the boy, Kara had grown dependent on him. She even seemed to have developed feelings for him. They were married, and then, over time, because he was so good to her and her son, he believed that she had come to love him.

Kara is a tender, sensitive soul. She weeps for the inferiors like the Jews and the other subhumans. I hate them. They remind me of that sickening secret my mother told me about the Gypsy man who had fathered my brother. And who knows, he might have been my father as well. I am very manipulative like a Gypsy. I took my brother's identity and convinced the world that I am him. My grandmother thought my brother was the demon. But maybe it was not him. Maybe it is me. Maybe I am the demon spawn from the filthy Gypsy man. Oskar shivered to think this could be true. *But if it is true, and if I am a demon, then isn't it also true that demons are powerful? Superior? Maybe all truly superior men are spawned from demons. But I would never let anyone know these thoughts. Andrei will always remain a shameful secret I buried.*

Oskar knew how easily Kara could be upset by the harsh treatment of the subhumans. He made sure she knew nothing about his work at the camp. She must never find out about his treatment of the prisoners. She wouldn't understand that a man must be strong and courageous if he was going to hold on to his power. And Oskar never really felt strong, so he used violence and fear tactics to convince people he was powerful.

Now, his precious wife was pregnant with his child. A smile came over his face as he remembered the day she'd surprised him with the news that she was carrying his baby. He'd just picked Kara and Karl up from the train station after her visit with Anka. It was Bertram's day off, so he was driving. She'd whispered to him that she had a surprise for him. And then all the way home he'd tried to guess the surprise, and she'd giggled, refusing to tell him what it was.

But later that night when they were alone and after he'd made love to her, she told him. "I'm going to have a baby," she'd said. *Oh, how my heart swelled with love and pride that night. I was awestruck. It seemed almost unreal that we were going to have a child. I felt as if I were dreaming. All I could say was, "Kara, a child. We are going to have a child. My child. My own flesh and blood." It wasn't that I didn't like her son, Karl. I did and I do. I know Karl adores me. But there is nothing like a child of your own. Hopefully Kara will give me a son. Once my son is born, I will teach him everything I know. I will make sure he is accepted in the best of circles. A son to call my own.*

I've had to work hard to find ways to rise in the party. But it will all pay off when my son is born. He will be accepted by the upper echelon in the party because of my brilliant tactics. I remember how foolish I felt when I had to lie to Kara. We were in Warsaw searching for Karl. I needed to impress her, so I told her that I was a good friend of Himmler's, and that Himmler would help me find her son. She believed it, swallowed the whole thing without question. But it gnawed at me that I had to lie. I wanted that lie to be true. It drove me mad to know that I had never even met the reichsführer. It had driven me so crazy that I decided it was something I must do. So I used my superior mind.

Asking questions but, of course, not too many, I slowly learned everything there was to know about Himmler. He laughed softly so as not to wake Karl. *And what did I learn? I learned that Himmler is no better than I am. He didn't come from a wealthy family. He was nothing but the son of a chicken farmer. And his wife is only a nurse. Then I waited, like I always do, until the right moment. It came when I heard that Himmler was coming to Auschwitz. I remember the look my superior officer at the time gave me when I said that I would like to meet the reichsführer. That pompous ass refused. He said I was too low to even think about meeting Himmler. So, of course, I reminded him that I knew of a homosexual episode he'd had with a prisoner. The look on his frightened face was perfect. I knew I had him. I knew he would do whatever I asked. And he did.*

He made the introduction as soon as Himmler arrived. Of course, a few months later, he was quietly transferred. But I didn't care. I'd gotten what I needed from him. And once he was gone, I was promoted, and then I set out to learn what I needed to know about my new superior officer, just in case I needed a favor from him in the future. Once Oskar was introduced to Himmler, he used all that he knew about the man to win Himmler over. He was an easy mark. *All I had to do was flatter him, and he was eating out of my hand.* And once he'd been befriended by the reichsführer, he set his sights even higher. He'd used the connection he'd made with Himmler to find a way to meet and impress the führer himself. And once he'd met the führer, he used every ounce of charm he had to win him over. And that was how he had been invited to Hitler's very exclusive birthday party that night.

Oskar held the bottle of wine up to the light and admired the picture of the führer on the label. *How handsome I looked in my uniform standing there rubbing elbows with Himmler and Göring. I truly am a perfect example of Nietzsche's superior man,* he thought. *And I was chosen by the führer as one of the few officers to be called up to the podium tonight to receive this bottle of wine with Hitler's picture on it. The look of envy on everyone's face was priceless when Hitler gave me that bottle in front of everyone.* He sighed; it was such a pleasant memory that he knew he would revisit it often. *I deserve this. I have taken what is rightfully mine because I am superior to all of these fools. I might even be superior to the führer himself. But oddly enough, I have heard that he reads Nietzsche too. I've heard he has made mention of Nietzsche many times. So perhaps we are equal, the führer and myself.*

What a night that was. "She is a true Aryan beauty," Hitler said when he saw Kara. Then he looked at her pregnant belly and added, "And how proud you must be that she will bear your perfect Aryan child for the future of the Reich." The only problem with that perfect night was the whispered, nagging gossip that everyone had heard but no one openly discussed. They all had a growing fear that Germany was losing the war. Oskar didn't give a damn about the fatherland, not really. But he had put all his energy and efforts into the Third Reich, and if it should fall, he knew for certain he was not going to fall with it. He would have to find a way to get out if he was sure that things weren't going to turn around.

Since he'd left that little mining town where he was born, he'd manipulated his every circumstance. Things had never come easy to him. Everything he'd achieved had taken careful planning and executing. But he'd risen far higher than men who were born under better stars, with more opportunity, and this was because he believed wholeheartedly that he was the superior man. So he knew if the time came when there was no hope for Germany, he would escape and start over somewhere else.

It would be shame if the Third Reich fell, because he really enjoyed the home he'd been awarded for his good service to the party. The furnishings were of the highest quality, and the taste in decorating was impeccable. He knew it had been the home of a Jewish family, wealthy and privileged. They'd been arrested and were probably already dead, so, of course, they were unlikely to ever return. This was information he did not share with his wife. He knew she would not, could not, continue to live in this house if she knew the truth. *So why should I tell her? Kara enjoys the benefits of being my wife. The wife of an SS officer living in Poland, who has access to anything we might want or need. And I love to indulge her.*

In fact, for her birthday recently, he'd had a garden installed in front of the house by Jewish prisoners. It was a magnificent flowering garden that attracted the attention of all the other German families in the area. Oskar mused as he gazed out the window at the garden, *And to think, I chose the right two Jews to plant it. Kara is going into town to visit the doctor next week so he can check on her pregnancy. While she's gone, I'll bring the Jews back and have them nurture the plants, so they continue to bloom.* He had to be strategic about the upkeep of the garden. *Kara must never see these prisoners. It would make her question everything. She must never have an opportunity to speak to them and learn of the camps and all that went on there.*

He knew she would be appalled. She might even leave Poland and divorce him. *No, it must never happen. I must make certain that she never finds out what I do for work. And no matter what, she must never know that it was me who had staged the entire kidnapping of her son.* He took a deep breath. It was, he had to admit, exhausting. But he was too deep in it to change a thing. *What a web of secrets. What a web of lies.*

There was no denying that he enjoyed the power he wielded over the subhuman prisoners whom he commanded: Jews, Gypsies, political prisoners. He especially hated the Gypsies, with their dark, swarthy complexion and their hypnotic violin music. They terrified him. The blood that ran through their veins might also run through his own. He hated to think about that.

Before he'd been transferred for his temporary stint at the mine, he'd worked at Auschwitz where there was a large Gypsy camp. When he walked past that camp and heard them playing their music, the tender notes from the violins drifting through the air, thoughts of shame overwhelmed him. He knew that the Gypsies were permitted to keep their instruments because they had been given a job. They were allowed to practice while they were in their block, but then they were forced to play while the other prisoners were herded into the gas chambers. It was decided among the superior SS officers, that the music helped to keep the prisoners calm. Sometimes Oskar would want to go to the Gypsy camp and kill one of the Gypsies. He longed to destroy one of them and then thereby kill the shameful secret that haunted him. But he dared not because he feared them too. In his mind he heard his grandmother's raspy voice say, "Magic, they are evil, spawns of the devil." Oskar shivered.

My brother was magic, but he was no spawn of the devil, Oskar would think as he walked quickly by the camp, staying as far away from the Gypsies as he could. Instead, he put his focus on the Jews. Oskar relished the fact that he was their master. Some of them, he knew, and he couldn't understand how or why, they still believed in the god of their religion. But in his mind, he felt that he was their true god. And for a boy who had grown up weak, afraid, and dependent upon his brother, this was quite a welcome change. When he thought about it, laughter bubbled up inside of him. *I am powerful. They fear me. They must do as I say, or they could face death. I decide who lives and who dies.*

Once when he'd walked through the camp, he heard them in their block singing in a strange language, worshiping their god. They knew this was forbidden, and he'd caught them in the act. Standing tall as he entered the block, he frowned at the group of pathetic Jews who sat in a circle praying. It gave him a rush of excitement to see the terror come over their faces. But that day, he remembered, had been a good day for him. And he didn't feel much like killing or punishing anyone. So instead of disciplining them, he said, "You Jew swine are the dumbest of people. You still worship a god who has abandoned you and left you here at the mercy of a stronger more powerful god. Do you know who that is?" None of them answered. Oskar laughed again, louder this time, then he said, "It's me."

Shaking his head, he walked out of the bunker and left them. Then he walked back to his office. His chest swelled with conceit as he took a bottle from the drawer of his desk and poured himself a glass of schnapps. *It's all up to me, whether they live or whether they die. If I feel generous for some reason, I just might give them an extra piece of moldy bread instead of throwing it in the trash. And if I have a bad day and feel angry, I could choose to beat one of them until his life seeps out of his broken body. The future of each of these men lies in my hands. Ahh, I truly am the superior man.*

Kara came out of the bathroom with her long, blonde hair loose and hanging about her shoulders. *She looks like an angel with that golden halo,* Oskar thought as he felt the breath catch in his throat.

"Have a glass of wine?" he asked.

"Oh, no thank you. I had quite enough at the party tonight," she said.

"Well, I have wonderful news."

"What is it?"

He handed her the invitation. She read it.

"Oh, Oskar, this is wonderful news. But what shall I wear? I didn't bring many dresses."

"It doesn't matter what you wear. I know you'll outshine every woman at the brunch."

CHAPTER SEVENTEEN

THE FOLLOWING morning at exactly ten thirty, there was a knock on the hotel room door. The Lerches had gotten up early. They were dressed and ready to go.

"Good morning, Oberstrumführer, Frau Lerch," an SD officer said. "I am with Hitler's Secret Service. I'll be escorting you up to the Eagle's Nest. Are you ready to leave?"

"Yes and thank you," Oskar said. Then he turned and smiled at Kara.

"Then please come with me."

Kara took Karl's hand, and they followed the SD officer. Oskar had been correct; they'd boarded an elevator that was inside the mountain. Kara turned to Oskar. "This is a little scary," she whispered, "and it is terribly cold."

"Nonsense, it's fun and it's an adventure. We are pure Aryans; we can brave the cold," he said, then turning to Karl, "Isn't that right, son?"

"Yes, Vater, we are pure Aryans. And this is fun! Besides, I am not scared as long as I am here with you, Vater. I think you are the biggest, strongest man in the world."

"That's a good boy." Oskar ruffled Karl's hair. "You know I'll always protect you, don't you?"

"Yes, Vater."

When they stepped off the elevator at the top of the mountain, Kara gasped. The view of the Alps was magnificent. "Oh, Oskar, it's heavenly," she said.

He pointed. "Look over there, that's Salzburg."

She turned her head to see the city, then she turned back and smiled at him. "This is spectacular."

"I knew you would love it."

Just then they were greeted by Eva Braun, who wore a traditional German dirndl skirt and embroidered blouse. "Welcome, I'm so glad you could come."

"Thank you so much for inviting us," Kara said.

"Follow me inside, please."

They did as Eva requested, and she brought them into a room with large picture windows, where they could admire the view. There was only one long table, and in the center was a vase with bright yellow sunflowers.

"This is lovely," Kara said. "I simply adore sunflowers."

"Of course you do; they are the official flower of the Reich," Oskar said.

"Please, won't you sit down? The rest of the guests are already seated, and the führer will be here in a few minutes. This is a rare treat because he almost never comes up to the Eagle's nest. He's only been here a handful of times," Eva Braun said.

"Well, we are certainly honored," Oskar said.

Eva Braun showed them to their seats next to Dr. Goebbels, his wife, Magda, and their six children. There were only a handful of top SS officers and their wives present at the table. They waited eagerly for the führer, who arrived accompanied by his bodyguard Martin Bormann and his German shepherd dog. Everyone stood and saluted him when he took his seat at the table. He greeted the guests humbly, in a soft voice. Kara thought he was a much different man privately than he was when he was speaking publicly. She'd always thought he was loud and aggressive, but today he was quiet.

A band played traditional German folk tunes, and the banquet was overflowing with lavish foods.

As they sat eating, Bormann asked Oskar, "How do you like the hotel?"

"It's very nice," Oskar said.

"Of course, we arranged for you two to have one of the best rooms. You do have a bathroom in your room, don't you?"

"Yes, and the room is lovely. The view is exceptional too. Of course, nothing compares to this," Oskar said, indicating the view from where they sat.

"I know, the Eagle's Nest is a special place," Bormann said. "That's why I commissioned this retreat for our führer."

"The Hotel zum Türken has quite a story behind it," Dr. Goebbels said.

"Oh?" Oskar said.

"Yes, in 1933 it was owned by a man by the name of Herr Schuster. One night, several SS officers were at the bar there; they were drinking. I suppose they were loud and carrying on a bit. But would you believe he tried to throw them out? He said he didn't want them in his hotel. The nerve," Goebbels said.

"I was there," Bormann said. "Schuster was an arrogant lout. I told him he had better sell us the hotel. He refused. That's when I decided that he needed to be taught a lesson. So, I had him arrested. Three weeks of torture in Dachau put him right. After that he agreed to sell it to the party. And that's how we acquired it."

Oskar glanced at Kara. She'd put her fork down. Her face had gone pale. Eva Braun must have seen it too. She smiled and said, "Let's not talk about torture on this beautiful day."

"I'm sorry, Eva. I didn't mean to put a damper on your gathering. I just thought everyone should know a little about the history of the hotel."

"I completely understand." Eva smiled. Then she added, "More beer or wine, anyone?"

And the band began to play another tune.

Once everyone had finished eating, they all gathered into a large living room with comfortable chairs and sofas. A young blonde girl with braids wrapped around her head served them glasses of schnapps as they enjoyed the warmth of a roaring fire. The band now played sing-along music, and everyone joined in. Karl and the other children sat on the floor in the corner together.

When the band stopped to take a break, Oskar said admiringly, "That's a magnificent fireplace. "What is it made of?"

"Red marble," the führer answered. "It was a gift from Mussolini."

"Poor man that Mussolini is. He's a bit of a fool, I'm afraid. His own people seem to be turning against him. Still, at least he is our ally," Dr. Goebbels said.

"It's a good thing that the German people are devoted to our führer. That would never happen here," Martin Bormann said confidently.

Hitler glanced over at Bormann. Oskar thought he detected myriad emotions running across the führer's face. Distrust, disbelief, sadness, but most of all anger. Hitler muttered, "Hmmm," and nodded in acknowledgment at the remark, but he did not offer any other comment.

Oskar saw the look on Hitler's face, and he thought, *Look at Hitler. He's not so sure of himself. I think he is worried about being overthrown. If I were to wager, I'd bet he is remembering how Henning Von Tresckow tried to kill him last month with that bomb. All of the men here know what happened, yet not one of us would dare mention it. But, to win his favor, I'll propose a toast.*

Oskar stood up. He held his glass of schnapps up high in the air and said, "To our führer, and to our Reich. May we reign for a thousand years."

Everyone raised their glasses and in unison said, "Prost! Heil Hitler."

Adolf Hitler smiled and nodded his head at Oskar.

CHAPTER EIGHTEEN

WHEN ABRAM and Moishe were called to the office of the oberstrumführer one evening after they returned from the mine, they shot a frightened glance at each other. But they had no choice but to follow the guard who escorted them silently to the office. As they walked through the camp, Abram was worried that somehow Oberstrumführer Lerch had learned the truth about Abram, Kara, and Karl. This was a truth that Abram had learned only last month when he and Moishe had gone to the oberstrumführer's home to build a garden. Abram was Kara's lover before he was arrested and until he saw her and his son, Karl, living with the oberstrumführer, he had no idea what had happened to his family. But when he saw them, and he saw that they were alive, he vowed to God that he would do whatever he must in order to reunite with his loved ones.

Abram was trembling now as he and Moishe entered the oberstrumführer's office. However, he was not worried as much about himself as he was about Kara and Karl. If this evil man had learned the truth, what would he do to Abram's family? Abram would rather die than see Kara or Karl hurt.

Behind the desk sat Oberstrumführer Lerch, with a genuine

smile on his face and two hunks of bread on the desk in front of him.

"Good evening," he said, handing one piece of bread each to Moishe and Abram. Although they were both starving, neither of them took a bite. They watched Lerch skeptically. "Sit down," the oberstrumführer said as he nodded, motioning to the chairs. "Go on. Sit."

Moishe and Abram shot each other a look but they sat.

"You boys did such a good job on that garden you built for my wife that I wanted to let you know that you will be going to my home next week to maintain it. And I thought you might enjoy a bit of extra bread as a reward for your good work."

"Thank you," Moishe and Abram muttered without looking directly into the oberstrumführer's eyes.

"That's all," Oskar Lerch said. "You stink so bad that I can't bear to have you in my office." Then looking over at the guard who waited quietly at the door, he instructed the man, "Take them back to their block now."

Without hesitation, Abram and Moishe stood up, tucked the bread into their shirts, and left the office. The guard nudged them with the butt of his rifle and they walked quickly back to their block. Once they were alone, Abram whispered, "Do you think he knows about me and Kara?"

"I don't think so. If he did, he would have done something to us."

"Possibly. Or he could be playing a trick on me. You know how they are. They love to do that," Abram said. "They love to play with people's hearts and their emotions."

"I don't think so," Moishe said as he began to gobble the bread he'd been given.

"It's crucial that he does not find out anything, or he might hurt Kara or Karl."

"I still can't believe that the oberstrumführer's wife is your Kara. And the boy who was with her is your son. Are you sure you weren't just imagining these things? Sometimes our own minds play tricks on us. We miss someone so much that we think we see them when, in fact, it is not them at all."

"Moishe, I am sure. I am sure that is my Kara and the boy with her is my son, Karl. Yes, he is older. But it is him. I would know my son anywhere."

"I can't figure out how she could have come to be married to the oberstrumführer? I can't understand it. Are you sure it was them and not just a woman and child who looked like them?"

"Oh yes, I am certain it was them. I don't know what happened. I can't understand how she ended up with him. I have millions of questions too. But this I know. I know it was her."

"She's Jewish?"

"No, she is not. But, of course, my son is half Jewish. And I fear for him because of it," Abram said. "The oberstrumführer has taken so much from me, but the worst thing he has done is that he has stolen my family. When I think of his filthy hands on my Kara, it tears me to pieces."

Moishe nodded. Then with a mouth full of bread, he said, "Maybe this is God's way of shooting life back into you. No?"

"What are you talking about?"

"Until you saw Kara again, you had lost all hope. Every day was a struggle to keep you from finding a way to kill yourself. Now, there is a driving force inside of you again. You want to live."

Abram took a deep breath and contemplated what Moishe was saying.

Then Moishe went on, "What if she married him to find you? What if she has been searching for you?"

"Anything is possible in these terrible times in which we live," Abram said. "Anything at all."

"Next week, we'll be at the house again. You will have an opportunity to see her," Moishe said. "Perhaps even to speak to her."

Abram's heart raced. As hungry as he was, he couldn't eat. "Can you imagine?" he said, his voice barely a whisper.

"I can," Moishe said.

"But as much as I want to speak to her, I would rather die than put her or my child in danger."

"That's true. You know, she could be a very clever girl, and that's why she is with him."

"She is a very smart girl," Abram said.

"Well, wouldn't marrying an oberstrumführer keep her and her half-Jewish son safe from the Nazis?" Moishe said.

"Yes, you're right. It would. When I saw her with him, I was so hurt that I wasn't thinking straight. But, you're right, that would be the smartest thing she could do. Being married to him, no one would ever suspect Karl of being half Jewish. She could protect his secret."

"Exactly," Moishe said.

CHAPTER NINETEEN

KARA WASN'T FEELING WELL. Although she was only in the first trimester of this pregnancy, it was already hard on her. She had constant heartburn and morning sickness that lasted all day. Instead of gaining weight, she was losing. Oskar insisted that she see the doctor each month so he could monitor her condition. And the last time she'd gone to see him, the doctor was concerned about her weight loss. If she could have, she would have slept all day, but even though she was tired all the time, she forced herself to get out of bed for Karl's sake.

Each morning she rose and got him ready for school. Preparing breakfast for Karl and her husband was exhausting, but she felt certain that it gave them both a solid start to their day, so she made the effort. However, once they'd both gone off to school and work, she lay down and slept so deeply that she often didn't awaken until Karl returned home. Then she would remember that she'd forgotten to eat that day, and although she had no appetite, she forced herself to sip on a cup of tea and eat two slices of dry bread. Keeping it down was another story. Many times, she vomited as soon as she finished eating.

There was no doubt in her mind that Oskar loved her. He was a good man, a kind man, who treated her and Karl with such tenderness that it brought tears to her eyes. And yet, deep in her heart, hidden away, unseen by anyone, was the love she felt for her first and only love, Abram, Karl's father. Even if he was dead, and she believed wholeheartedly that he was, she could never let go of those feelings. Abram had given her hope and taught her to love after her abusive father's mistreatment of her, which had left her believing that all men were horrible sexual predators.

Abram had changed her mind about men with his soft, gentle, and understanding ways. Sometimes she would still dream of him, dreams so vivid that she could almost feel his arms around her, his kiss on her lips, his eyes locked on to her own. When she had these dreams, she would awaken with tears covering her cheeks, and a longing for the past that was so strong, it left her feeling angry and helpless with a deep empty pit in her stomach.

On his days off, Oskar made every effort to help Kara with everything she had to do in the house. Most German officers would not have considered doing the work of a hausfrau, but Oskar loved Kara, and he would move heaven and earth for her if he could. Nothing was too hard. He tried to do the wash, and he prepared food to the best of his ability, which was lacking. Karl, who was a precocious six-year-old boy, told his mother as much. "I hate it when Vater cooks. The food is terrible, and he expects me to eat it."

Kara would ruffle Karl's blond hair and say, "You wouldn't want to hurt Vati's feelings, would you?"

To which Karl replied, by shaking his head and whispering, "No, I guess I'll just try to eat it."

Kara looked at the calendar to assure herself that she had a doctor's appointment today. *Yes, I am right; it's today,* she thought. *I hate to go there. He is going to be so angry with me because I think I have lost more weight.* She shook her head as she walked toward the bathroom to wash her face and brush her teeth. But she was stopped by the ringing of the telephone. *It's probably Oskar calling to make sure I haven't forgotten the appointment today,* she thought as she walked over to the phone and picked up the receiver.

"Allo," she said.

"Kara, it's me." She recognized her sister Anka's voice.

"Anka, how are you?"

"I'm all right. But I had no idea how difficult it was going to be raising a child." With Oskar's help, Anka and her husband, Ludwig, had recently adopted Gretel, an infant, from the home for the Lebensborn.

"Yes, it certainly is a lot of work," Kara agreed. "I remember when Karl was an infant. It can be exhausting."

"I need your help. Sometimes she just cries for no reason, and she won't stop. It unnerves me."

"Check her to see if she's hungry or wet. If she's not, just walk with her or rock her."

"I've tried. I need to see you. I want to see if you can help me figure out what I am doing wrong. Ludwig has a few days off; we were thinking we might come for a visit."

"Of course. Oskar and I would love to have you," Kara said. But it wasn't exactly true. Kara loved her sister. After all, with the miserable parents they'd had, Kara had practically raised Anka. However, Anka had grown up to be needy, dependent, and often downright selfish. And now, with Kara not feeling herself, she didn't think she could manage to take care of Karl, her husband, her sister, and her sister's child. And she knew that this was exactly what would happen when Anka came to visit. Still, she couldn't find it in her heart to deny her sister's wish to see her. "So, when are you planning on coming?"

"Sunday afternoon. We'll stay until Wednesday if that's all right."

Sunday, Monday, Tuesday, if they're leaving Wednesday that's only three days. That won't be so bad. "It sounds splendid," Kara said, forcing herself to sound enthusiastic. Patches, the dog Oskar had purchased for Karl, nudged Kara's hand. She reached up and scratched between his ears. Before Oskar had brought Patches home, Kara had been afraid of dogs. But Patches had found his way into her heart, and now she adored the silly mutt. Glancing at the clock, she realized she had to leave the house, or she would be late to her doctor's appointment. "Sunday through Wednesday would be perfect. But I'm sorry I have to hang up now. I have an appointment, and I can't be late."

"What kind of appointment?" Anka asked, concerned.

Kara hadn't told her sister about the pregnancy yet, and she didn't have time right now. "I'll explain when I see you."

"Is everything all right?" Anka asked, a slight tone of panic in her voice. "You're not sick, are you? If you need me, I'll come earlier."

"No, no, you wait for Ludwig to bring you and the baby. Please don't worry about me. I promise you everything is fine. But I must go now."

"All right, then I'll see you on Sunday. I love you, Kara."

"I love you too, Anka."

Kara didn't have time to freshen up. She was running late now. So she grabbed her handbag and dashed outside.

Bertram, the Lerches' driver, stood outside the black automobile waiting for Kara. He'd returned to the house after driving Oskar to work to be available to drive Kara to her appointment. He was a middle-aged man who never said much. Oskar had hired him after firing their previous driver, a young, handsome man who was always eyeing Kara. Kara gave Bertram a quick smile as she and Karl got into the car. "I'm sorry it took me so long to leave the house; my sister called."

"I understand, Frau Lerch. But we must hurry, so you're not late for your appointment," Bertram said as he closed her door.

She nodded. He got into the car and began to drive quicky but carefully toward town. Bertram was always considerate and never asked her any questions. Yet he somehow made her uncomfortable. He seemed to be watching everyone and everything. And she knew, because Oskar had told her, that he was very devoted to the Nazi Party.

They drove through town quietly and stopped to drop Karl off at school. She was glad he didn't chatter like some of the other servants Oskar hired, because her mind was on Anka. She was dreading her sister's arrival. She wasn't feeling well enough for all the work that would be involved in helping her sister.

CHAPTER TWENTY

THE OPEN-BED TRUCK carrying Moishe and Abram pulled up in front of the oberstrumführer's home just as the car carrying Kara and Karl away to her doctor's appointment turned the corner. Forced to exit the truck quickly at gunpoint, Moishe and Abram were commanded to start working on the garden.

"You have only a couple of hours to finish this job. And it better be finished in time. And it better be done well," the guard said. "So mach schnell."

Moishe and Abram shot glances at each other, and between those glances Abram looked at the windows of the house. He didn't know that Kara was not inside. And he was on edge. Just the very idea that Kara was so close to him, right inside that brick building, made his palms sweat and his heart tighten. *I have to see her. I have to look at her and touch her with my eyes. But maybe it's best that she doesn't see me. I don't want to do anything to her that might make her life more difficult. Right now, she probably thinks I am dead,* he thought as he worked pruning and planting, removing the dead plants and replacing them with new ones. Abram didn't know how much time passed. He worked robotically without thinking about what he was doing. His mind was on Kara, and his eyes continually drifted back to the house.

"It's time to go. I must admit the garden looks good. Now, get in the truck." The guard nudged Abram in his bony ribs with the butt of a rifle. Then he nudged Moishe.

Abram looked over at Moishe, who nodded subtly. They both climbed into the bed of the truck. Then the guard jumped in the back, and the driver drove away.

When they arrived back at the camp, Abram sat down on his cot. "I thought for sure I would see her today. I am so confused. I want her to see me. I want her to know I am alive and that I love her, and I love our son more than anything in the world. And yet I am afraid that if she sees me, it will hurt her to know that I am alive. I would rather die than hurt her." He hesitated for a moment. Then in a soft voice, he said, "I am also worried that maybe she doesn't even love me anymore."

"I know. You have so many questions, so many emotions, and who could blame you?"

"I am starting to feel despair again. Like it's all hopeless."

"I know. But you must not lose heart. God has a plan. I'm sure we are going back there to work on the garden again," Moishe said, trying to manage a smile.

"How can I not lose heart? When I think of the woman I love lying beneath that terrible man, I feel like dying. I don't where God is, or what he is thinking. How could he abandon his people in a place like this? You tell me, Moishe. You tell me where God is?"

"I don't always understand why God does what he does. But I know he has a plan."

"But what is that plan? How can we possibly understand it when we see men being beaten to death right in front of our eyes?"

Moishe shook his head. "Don't lose faith, Abram. Losing faith is one of the most dangerous things you can do. Then you give the Nazis complete power over you. Right now, they might have control of your body, but you control your mind and spirit. Don't give them that too."

"I know what you're saying. I know you're right. But, my wife, the only woman I have ever loved, the mother of my child, is living with a monster, who murders Jews for fun. How am I supposed to feel? I ask myself, why? Over and over, I ask myself why she married him?"

"I told you before, that I think she probably married him to protect herself and Karl." Moishe touched Abram's shoulder.

"I have thought of that, and I know you are probably right. She had no choice but to find and marry one of them. It would be the only way she could protect Karl and herself. But believe me, that makes it even worse. I can't protect her or my son. I am good for nothing. I can't protect anyone. I am stuck here in this hell. No longer even a man, just a broken piece of flesh that . . ." Abram's voice cracked. He didn't want to cry. *Men don't cry*, he thought, but the tears came anyway. They fell down his face. Moishe looked away, not wanting to embarrass his best friend. But then he turned back to Abram and said, "There's no shame in crying."

Abram nodded, wiping the tears from his cheeks with his uniform sleeve. "Things just shouldn't be this way," he said. "I owe her so much more." Then he added, "And if she doesn't love me anymore"—his voice cracked—"maybe it's best for her."

Moishe didn't say anything; he just patted Abram's shoulder.

CHAPTER TWENTY-ONE

DR. KAISER, the doctor who served the German community in Poland where Kara lived, was a man of small structure. The skin on his cheeks and chin hung lifelessly. His face was deeply lined, and his cheekbones jutted out like giant waves rising on the water. Smiling at her gently with colorless lips, and fixing his pale rheumy blue eyes on Kara, he said gently, "Frau Lerch, you are losing too much weight. You should be gaining. This is not good."

"I know. I try, Dr. Kaiser, but I can't eat. I feel sick all the time."

"You must try harder. For the sake of your unborn child. For the sake of your husband who loves you, and, of course, for the sake of the fatherland. This is a pure Aryan child you carry in your womb."

She nodded. "I am trying. I promise you; I am trying. But as soon as I swallow, the food comes back up."

"Are you getting outside, getting enough fresh air? How about exercise?"

"Not as much as I should. I am so tired, Doctor. I always want to lie down, and as soon as I lay my head on the pillow, I fall asleep," Kara said. *Oh, how I wish I had a bowl of Hoda's matzo-ball soup. She always made it when one of us wasn't feeling well, and it always helped. I can still remember how comforting that hot soup was. Dear God, I hope Hoda is all right.*

The doctor gave her a firm look. "I want you to make an effort. No matter how exhausted you feel, you must take a walk every day. This will help build your appetite and will also make sure you get plenty of fresh air."

"Doctor, I'm afraid that the smell outside makes me sick to my stomach. Oskar says it's from the chemical plants that are nearby. But it is an absolutely nauseating odor."

"I understand. But the smell won't hurt you. And, for the sake of your unborn child, you must try to get some exercise and fresh air."

She nodded. He hadn't told her anything new. "Well"—she tried to smile—"my sister is coming to visit next week. I'm sure she will find a way to get me out of the house," Kara said.

"Yes, the more you can get out, the better."

"She likes to get out and do things. So, I am sure she will not only have me walking, but we'll be shopping and going to the beauty salon."

"That will be good for you. I want you to come and see me again in three weeks. When you come next time, I'd like to see you gaining some weight. All right?"

"All right," Kara answered, hoping that maybe the doctor was right. If she got out more, she might have more of an appetite. But right now, she couldn't imagine eating a single bite of bread.

CHAPTER TWENTY-TWO

EARLY ON SUNDAY MORNING, Anka arrived with Ludwig. He was carrying Gretel in his arms. Patches began barking even before they reached the door. Oskar lay beside Kara, sleeping soundly. Kara opened her eyes as soon as she heard Patches barking. Then she heard the knock on the front door. She knew it was the day Anka was scheduled to arrive. But she hadn't expected her to come so early. Grabbing her robe and flinging it on, she ran down the stairs and opened the door.

"Kara!!!" Anka said as she hugged her sister tightly. "How are you? My gosh, how I missed you." Then she was quiet for a moment. "You're so thin. You've lost a lot of weight."

"Yes, I have."

"Are you ill?"

"No, I'm fine." Kara managed a smile. "Come in and sit down. Ludwig, let me go and get a blanket, so you can put the baby down. She must be heavy."

"What about the dog?" Ludwig said, eyeing Patches suspiciously. "Won't he hurt the baby?"

"No, he is as gentle as can be. I promise you, there is no need to be afraid of Patches. He won't hurt anyone."

"Ludwig can't stay," Anka said as she plopped down on the sofa. "He was supposed to be off from work for a few days, but he was called in. So, he has to go right back home."

"Oh, I am so sorry. We would have enjoyed having you," Kara said, trying to sound full of life and enthusiasm, but the truth was she was tired. "Do you have to leave right this minute?"

"In an hour or so," Ludwig said.

"How about some coffee and some breakfast before you go?" Kara offered.

"That sounds wonderful," Anka said. "I'll help you prepare everything."

Kara smiled and walked into the kitchen.

"Everyone is still asleep?" Anka asked.

"Yes, Oskar and Karl are still sleeping. I am surprised Karl didn't hear the dog barking," Kara said, "but he is probably exhausted. Yesterday, Oskar took him fishing. They were gone from early in the morning until it started getting dark. I'm sure spending the day in the sun tired him out."

"Oskar likes to fish?"

"Not really," Kara laughed. "He does it for Karl."

"He's a good husband and father."

"Yes, he is," Kara said.

"And, you are so lucky; he's handsome too."

Kara let out a laugh. "I guess he is. I can't believe you still care about looks. I don't even think anymore about him being handsome.
"

"Of course you don't. That's because he is. But still, I don't know how it doesn't affect you. If he were mine, I would be making love to him all the time. He is quite a catch. Handsome, successful. What more could you want?"

"Ludwig is a good husband."

"I suppose. But he's not handsome or tremendously successful," Anka moaned.

"Most importantly, he loves you. I know that for sure."

"Yes, I just wish I felt the same toward him," Anka whispered. "There's just no magic with us. I'm bored. I feel like I've been cheated out of love and romance. I feel like I am stuck with a boring man. Do you know what I mean?"

"I know what you're saying. But you haven't been cheated. Ludwig would do anything for you."

Anka put her lips to her sister's ear and whispered very softly. "But he's not exciting like the men we used to read about in those forbidden books." Then she added, "Oskar is like one of those men. He's wildly handsome, sexy . . ."

Kara shook her head as the coffee began to percolate.

"Is he good in bed?" Anka asked, still whispering.

"Anka! What a question."

"I'm your sister. You can tell me anything."

Kara laughed, "I don't want to talk about this."

"Well, I'll talk about it. I will tell you that Ludwig is not! That much I can assure you." Anka's voice was a mixture of sarcasm and sadness.

"Shhh, he'll hear you," Kara said. "He's right in the other room."

"I don't give a damn."

"Anka, what is it?" Kara put the cups down on the counter and faced her sister.

"We're talking about separating. Things have not been the same since we adopted the baby."

Kara stared at her sister. There were so many things she wanted to say but couldn't bring herself to say them. Anka looked so tired and sad. It was not like her to be anything but carefree. Kara knew Anka had never loved Ludwig. But she thought they were well suited to each other. Although Anka was childish and demanding, Ludwig overlooked her shortcomings. He gave her whatever she asked for, including adopting a child. So why would she want to leave him now? What had happened? "Is that why Ludwig is not staying here with us. Does he really have to return to work? Or is he just returning home?"

Anka nodded. "That's why he's leaving. We need time apart from each other." Her eyes became glassy with unshed tears. "I don't know what to do, Kara. I'm just not happy. I want more from life. I want love, and romance, and excitement. Do you understand?"

Kara nodded and took her sister into her arms. She understood Anka better than anyone. Anka depended on Kara. It had been that way since they were small children, and Kara had been like a mother to her younger sister, sheltering Anka from their abusive father and the guilt their submissive mother laid on them. Now, as adults, whenever Kara was around, Anka seemed to become a child again, leaning on her sister for everything. "We'll work this all out. Don't you worry," Kara assured her sister, although she wasn't sure if she would be able to. "Don't cry. Everything will be all right."

"Oh, Kara, what would I ever do without you?"

Kara touched her sister's shiny blonde curls and said, "Don't even think about that. Why don't you have a nice cup of coffee, and I'll finish preparing breakfast for you and Ludwig before he leaves."

Anka nodded. Kara got up and poured her sister a cup of steaming coffee. Then she started cooking.

After Kara finished scrambling some eggs and buttering bread, she went into the living room where she found Ludwig rocking a sleeping Gretel in his arms. "Come and eat. I made breakfast," Kara said.

"No, it's all right. I should be going. Do you have a crib for her?" he asked.

Kara nodded. "I had to use a dresser drawer because I didn't have one. But I filled it with blankets so it's very cozy. She'll be very comfortable. If I would have had a little more time, I would have purchased a crib. I'll make sure to get one for the next time you come to visit. Come, follow me. I'll show you where it is."

Ludwig followed Kara into a bright cheery room with a drawer filled with blankets that stood beside a small bed. He lay the sleeping child in the drawer. Kara looked down into the baby's face. "She is quite a beauty," Kara marveled.

"Yes, she is. Isn't she? Blonde, blue eyed. A perfect Aryan daughter. The Lebensborn is very careful about breeding children, and you can tell when you look at her. She is perfect," Ludwig said.

Kara didn't particularly like the idea of breeding children. But she didn't want to discuss that with Ludwig right now. He looked so sad that Kara almost put her arms around him. But she stopped herself. It might give him the wrong idea. Instead, she just smiled. "Are you sure you can't stay for a day or two?" she asked, hoping he might change his mind and try to work things out with her sister.

"No, I really can't. It's my work. I'm sure you understand."

"Yes, of course."

The baby was sleeping soundly, so they walked out of the room and quietly closed the door. Kara hoped Karl wouldn't wake the baby when he got up. He was always noisy and full of boundless energy first thing in the morning. Descending the stairs, Kara thought about all the things she wanted to ask Ludwig. She longed to intervene, to somehow help him and her sister solve all of their problems. But she didn't know how. So she remained silent.

Without saying goodbye to his wife, Ludwig went to the door. "Well, I must be going. Please tell Oskar that I am sorry I couldn't stay to visit with him," he said.

"He should be awake in less than an hour," Kara said, almost pleading.

"Yes, and I would love to stay and wait for him, but I must get on the road. I have to get back to work." He gave her a sad smile. It was so sad that she had to look away.

"I'll tell him that you send your good wishes."

"Thank you, Kara," Ludwig said. "Take care of her."

Kara nodded. Ludwig walked out the door closing it quietly behind him.

CHAPTER TWENTY-THREE

THE HEAT OUTSIDE WAS RELENTLESS. All day long, Abram sweated as he labored in the mine. But his thoughts were about Kara. He was concerned that his mind was playing tricks on him, and he hadn't really seen her when he and Moishe were working on the garden at the oberstrumführer's house. Doubt began to creep in. *Could I have been mistaken? Maybe I only thought I saw her the last time we were there. Maybe it was just a vision. I think of her so often that perhaps when I see a woman, I envision her as Kara. Hunger and this relentless heat can make a man see things that aren't there. Could it be possible that I am seeing things?*

He remembered sitting in the bed of the truck, exhausted from working on the garden. His finger was dripping blood because he'd cut it on one of the stones. Looking down, he'd watched the blood as it dripped onto the floor of the truck. The driver had started the engine, and they were about to pull away from the oberstrumführer's home when he'd heard her voice, clear as a silver bell. Raising his head up, he saw her standing beside their son, Karl. *No, it was no mirage. It was them, my wife and my son. I know every inch of Kara's face and body. The memory of running my fingers through her soft, golden hair has kept me from suicide on many nights as I lay on that cot. So where was she that afternoon? Probably out for the day cavorting with other Nazi wives?*

His thoughts were so confusing that he couldn't concentrate on his work. But he also could not stop for even a second, or he would be shot. When Abram hammered his thumb, he almost let out a cry. Not daring to scream and alert the foreman, who might beat him for slowing down for a second, he bit his lip against the pain and quietly cursed. He sucked in deep breaths until the pain was manageable.

Then the thoughts returned. *Is it possible that she saw me? Maybe she looked out the window and cringed because she didn't want anything to do with me? Dear God, maybe my wife has become one of them. Could my Kara have turned her back on the Jews? I know it would be easier for her and Karl if she did. Logically, if I think with my head instead of my heart, I know it would be better for her if she didn't see me, if she didn't ever find out that I am alive. They are safe, my wife and son. They are protected by the very man who torments me. I hate him. I would kill him in an instant if I could. But, at the same time, it does bring me relief to know they are alive . . . and safe.*

CHAPTER TWENTY-FOUR

As she always did, Anka unloaded all of her responsibilities on Kara's shoulders. It had been that way since they were young. Kara acted as Anka's mother. And even though they were now fully grown women, when they were alone together, they easily fell right back into the same familiar pattern. Kara took care of Gretel and Karl while Anka stood by and told Kara all of her problems. It wouldn't have been so bad for Kara had she not been feeling so sick. Anka talked incessantly about how angry she was with Ludwig, and Kara couldn't seem to find the right time to interrupt her to tell her that she was pregnant.

Little Gretel was a joy to Kara. Although it was a lot of extra work having a very young child around, caring for Gretel brought back memories of her life when Karl was small. As she changed a diaper or held the baby in her arms, inhaling the sweet scent of her soft skin, Kara's mind would travel back to the golden days she'd spent with Abram. She thought about how they'd watched little Karl as he slept. Together they examined his tiny fingers and ears, marveling at the wonders of their child. It was a bittersweet feeling that made her heart ache with tenderness followed by tears of loss.

Each morning since Anka arrived, after Oskar left for work, she and Kara had breakfast. Then Anka went outside to sit under the large weeping willow tree in the yard and stare out at the garden while Kara fed the children. A week passed. Anka was supposed to have left after a few days, but Kara began to realize that her sister had no intentions of returning home. She needed to talk to Anka, to find out what happened between her and Ludwig to break them up, and she also needed to know whether Anka intended to stay with her indefinitely. With a blanket in one arm and the baby in the other, Kara called out to her son who was playing with the dog in his room, "Karl, bring Patches, and come outside with me, please."

"Can I bring his ball, so he can fetch it?"

"Yes, of course."

Karl, with the dog at his heels, followed his mother into the yard.

"Please keep an eye on Gretel while you play. All right? Make sure that the dog doesn't step on her," Kara said as she laid the blanket on the ground under the shade of an oak tree and then carefully placed Gretel on the blanket.

"Yes, Mutti. I will," Karl said.

She ruffled his hair. "You're such a good boy," she said, remembering with a smile, how when he was just a small child, people often mistook him for a girl because she had refused to cut his hair. Now he was looking more and more grown-up every day. He resembled her mostly, but there were times when she would see tiny bits of Abram in the way he walked or the way he looked at her. Kara let out a sigh. *Oh, Abram, we were doomed from the start. And yet, I don't regret a single moment with you.*

"Fetch the ball!" Karl was telling Patches, who had settled next to Gretel with his muzzle in her lap.

"He won't fetch today, Mutti."

"Maybe he doesn't feel like it. So, why don't you sit with Patches and Gretel, and tell them a story, like I tell you stories."

"Good idea," Karl said. Then he began, "Once upon a time . . ."

As Kara walked over to Anka, her mind flashed back to their childhood when the two of them had hid under the covers, and she told Anka stories. No wonder my son is so good at telling tales. *His mother was a storyteller, and his father was a bookseller.* She and Anka had shared a room when they were living with their parents. From that room, they could hear when their parents were fighting and screaming at each other. It happened often. And on the mornings following one of their screaming matches, their mother had bruises or black eyes. They came to know that their father was beating their mother, and the sound terrified them. Anka had clung to Kara during those nights. She would tremble, unnerved by the sounds. That is how story time began. In order to distract her sister, Kara had told her stories or read her books. So began the love they shared for literature. And it was that love that had led her to Abram. The greatest love of her life.

Kara plopped down on the grass beside Anka. "How are you feeling?"

Anka shrugged. "Confused."

"I know you are angry with Ludwig. But you still haven't explained why. Do you want to tell me what happened?" Kara said, taking Anka's small white hand into her own.

"Ludwig had an affair."

"What?" Kara was genuinely shocked. She'd never thought Ludwig would cheat on Anka. Not in a million years. He adored her. In fact, he adored her so much that he put up with her constant badgering of him. "I don't believe it."

"I didn't believe it either. I would never have thought anyone would want him. But I know the truth, and you can believe it. He cheated on me," Anka said.

"Oh, Anka. I'm so sorry."

"I never loved him. So, why do I care so much?" She shook her head. "What does she have that I don't? Is she prettier than me? I've seen her, and I don't think she is. Is she smarter? Perhaps. I don't know how smart she is. If she is, what is she doing with Ludwig? Boring, boring Ludwig."

"I am so sorry."

"Kara, I am so hurt. How could he do that, when he had me?"

Kara didn't know what to say, so she squeezed her sister's hand. "Men cheat for millions of reasons. Do you know the woman?"

"You are never going to believe it, but it's a girl who he met at the Lebensborn when we were there to fill out the papers for adoption for Gretel. Her name is Aloisa Altner; she works there. He would go to see her in Munich, taking time off work and leaving me alone with the baby for days. What nerve."

"When you found out about it, did he end it?"

"That's just it. No, he refuses to end it," Anka said, then she let out a long breath. "When I confronted him and asked him where he goes all the time, he didn't even try to deny it. He said, 'I've met someone else. I am sorry.' That's what he said." Anka shook her head. "Then do you know what else he said to me? He told me that she cares for him. He says she respects him the way I never did. He claims he got tired of my constant criticism of him." Tears began to run down Anka's cheeks. "Was I that bad to him?"

"You weren't kind to him, Anka," Kara said as gently as she could.

Anka huffed. Then she said in a small voice, "I suppose I wasn't. But it was hard to be kind to him. He got on my nerves; he could be such a damn fool most of the time."

"I'm so sorry."

"I hope it's all right; I need to stay here with you for a while. I don't know where else to go. But I can't stay in that house with him, knowing he is seeing that other woman."

"Of course it's all right. You're my sister. You can stay with us as long as you like," Kara said. She was tired and feeling ill. But she would never turn Anka away no matter how hard things were for her. *She is my sister, my blood. She took Karl and I in when Abram was arrested.*

"I need a distraction. Can we go shopping one day this week perhaps?" Anka asked, her blue eyes shining like a child's.

"Of course. We'll take the children with us."

"I would love to leave them at home with a sitter, but I am sure that there is nothing I can say that would convince you to do that," Anka said.

Kara shook her head. "No, you're right. I would never leave the children with strangers. Not after that terrible fiasco I went through when Karl was kidnapped. I am so grateful to have him back that I never let him out of my sight."

"I understand." Anka looked a little disappointed.

"However, we can still go," Kara said, trying to make Anka feel better. "You'll see; the children won't be much trouble. I'll ask Oskar if we can use his driver for the day. I'm sure he won't mind."

"Oh, Kara you're so lucky." Anka sighed. "You've always been luckier than me. You have a handsome SS officer for a husband. When you walk down the street with him, the women look at you with envy. And not only that, but he loves you so much. I wish I had a man like Oskar."

"Let's not think about men today. Let's just enjoy the sunshine. Look at the children," Kara said, pointing to Karl who was telling Gretel a story. "They are getting on so well. Karl is so grown up and so good with the baby."

"I was afraid of the dog at first. The only dogs I know of are the guard dogs that Ludwig tells me about. And they are vicious, but she seems so sweet."

"Patches?" Kara laughed. "She is such a sweet animal. I was afraid of dogs, too, before we got her. Now I love her. She's like a member of the family. I talk to her when I feel down. And she listens, but she never offers advice."

"I'm sure she doesn't." Anka laughed. Then Kara laughed too.

"It's going to be all right," Kara said. "You're here with me now. I'll help you like I always have."

Anka pulled her sister into an embrace. "Kara, I don't know how to thank you."

"Stop that. You know you never have to thank me. I'm your sister. That's what sisters are for. When things go bad, we are there for each other, right?"

"Right," Anka said.

CHAPTER TWENTY-FIVE

THAT NIGHT when Kara and Oskar were alone in their room, she turned to him, and in a whisper, she said, "Anka and Ludwig are having serious problems in their marriage."

"What's wrong?" He sat up on one elbow. He'd been lying in bed waiting for her to come to him. Opening the covers for her and patting the bed, he waited while she climbed in beside him.

"He is having an affair, I guess."

"Ludwig? With another woman? I'm surprised."

"Yes, I was surprised too. But he was, and from what Anka says, he still is. Would you believe it's the woman from the Lebensborn who assisted them in the adoption?"

Oskar tensed up. He was caught off guard. Hardly expecting this, his voice was filled with more concern than he would have liked. "Which one? What was her name?"

"Aloisa Altner," Kara said. "I am pretty sure you know her. She is the same woman that you introduced them to when they went to adopt Gretel."

A shiver ran down Oskar's back. For a moment frown lines appeared on his forehead, but then he seemed to catch himself and smiled at Kara. "I can't imagine Ludwig and Altner. What a strange situation." There was a nervousness about him that Kara had not seen before.

"Seriously, why are you so upset about this?" Kara said.

"I'm not upset." He forced himself to let out a short laugh. "I'm just shocked, that's all. Ludwig is such a dull man. I wouldn't think a girl like Aloisa would be interested in him."

"You seem upset."

Oskar cleared his throat. "I feel bad too, because it was me who set up the entire adoption. I wouldn't want to be responsible for their breaking up."

"Nonsense. Of course, it's not your fault. You had nothing to do with this part of it. Ludwig is a full-grown man; he should know better."

Oskar gave her another strained smile. "He should, and so should she."

There were a few moments of silence. He touched her arm. She glanced over at him. She knew by the look in his eyes that he wanted to make love. But before they began, she wanted to make sure she had the use of their driver so that she could fulfill her promise to Anka.

"Oskar, is it possible that Anka and I can have Bertram drive us around next week? We want to go into town and do a little shopping? I was thinking perhaps on Monday if that's all right with you."

"Yes, of course," he said. "Anything for you."

She lay her head on his chest.

"Thank you," she said. He was gently rubbing her head. "And please don't feel badly about helping Anka and Ludwig with the adoption. You're not responsible for his cheating. This is something he chose to do."

When she'd first come to bed, he been ready to make love to her. Yearning for her, in fact. But now that she'd mentioned Aloisa Altner, a woman who knew his secret about kidnapping Karl, he was so filled with worry and anxiety, that his manhood had gone limp. *Damn, sometimes I am such a fool. What was I thinking? I was so stupid as to send Ludwig and Anka to meet with Aloisa?*

I know why I did it. I thought Ludwig was too ugly for Aloisa to even notice him. And as far as he was concerned, I thought Ludwig was too far gone on his wife to ever be interested in another woman. I assumed they would make the adoption, and that would be the end of it. But now she and Ludwig are lovers. And she knows far too much to be intimate with a man who is so close to my family. If Kara ever finds out that I arranged for Karl to be kidnapped, she would never forgive me. I would lose her forever. Now I must do something before Aloisa feels close enough to Ludwig to tell him all that she knows.

He leaned over and kissed Kara. "Good night, darling. Sleep well," he said. Then he turned off the light and lay on his side, facing away from Kara. *Who would ever have thought that a simpering fool like Ludwig would have found a way to get a girl as attractive as Altner into his bed? Well, I must put a stop to it. That's all there is to it.*

Oskar couldn't sleep. His mind was racing with ideas.

The following morning Oskar got up early for work. Kara stirred in bed. She felt that his side was empty. Stretching, she got up. He was in the kitchen sipping a cup of coffee. "Do you feel all right?" she asked.

"Yes, I am fine, darling. I just didn't want to wake you. I have an early meeting."

"I would have gotten up to prepare your breakfast," she said.

"It's all right. You're having a baby. You need your rest."

"Can I prepare something for you now? I'll be quick."

"Not necessary. I have to get going."

"Are you sure, because I don't mind."

"Absolutely." He smiled and gently touched her cheek. "I'll see you this evening. Go back to bed and get some rest."

She nodded and went back to bed.

When he arrived at his office, it was quiet. His secretary hadn't arrived yet. During the night, he'd made a plan, and now he sat with his hand on the phone and a cup of coffee growing cold beside him. *I always liked Aloisa. And I don't want to kill her. Killing a young, pretty Aryan woman is a hell of a lot different than killing a Jew. I could get into a lot of trouble for this. But if she is sharing Ludwig's bed, there is no telling what secrets she will reveal to him when they are in the throes of passion. And I just can't take the risk.*

Oskar tapped on the desk for a moment. He checked the clock. It was still early; she might not even be at work yet. *But I must try. I would prefer to talk to her before anyone else comes into the office.* He picked up the receiver: "Operator, how may I help you?"

"Connect me to Steinhöring, the home for the Lebensborn in Munich."

"One moment, please, I'll connect you."

He waited a few moments, and then a woman's voice said, "This is Steinhöring. How may I help you?"

"This is Oberstrumführer Lerch. I need to speak to Aloisa Altner."

"I'm sorry, she's not at work yet. I expect her in about an hour. May I leave her a message?"

"Tell her to call me as soon as she gets in," he said. "She has my number."

"Yes, Oberstrumführer. I will give her the message."

"That's all, then," he said and hung up the phone.

Oskar was still sitting at his desk a half hour later when the phone rang. He picked up the receiver with trembling hands. "Oberstrumführer Lerch here."

"Oskar, it's Aloisa."

"Aloisa." He forced himself to sound casual, but inside he was churning with worry. "I am coming to Munich in a couple of days; I would love to see you. I need to talk with you about something."

"Of course," she said, then added, "Is something wrong?"

"It has to do with our little secret."

"You mean our secret about the little boy?"

"Yes."

"Has something happened?"

"I can't talk on the phone. We'll discuss this when I see you," he said and hung up the receiver.

CHAPTER TWENTY-SIX

ALOISA HELD her breath for a moment. She felt uneasy, although she wasn't sure why. Oskar had sounded perfectly fine. Yet she felt goose bumps rising on her arms. Something wasn't right. Every instinct in her body told her that. Since she was a little girl, she'd been able to sense danger. And that was what she was feeling right now. Once she and Ludwig had become lovers, she had come to trust him. He was always kind and willing to listen. She leaned on him in a way she'd never leaned on anyone before. And right now, because she was feeling uneasy, she decided she needed to talk to Ludwig about this. So she picked up the phone and called him.

"Darling, it's me," she said. "I need for you to come here to Munich as soon as you can."

"Why? What is it?" he said. "Are you all right?'

"I will tell you when I see you. I could be crazy. I mean, it could be nothing. But I have this terrible feeling that I am in danger. How soon can you get here?"

"I'll call in to work, and tell them there has been an emergency. Then I'll get right into my car and leave immediately," he said. "I'll be there as soon as I can."

"All right. I'll bc waiting."

CHAPTER TWENTY-SEVEN

THAT NIGHT, as they lay in the darkness side by side in their bed, Oskar told Kara he was going to have to leave for a short while on a business trip to Munich.

"Munich? You're going to Munich?" Kara said, suddenly worried about being without him when she was feeling so poorly. This pregnancy was much harder on her than her pregnancy had been with Karl. "For how long?"

"A few days. I leave tomorrow. I'll miss you terribly. But it's business. I'm sure you understand."

"Of course, darling," she said, pulling herself together. *I'll be fine. If I need anything, Anka will be here with me.*

"I'm so sorry I won't be here with you to help you entertain your sister. I know she's in a bad way and will need to be distracted."

"Don't worry about Anka. I'll take care of her. You just get your business done. And besides, I will feel better about using the driver to go shopping if you're out of town and I know you don't need him."

"You can use Bertram to drive you whenever you need him. Even when I am not away on business. He can always drop me off at work."

"Yes, but whenever I use the driver, I'm concerned that you might need to leave work early or you might need to leave work and go somewhere . . ."

"My wonderful, thoughtful wife," he said, kissing her head. "This is the perfect time for you and your sister to have a full day of shopping. I'll leave you plenty of money. Do you plan to go tomorrow?"

"I think that would be best. Anka needs to get out, and she loves to shop."

"So, of course you'll take the children?"

"Yes, we'll make a day of it. And since you're going to be out of town, we will stop and have dinner in town. There will be no need to come rushing home."

"Excellent idea. It sounds like a lovely day for you girls."

"Yes, I agree." Kara smiled. "Thank you for being so good to me," she said, but she thought, *I am glad he doesn't know how sick I have been feeling. If he did, he wouldn't go. And he might not want me to take Anka into town.*

"How else could I be, but good to you? I love you."

Leaning down, he kissed her forehead. Then ran his fingers down the side of her face. "You are so beautiful. Have I told you that before?"

She laughed, "Many times."

"Well, it's true," he said, then he got up. "I'll be right back," he said, and went into the kitchen to telephone his superior officer at home to ask for a few days off.

CHAPTER TWENTY-EIGHT

THE FOLLOWING MORNING, Oskar was packed and ready to go. After a quick breakfast, he leaned down to give Kara a long, slow kiss goodbye. "Have a good time shopping today," he said. "I left you some money on the night table in the bedroom."

She smiled at him.

The sun was fiercely hot in a clear blue sky as he went out to the car. He got into the vehicle and then looked back at the house and thought of Kara. She meant far too much to him for him to risk having Aloisa make a mistake and let his secret out. Sighing, he turned to Bertram. "Take me to the train station," he said.

His uniform was uncomfortable because it was growing hotter by the minute. If it weren't for his love for Kara, he would never have given up his automobile to take the train.

When they arrived, Bertram got out of the car and opened Oskar's door. Oskar climbed out and stretched, then he said, "Bertram, my wife and her sister are going to be taking the children into town today. You will drive them. It might be a very long day, so inform your wife that you won't be returning for dinner tonight. And, this is very important; I expect you to take good care of my family. Do you understand me?"

"Of course, Oberstrumführer," Bertram said. "No need to worry."

"Good," Oskar said, then he walked up to the ticket seller and purchased a one-way ticket to Munich. *I don't want to buy a round trip because I have no idea how long I am going to need to be there,* he thought, but he smiled at the seller, who was an elderly man with a full head of wavy, steel-gray hair and glasses. Then he went to a public telephone and called his office.

"Berni?" he said when his new secretary, a petite young blonde, answered the phone. Oskar had become much like his superior officer in that he changed secretaries often. That was because he seduced them, and once he'd slept with them, he couldn't bear the sight of them. They always became desperate, longing for his affections. So he let them go and started over again.

He'd overheard the other male officers talking. They said that when a man slept with plenty of women, he would find it easier to control his need for one special one. Oskar felt that he was too dependent on his wife. And so, he slept with other women, hoping it would help him not to need her so much. But it didn't work. Every woman he took to his bed made him think of how much he loved Kara. And although he only chose the prettiest girls he could find, in his heart and mind, they all paled in comparison to Kara.

"Yes, Oberstrumführer," Berni said.

"I will be gone for several days on business. I will keep in touch with you in case you need to tell me anything of importance. So, make sure you write everything down."

"Yes, Oberstrumführer," she said.

So meek, so humble, so afraid of me, he thought. Then he said, "Now, I want you to go and find the guard by the name of Albert Schiller and put him on the phone. I don't have long, so mach schnell, won't you?"

"Yes, please hold the phone for just a moment. I'll go and see where he is."

It was almost three full minutes before a male voice said, "Yes, Oberstrumführer, this is Schiller."

"I want you to get ahold of those two prisoners who built the garden for my wife and take them over to my house this morning. You might need to purchase some new rosebushes because the old ones look like they're dying. Make sure the Jews revamp the garden, so everything looks alive and blooming, then get them out of there before my wife and her sister return from shopping this evening. You know my rule. Yes?"

"Yes, Oberstrumführer." Then he repeated the rule: "Your wife is never to see the prisoners. She is never to know anything about the camp. Nothing about your work or what we do here."

"Very good. That's right. Make sure you keep that rule. I must go now. Do as I say."

"Yes, Oberstrumführer."

Oskar hung up the phone. Then he walked over to man who was selling newspapers. He purchased one and then found a bench in the shade where he sat down to wait for the train. Flipping through the pages of the newspaper, Oskar's mind kept drifting; he couldn't concentrate on reading. There was just too much at stake with the mission he was about to embark on. He felt a burning in his throat. Lately he'd been getting heartburn every time something made him nervous. *I'm not afraid to kill the girl. And if I get caught, I would probably be able to use my connections to get out of it. But Kara will find out.*

The screech of a loud train whistle startled him, and he looked up as the train pulled into the station.

A porter yelled, "All aboard for Munich."

Oskar folded his newspaper and boarded the train.

Beads of sweat from the relentless heat formed on Oskar's brow as he glanced around the train car. He saw fear and respect in the faces of the other passengers, who lowered their eyes as he passed. *It's this uniform. It commands respect.* He took a window seat and waited for the train to pull out of the station. Men and women with suitcases, a young woman with a small child, two old men, all boarded the train. No one sat beside Oskar. When they saw him, they cast their eyes down, not daring to look directly at him.

After several minutes, the train rumbled and began to move. Oskar looked out the window and thought about Kara. It was a long ride, and that would give him plenty of time to think. She was just starting to care for him, to trust him. His plan had worked, kidnapping and then rescuing Karl had made her see him as her hero. But if she ever found out that he'd manipulated the entire situation, he was certain she would leave him in an instant. The love Oskar felt for Kara was obsessive, and he had tried hard not to be so intense. He'd tried to ease the severity of his need by throwing himself into his work and by sleeping with other women, but nothing had eased the intense desire he had to possess his wife. He wanted all of her to be his, her every thought, her every move.

No matter what he was doing, his mind was constantly on her. And although she'd come to care for him—she even said that she loved him—deep in his heart he never felt that she was entirely his. She'd given him no reason to feel this way, yet he did. "It's not good to love a woman too much," he recalled his mother saying when he and his brother were young boys. How he wished he could sit down with his brother and talk to him face-to-face right now. Oskar had been the only person he could ever trust fully, the only person who had ever understood him completely. Oskar was stronger, and Erich felt that if Oskar were alive, he would know what to do, how to make Kara give herself to him fully.

But Oskar was gone. *He* was now Oskar. They had merged into one body. And although taking his brother's name and his achievements had given Erich some comfort, he still never felt complete. And he knew he would have given up anything: all the power, the success, and even his name, in order to have Oskar at his side advising him.

CHAPTER TWENTY-NINE

WHEN ANKA AWOKE, she found Kara in the kitchen feeding the children. Karl was sitting at the table with Patches on the floor at his side. The little boy was eating a plate of eggs and bread. Gretel seemed content in Kara's arms as she quietly sucked on a bottle.

"How do you always manage to get things under control?" Anka asked, smiling. "Do you know that when I am at home and things get out of control, I always ask myself, what would Kara do in this situation. But no matter what I try to do, everything always falls into chaos."

"I don't believe that," Kara lied. She'd been at Anka's home, and she'd seen firsthand that Anka couldn't handle things.

"I am just not cut out to be a hausfrau. I really want to fulfill my obligations to the führer to be a good wife and mother, but no matter how hard I try, I've never been able to manage things."

"You can, and you will. You're just going through a difficult time right now. Any woman in your position would feel the same," Kara said, trying to ease her sister's angst. It was difficult for her because she still wasn't feeling well. Her morning sickness was getting worse. It had woken her up this morning and she vomited. No matter what she did, she found it impossible to eat. Her head was throbbing, but she would never let on in front of Anka because she knew it would send her sister into a panic. Kara had always been the strong one, and right now Anka needed that strength desperately.

"She is pretty," Anka said.

"Who?" Kara asked, genuinely confused.

"The girl at the Lebensborn. The one Ludwig has been seeing."

"I saw her, but I don't remember what she looked like."

"You were so upset when you met her. I can imagine your mind was only on Karl," Anka said.

"Yes, I was. When Karl was missing, I couldn't think of anything but finding him again."

"Well, I remember her very well. When Ludwig and I went to adopt Gretel, she was there. She was so smug. And you know what?"

"What, dear?" Kara said, laying a rag over her shoulder, then laying Gretel on top of the rag and gently patting her back until she burped.

"She was flirting with Ludwig even then, even when we were so happy together because we were adopting a child. What kind of woman is she? This Aloisa Altner? A woman without a conscience. That's for sure. At the time I ignored her. I didn't care what she did because I never thought Ludwig would so much as look at another woman."

"I wouldn't have thought so either," Kara said.

"I wish you remembered her."

"I'm sorry. I don't."

"I would love to know if she was prettier than me."

"Anka, please. It doesn't matter."

Anka looked down at the table, then her eyes grew glassy like she might cry. "It matters to me. It matters a lot."

Kara lifted her sister's chin, so they were looking at each other eye to eye. Then Kara gave Anka a gentle half smile. "Listen, there aren't too many girls who are as pretty as you. I doubt this one was."

"So why did he do it? What did she have that I don't?"

"The truth?"

"Of course, I want the truth. I need to know," Anka said.

"You were always mean to him, always treating him disrespectfully. She probably adores him and makes a fuss over him. I mean, he has a good position. He has money . . ."

"Silly little fool that she is. He'll grow tired of her. I know he will. And then he'll try to come back to me. But when he tries to come home, I'll slam the door in his ugly face," Anka snorted bitterly.

"Why don't you try to calm down and have something to eat. You're making yourself upset," Kara said, then she added brightly, trying to change the subject, "After you finish breakfast, we can get dressed and then go shopping for a new dress for you. Would you like that?"

"Oh yes!" Anka beamed like a child. "Will you have breakfast with me?"

"I already ate," Kara lied. "You go on and eat now so we can get ready for our day."

"All right. I will."

CHAPTER THIRTY

AFTER ANKA FINISHED EATING, she went upstairs to get dressed while Kara got the children ready. Then she quickly washed her face and brushed her teeth. While Anka was deciding which dress to wear, Kara went outside and found Bertram sitting on the bench that Oskar had recently purchased for the garden.

"Bertram, please bring the car around, won't you? Anka and I are going shopping," Kara said.

"Yes, Frau Lerch."

In spite of all her crying and suffering, Anka looked radiant in a flowered summer frock with tiny pearl earrings. Her golden hair was caught up in a twist secured by a pearl comb. She wore just a dab of rouge and enough lipstick to make her lips look a shade deeper. "How do I look?" Anka asked Kara.

"Beautiful as always," Kara said. She was carrying Gretel in her arms as they all walked toward the car. Turning to Karl, Kara said, "Stay close to me all day. I don't want you getting lost for a minute."

"Oh, Mutti, I hate it when we go shopping with Auntie Anka. It takes her forever to find what she wants. We just go from store to store all day long. It's hot in the stores and boring."

"I know. But if you're good, I'll take you to a picture show on Saturday."

"You promise?"

"Of course, I promise," Kara said. "And you know I always keep my promises to you, don't you?"

"Yes," he said, but he looked like he was dreading the afternoon.

CHAPTER THIRTY-ONE

ANKA WAS ANIMATED, talking incessantly the entire ride. Now that Kara had a moment to get a good look at her, she realized that Anka had overdone her makeup application with too much red rouge and dark mascara. "I know what I'll do. I'll make him rue the day he ever looked at the silly girl. She's nothing compared to me. I'm far prettier." Anka snorted, then added, "I'll buy a new dress and change my hairstyle. And the next time I see Ludwig, I'll tell him what I really think of him. I'll tell him that he's so ugly, and so stupid that he isn't worth my time," she said almost too giddily. "Perhaps later we can go to the hairdresser?"

"Yes, perhaps. It is very hard on the children to sit in the beauty shop for hours. But we'll try."

"Well, I need a new hairstyle for when Ludwig comes crying back to me."

"Let's not worry about Ludwig today. Let's just try to relax and have fun. All right?" Kara said soothingly. The baby was hot in her arms. Karl was leaning his head on her arm, and this was just adding to the overwhelming heat. The windows were open, but even the breeze was hot. Kara felt woozy, but she hid her dizziness and the nausea she felt because she wanted Anka to have a good day.

"Bertram, would you please drop us off on the main street of town, "Kara asked.

"Yes, Frau Lerch."

They drove for a few more minutes before Bertram pulled the automobile over. He parked and got out to open the door.

"Where will you be? Where can I find you in case we would like to leave here and go to another stop?" Kara asked Bertram.

"I'm going to have something to eat at the café right over there." He pointed. "When I've finished eating, I'll come back to the car and wait for you here. There is no hurry. The oberstrumführer told me to expect this to be a long day."

"Yes, I do expect he is right," Kara said, "but if my sister insists, we may leave here and go to the beauty salon a few streets away. So I just wanted to know where to find you."

"I'll be right here at your service," Bertram said.

CHAPTER THIRTY-TWO

ANKA WAS tireless when she went shopping. Kara knew she would be, and if Kara had felt better, she wouldn't have minded. But today, all she could think of was getting home and taking a cool bath. They walked from store to store, where Anka tried on every dress in her size.

Meanwhile, Karl grew more and more restless. He was sweating and red faced. Kara had to reprimand him several times for kicking the chairs in the dressing rooms. Then he began hiding under the clothes racks and disrupting the customers who were shopping. Kara scolded him, but he was bored and continued to look for ways to misbehave. She knew he was doing it to get her attention, but she felt sorry for him because she, too, was growing tired of this shopping spree and wishing that her sister would buy something already so they could go home. Or to the salon, if Anka insisted, which she was sure Anka would. Gretel was fussy from the heat, and when Kara tried to give her a bottle, she refused.

"I think she's wet," Kara said. "I'm going to take her to a bathroom so I can change her."

"Oh dear. That baby is always needing something. She never

gives me a minute's peace," Anka said, then she shook her head. "All right. I'll keep an eye on Karl."

Kara had a quick memory flash across her mind. It was of the day of Karl's disappearance. A shiver ran up her spine. Then she said, "No, it's fine. Just go ahead and finish trying on those dresses you brought into the dressing room. I'll take Karl with me."

The bathroom was small and airless. Kara began sweating as soon as she closed the door.

"It smells bad in here," Karl said, then he gagged.

"I have to change Gretel, or she's going to get a rash. She's soaked."

"Why doesn't Auntie Anka take care of her? She is her child. But she never does anything for her. You know what I think? I think Auntie Anka is lazy."

"That's not nice," Kara said. But even though she didn't tell him her thoughts, she agreed with him. "Now, do you have to use the toilet? Because this would be a good time to do it."

"No, Mutti. I want to get out of here. The smell is making me want to vomit."

"I know." She opened the door to let some air in. Laying Gretel on a wooden table, she began to remove her diaper.

"Can I wait in the hall?" Karl asked.

"Absolutely not."

Grabbing a thick cloth from her bag, she quickly changed Gretel's diaper. "You could help me though. I need to pee. Can you watch Gretel for a moment? You're a big boy, you're much older, and I know I can trust you."

Little Karl's chest swelled with pride. "I'll make sure she doesn't fall off this table," he said. "I'll keep a hand on her."

"All right. But you must not look away from her for even a second, all right?"

"Yes, I promise."

Kara closed the door, and Karl held on to Gretel while Kara relieved herself. She found that as her pregnancy was advancing, she needed to urinate more frequently. *I feel awful. I just wish Anka would find a dress already so we could go home. I'm exhausted, and knowing her, we have only just started. She's going to want to get her hair done and buy some accessories. I don't know how I am ever going to get through this day taking care of these two little ones feeling the way I do.*

Sweat began to form on Kara's face. A wave of hot nausea came over her and she gagged.

"Mutti? Are you sick?" Karl asked.

Kara wanted to reassure her son that she was all right. But she couldn't answer. The room was spinning. But she nodded her head and tried to give her son a reassuring smile. Bile rose in her throat. She pushed it back. Then grabbing on to the wall to steady herself, she stood up and tried to adjust her undergarments and her dress. Kara's entire body was shaking. Then Karl screamed, "You're bleeding, Mutti. You're bleeding pee." He pointed to the small pool of blood that had formed on the floor beneath Kara's feet.

The room was spinning harder now. "Get Auntie Anka. Hurry," Kara said. "Take Gretel with you . . ." Then Kara passed out and fell on the bathroom floor.

CHAPTER THIRTY-THREE

KARA AWOKE in the back of the automobile. She searched frantically for Karl and Gretel. She breathed a sigh of relief when she saw that both of them were sitting at her side. Karl was holding Gretel in his arms. Anka sat on Kara's other side; her face had lost all its color. "Kara," she said, "I'm scared. Are you all right?"

"I'm fine," Kara said.

"I'm taking you to the hospital," Bertram offered.

"No, you must not. Please take me home and send for the doctor. I can't leave the children and stay in a hospital."

"I'll be there," Anka said.

"Yes, I know," Kara said, but she thought, *You are not responsible enough for me to trust you to take care of the children. I have to go home and call Oskar. When he comes home, I'll go to the hospital if I need to. But not before.*

CHAPTER THIRTY-FOUR

WITH OBERSTRUMFÜHRER LERCH AWAY on business, the guard and the driver who brought the prisoners from the camp to take care of the Lerches' garden, could be less diligent. When Lerch was around they dared not step out of line. But now that they were sure he was gone out of town, they made a deal between themselves to make their day more pleasant. The guard wanted to leave early that evening. His brother was in town, and he wanted to take him out for a few beers. So he asked the driver if he would cover for him and complete the day's work without him. In exchange, the guard agreed to cover for the driver who wanted to see his girlfriend. "You take the truck for an hour or two over to your girlfriend's flat. It's right around the corner, isn't it?"

"Yes, it is, actually," the driver said.

"Well, take a few hours off after you drop me and these two stinking Jews off at the oberstrumführer's home."

"Yes, that would be very nice," the driver agreed. He and the guard were good friends. So the guard knew that he was having an affair with a married woman, and this would be a good opportunity to see her during the day when her husband was at work.

The truck driver maneuvered the truck carrying Abram,

Moishe, and the guard up to the front of the Lerches' home. Abram felt his heart race. Inside that house was the woman he loved, his son, and the man he despised more than anything in the world. For a moment he had a fantasy. He saw himself overtaking the guard and stealing his gun. But he knew he wouldn't dare. The gun was pointed directly at Moishe's head. *No, I can't put Moishe at risk like that. Besides, as much as I want to see Kara, I don't want to do anything that would hurt her in any way either.*

"Let's move. Come on, get off the truck and start working. Mach schnell," the guard said, using his gun barrel to edge the prisoners forward.

Abram and Moishe jumped off the bed of the truck and ran over to the garden. Without looking back at the truck, they began their work.

The driver pulled away. He was on his way to see his lover.

Abram had just finished digging up and removing a dead rosebush. His face was scratched up from the thorns. He went back to the street where the driver had left a heavy pot with a fresh bush inside it. He dared not drop the pot, but it was so heavy. His body was covered in sweat, and the thorns were piercing his flesh, when Bertram pulled up and parked the automobile in front of the house.

The little boy with the golden hair, who Abram knew was his son, Karl, jumped out first, even before the driver had a chance to turn off the car. He held the door open. Abram was mesmerized. His eyes were fixed on the child. Looking at him now, Abram was even more certain it was Karl. *That's my son.* Abram's heart thundered in his ears.

"Mutti, let me help you," Karl said.

Then Kara got out of the car. Her dress was covered with dried blood. When Abram saw the blood, he stopped working. He was stunned. He forgot that he had decided to stay away from Kara and ran over to the automobile to see if she was all right.

"What the hell are you doing?" the guard said angrily to Abram. "Come back here this instant or I'll shoot."

CHAPTER THIRTY-FIVE

Ludwig was tired from working all day. But he'd never heard Aloisa sound so uneasy. She was usually calm, even when he was unable to get time off work or away from home to come to see her. But she'd sounded desperate on the phone, so even though he was exhausted and would have preferred to leave in the morning, he left immediately and drove through the night to Munich.

Ludwig had never been one to exude charm, and he wasn't well liked by his superior officers at work. They'd been complaining that he was taking too much time off. So when he telephoned to say that there was a family emergency and he would need a few days off, his superior officer grunted and said, "You're lucky that we still keep you. I expect you to return to work in three days, or don't come back at all."

"Thank you so much. I'll be there," Ludwig promised.

Not only was he tired, but he was hungry. It had been hours since he'd last eaten, and his stomach growled, but he didn't stop to eat or rest. Instead, he drove the car as fast as it would go directly to the home for the Lebensborn to speak with Aloisa. No matter what it was that she had to tell him, he would find a way to make it all right. If she'd lost her job, he would send her money.

It was true that he didn't love her the way he loved Anka. He doubted he would ever love anyone that strongly again. And perhaps that's a good thing. *The love I feel for Anka is so consuming that it has almost destroyed me*, he thought. But he cared deeply for Aloisa. She made him feel like a man. She made him feel important. In fact, she'd treated him better than anyone else had ever treated him. So now that she needed him, he was going to be there for her.

When Ludwig arrived, Aloisa was sitting at a desk with a pile of papers in front of her. Ludwig rushed to her side. "Can you take a lunch break?" he asked.

"It's almost three o'clock. But I am sure that I can arrange it. I'm so glad to see you." She smiled and touched his hand. "I'm so glad you came so quickly. It's important that we talk. So, wait here."

Ludwig sat at the desk, waiting. His hands were clammy.

A few minutes later, Aloisa returned. "Let's go," she said, taking her handbag out of the desk drawer. It was a beautiful brown leather bag that Ludwig had given her as a gift the last time he'd visited. It was a high-quality item that was well made. Aloisa cherished it; she had never owned anything as nice.

They walked outside into the afternoon sunlight.

"Have you eaten?" he asked.

"I don't want to talk inside of a restaurant. I don't want to risk anyone overhearing what I am about to tell you," she said.

Ludwig glanced down at her. She was a lot shorter than he was, and that made him feel even more protective. "Whatever this is that's bothering you, I can see that you're very frightened," he said with concern in his eyes. "I could tell something was really wrong when we were talking on the phone; that's why I got here as quickly as I could. But I never expected you to be so unnerved. What the hell is it?"

She put her arm through his, and in a voice just a little above a whisper, she said, "Yes, I am terribly frightened. Let's cross the street. We can sit on a bench in the park. It's usually quiet this time of day. Most of the people are working, and the children are in school or taking naps. We should be able to talk there."

He followed her. They sat down on a bench under a tree. Then he took her hand in his and lifted it to his lips. Kissing it, he said, "Please, tell me what's wrong. Is it your job?"

She shook her head. Then her voice cracked as she asked, "Does Oskar know about us? About you and me?"

"My brother-in-law? You mean that Oskar?"

"Yes."

"I am not sure. I mean I never told him. He might know," Ludwig said uncertainly. "I was going to tell you that Anka and I have separated, and she has gone to stay with her sister. So, Oskar may know about us if Anka told Kara. And my guess is she probably did. Why?"

"You told Anka about us? You told her we are seeing each other?" She was speaking fast, and her voice was high pitched.

"She knows because she found the love letters you sent to me. I am a sentimental fool. I kept them in my drawer."

"Then she knows everything?"

"Anka? Yes. She knows, and it's probably for the best. We should have separated long ago. She and I were never happy together. I told you when we first met. I tried everything to make her happy, but she never loved me, Aloisa. Not the way you do. You make me feel like life is worth living. I didn't realize what it would be like to have someone love me. I spent all of my time loving her, but she never gave anything back—"

"Ludwig," she interrupted him, "there is something I must tell you. But I am so afraid to tell you," she said. And when he looked at her face, he saw that a deep furrow had formed between her brows.

"Tell me. You know you can tell me anything."

She sucked in her breath. "Do you remember when Karl went missing?"

"Of course. It was a terrible nightmare for everyone in our family. We weren't sure we would ever find him again."

"Well . . ." she hesitated. "There is something you don't know. No one knows this. And I was told no one must ever find out. Especially not Kara."

"Go on," he said.

"Karl wasn't kidnapped. Oskar orchestrated the entire thing. He arranged to have Karl taken from that old woman's apartment. It was to be made to look like a kidnapping. Then he was to be sent to us at the Lebensborn."

"But why would Oskar do that?"

"He had a plan. He wanted to make Kara more dependent on him. He was there to help her search for her child. And then when Oskar found Karl and brought him home, he became her hero. She fell in love with him, just as he knew she would. And then he married her. This was all in his plan."

"Are you certain of this?" Ludwig was shocked.

"Very sure. Because I was a part of the plan. That's why I am so frightened. If Oskar knows about us, he will be afraid that I might tell you about what he did."

"And so then, why are you are telling me?"

"I am telling you because Oskar called me yesterday, right before I called you. He is coming here. He said he wants to talk to me. But if I know him, I think he is going to try to keep me quiet. He might offer me money. Or he might try to kill me. I don't know what he'll do. So if anything should happen to me, you'll know it was him."

"It's hard to believe that Oskar would do something so devious. He seems like such a good man."

"You don't really know him. He can be very charming, but the truth is he's manipulative. And I believe, if he is provoked, he can be dangerous."

"How did he get you to cooperate in such a terrible plan?"

She shook her head and sighed. "I am ashamed to admit this, but I did it for the money. He paid me. I didn't earn enough at my job. The extra cash helped me to purchase a few things I needed. I know it was wrong. But at the time, I didn't know you or the little boy. I am ashamed to say, but because you were all strangers to me, it didn't make any difference. I just went along with him because he paid me well."

"Aloisa," he said in a soft voice, shaking his head.

"I feel awful. Like a terrible person. Do you still love me?" she asked.

"Of course I still love you. Love doesn't just disappear."

"Oh, Ludwig. I was worried you would think I was horrible. I was afraid you would break things off with me."

"Never. Still, this is all so shocking to me. But I believe you. So, in light of what you have just told me, I think you should come home with me. You can quit your job. I promise you; I will take care of you. In my house you will be safe."

"What if Anka decides to come home? What then?"

"Then I will get you an apartment, and I'll move in there with you," he said. "Anka and I are through."

"Do you still love her?"

He wanted to lie, but he couldn't. "I'll always love her, Aloisa. But she was not good for me. And I wasn't good for her. She was so unhappy." He touched her face, gently running his fingers down the side of her cheek. "Come home with me."

"I don't know. I need to think this through. If I leave here, then my career will be over for good."

"You will have a new career. You'll be my hausfrau."

She looked into his eyes. "I can't do it. My supervisor says I am up for a promotion. I have worked so hard for this."

"Yes, darling, I realize that. But your safety . . ."

"Here is what I am thinking. If I tell Oskar that I already told you everything and that should anything happen to me, you will know it was him, I believe he will be reluctant to hurt me. Don't you agree?"

"I hope so. You're important to me and I hate to take chances like this. I would rather you just left here with me."

"I don't believe he would do anything knowing that you would turn him in to the authorities," she said. "How long can you stay?"

"I have to head right back. I can't be away from work any longer. My job is on the line. But I'll return as soon as I can."

"Kiss me," she said. "I want to feel your lips on mine."

He leaned over and put his hand in her hair drawing her face to his. Then he gently kissed her. *I am such a different man with her than I was with Anka. She makes me feel like she wants my affection. Anka was always pushing me away.* "I can't stress this enough; I just really wish you would come with me," he said. "I am afraid for you. I don't want to lose you."

"I've worked so hard for this promotion. I am finally being considered for it. How can I just leave it all behind?"

He nodded. "I still find it so hard to believe that Oskar would have done such a thing."

"He did because he wanted Kara to fall in love with him. He is quite the schemer. And it worked, didn't it?"

"Yes, I suppose it did. There was a time I might have understood how someone could do something so terrible to gain the love of another person. I was desperate for my wife's love. But now that I have you, I finally understand that love can't be forced. It must be given freely, or it will never be real, never be meaningful."

She took his hand. "I wish I didn't have to go back to work. I wish we could spend the afternoon in bed."

"Yes, so do I."

"Can't you just stay the night?"

He looked into her eyes. "I suppose I can spend half the night. I'll leave before dawn. At least that will give us some time together."

"Take the key to my apartment. I'll meet you there after work," she said, leaning over and kissing him.

CHAPTER THIRTY-SIX

WHEN ABRAM SAW Kara covered in blood and the panic on his son's face, he forgot that he was a prisoner. He forgot that a guard held a gun to his head. All he could see was the woman he loved, bleeding. And he ran to her.

The guard was so shocked he didn't shoot.

"Kara . . ." Abram said softly.

She could hardly stand up, and she was holding on to the side of the automobile. Then she looked up and into his eyes. "Abram? Abram?" she said. "Is it really you?" Her hands were trembling as she reached for him. "Am I dead?" she asked in a small voice.

He shook his head. "No, you're not dead. And yes, Kara, it's me."

"Prisoner, get away from her. Come over here and get back to work or I'll shoot," the guard said. He was nervous. Not only was the prisoner acting strangely, but he couldn't help but remember and fear the words of the oberstrumführer: "My wife must never see the prisoners." He pulled his gun on Abram. But he was afraid to fire in front of the oberstrumführer's wife.

Kara looked at the guard, stunned. "Who are you? What are you doing here? Put that gun down immediately."

"Your husband said . . ."

"My husband. What has all of this got to do with my husband?"

Now the guard was at a loss for words. She was never to know anything about the oberstrumführer's job. *He made that clear. But what should I tell her now? I am standing in her front yard. A prisoner, filthy and wearing a uniform is speaking to her. I am in such terrible trouble,* the guard thought. *I dare not kill this man here in front of her. The oberstrumführer would not like this at all. Not at all. But I don't know what to do.*

The guard didn't answer Kara's question. He just shook his head.

"I am confused." Kara was holding her head. "But I plan to speak to this man," she said, indicating Abram. And then to the guard, she said, "And as for you, I want you out of here. Get off my property."

Kara turned her attention back to Abram. "Abram, you are alive," she said incredulously.

"Yes."

"It's a miracle. I feel like I am dreaming. How did you find me?"

"Kara . . . I am a prisoner. Your husband is the oberstrumführer at the mine where I work. Several weeks ago, I was brought here to your home, to build you a garden. At the time I didn't know it was for you. But then I saw you . . . and Karl. Oh, Kara . . . today I was brought back here again to maintain your garden. And I wasn't going to speak to you because I knew you were safe, but then when I saw the blood on your dress, I couldn't help myself," he said. His voice was choked up. Then he touched her hand with his own trembling one. Tears flooded his face. "Why are you covered in blood?"

"I am feeling so ashamed. I am pregnant. I think I might be losing the baby." Then she reached out gingerly as if she were afraid he might disappear and touched his arm. "But you're here. You're real. I can't believe it." Then she put out her arms, and he took her into his embrace. She began to weep.

"Please, Frau Lerch. Don't touch this man. He is probably full of lice and disease. I don't know what is going on here. But I must take him away," the guard said. "Your husband will be furious."

Kara was woozy, and she felt like she might faint again. "Stay away from him and from me," she said, her voice deep and commanding like a cat growling.

"Mutti"—Karl tugged on his mother's arm—"what is going on. Who is this man? Why is he so dirty and skinny? He scares me. He looks like a skeleton."

Kara looked down at Karl. She touched his golden hair. *I think I am dying. If I die now, Karl will never know his real father. He will never believe Abram is his father unless I tell him. This might be my only chance.* She was trembling from the loss of blood. But in a small voice, she managed to say, "This man won't hurt you, Karl. You needn't be afraid. He's your father. This man is your father," she said, then she fainted.

Anka fell to her knees beside Kara. Her hand covered her mouth. She was terrified that she'd lost her sister. *My life will not be the same without her.* Tears covered her face. She was distraught, but even so, she couldn't understand why Kara had said that a Jewish prisoner was Karl's father.

CHAPTER THIRTY-SEVEN

KARA FELL TO THE GROUND. Abram immediately knelt beside her. Taking her hand in his, he felt her head: it was hot with fever. "We must get her out of the sun," he said.

Bertram and the guard exchanged a terrified glance. Although neither of them said aloud what they were thinking, they both knew that Frau Lerch must be protected at all costs. If she died while the oberstrumführer was away, he would go mad with rage and blame them both. For a moment, they forgot about Abram. Karl began to scream frantically, "Mutti, Mutti, get up." Abram tried to take the boy in his arms, but Karl didn't know him, and he pushed him away, continuing to scream, "Mutti, wake up. Please wake up."

Anka was screaming, "Bertram you must help her. Hurry. Bertram, do something."

"Help me lift her," Bertram said to the guard. "Be careful."

The guard silently cursed the driver of the truck for leaving. He could use his help now. But there was little time to waste; they had to get Kara inside.

For the moment, Abram and Moishe were forgotten. But Abram was so stunned and worried about Kara that he didn't run; he was frozen to the ground. As soon as Bertram and the guard carried Kara inside the house, Anka followed them carrying Gretel and holding tightly to Karl's arm.

Abram was lost in the moment. But Moishe saw the short window of opportunity. He knew that if they moved now, they would have a few seconds to escape. But they must act immediately. Moishe grabbed Abram's arm and shook him. But Abram stood stiff. Moishe pulled him, trying to wake him up, out of his dreamlike state.

"I have to go in there," Abram said. "She needs me."

"You can't go in there. The guards will shoot you for sure. You can help Kara right now by escaping. Listen to me." He put his hands on Abram's shoulders, then shook Abram hard. "There is no time right now for us to stand here and talk this over. We have to run, and run fast."

"But Kara. I can't leave Kara."

"If you stay, you'll be murdered. They'll shoot you. Or at best you'll be sent back to the camp. After what she said about you being Karl's father, they will want to get you out of the way. And you know they won't hesitate to shoot you. We have no choice, we must run. When we get away from here, once we're safe, we can make a plan. We can figure out a way to come back."

"She needs me. I can't leave her now. Even if it costs me my life."

Moishe stood still for a moment, then he slapped Abram hard across the face. "Abram! You'd better listen to me. I have no time to stand here and convince you. Just trust me. You must trust me," Moishe said, grabbing Abram's arm and pulling him. Finally, Abram began to run beside Moishe.

For a second Abram stopped and looked back.

"Run! Abram. This is our only chance. Run! Don't look back."

And they ran. Abram forced himself to keep going without looking back, but his heart ached, and he couldn't stop worrying about Kara.

The sound of gunshots in the distance paralyzed Abram. He

stopped for a moment and glanced at Moishe. "Don't stop running," Moishe warned, and he grabbed Abram's arm and pulled him forward.

And they ran.

CHAPTER THIRTY-EIGHT

OSKAR LERCH SETTLED into his hotel room. It was a quiet, comfortable room with plenty of light if he chose to open the shades, which, at the moment, he did not. He needed the quiet and darkness to help him gather his thoughts. *If Aloisa decides to open her mouth as lovers often do, Ludwig would be appalled at what I did. The self-righteous little idiot would feel it was his duty to tell Kara the truth. And he would stick his nose in my business. I would give that whore Aloisa money if I could be sure it would keep her silent. But as long as she and Ludwig are lovers, she is too close to my family for me to trust her to be quiet. I don't want to kill her. She's an Aryan woman; there will be an investigation. I would rather avoid all of it if I can.*

Oskar sighed aloud, then he thought, *Maybe she doesn't love him. Maybe she's just using him for money, in which case I can give her more if she's willing to stay away from him. I'll decide what to do once I am face-to-face with her. I need to speak to her to see exactly what her feelings are for Ludwig and if I can still trust her. Once I know this, I can decide what I must do.*

Oskar took a bottle of whiskey out of his suitcase and took a swig. The hot liquid slid down his throat, calming his nerves. He took several deep breaths. Then he picked up the phone and asked the operator to connect him to Steinhöring, the home for the Lebensborn.

It took almost five full minutes before the connection to Aloisa was made. And during that wait, he grew more unnerved. First, he was connected to a receptionist, then to some other woman, and finally to Aloisa.

"Allo," Aloisa said. When he heard her voice, he reminded himself to sound calm.

"Aloisa, Oberstrumführer Lerch here. I just arrived in town. I don't have any business until tomorrow. So, if you're free tonight I would love to take you to dinner." He made his voice as cheerful as possible.

"Tonight?" she asked. Ludwig had left that morning to return to work at the Wolf's Lair, and she'd been expecting Oskar's call. Just not so soon.

"Yes, if you are available."

"All right," she said. "Where shall I meet you?"

"I'll pick you up at your apartment. What's your address?"

"I would rather meet you at the restaurant. I could go there right from work," she said, not wanting to give him her address or to get into his automobile with him.

"That's fine," he said. "There's a nice little biergarten in the center of town. You might know it. It's got lovely outdoor seating with yellow umbrellas. Do you know the one I'm talking about?"

"I do, actually," she said. "I get off work at seven. I can be there at eight."

"Why don't I just pick you up at Steinhöring instead? It will be easier to drive from there."

There was nothing she could say. He was right. Of course, it would be easier, and anything she said now might give him the indication that she was afraid of him. And if she were wrong, and he didn't mistrust her, he might start feeling uneasy. She had no choice. "Sure, that would be fine," she said.

"I'll see you tonight," Oskar said, then he hung up the receiver.

Oskar took another swig from the bottle of whiskey. Then he sat in the dark room and gazed out the window. *I should probably make an appointment to share my Aryan sperm with at least one, perhaps two of the young women at the Lebensborn. Not that I am terribly devoted to creating a child for the führer. But it would make me look good to my superiors. But sex, unless it is with Kara, is boring without a challenge, and there is no challenge at the Lebensborn. The girls are willing and even eager to produce a perfect Aryan baby for Hitler. But I think it would be to my benefit. If I had a couple of visits with women at the Lebensborn, then it would look like that was the reason I came to Munich. And should I decide that I must dispose of Aloisa, it would be good to have an alibi. Just in case I should be questioned about this for any reason.*

CHAPTER THIRTY-NINE

ABRAM AND MOISHE ran across the well-manicured lawns of the homes owned by the SS officers, who worked at the camps. They ran through open fields and farms until they reached a patch of undisturbed land, covered in trees, plants, and wildflowers. There, hidden by a canopy of God's green leaves, both of them heaving and out of breath, they finally plopped down. Once Abram was able to catch his breath and speak, he said, "I'm really worried about Kara."

"I know."

"She needed me. I should have been there for her. But, like a coward, I ran."

"You are not a coward. And don't feel guilty. If you would have stayed, the guards would never have let you stay with her anyway. We would either be dead right now, or they would have taken us right back to camp."

"What if something happened to her. I mean . . . what if . . . dear God . . . what if . . ."

"I know what you're thinking. But for your own sanity you must not think like that. We have to believe she will be all right."

They were silent for a few minutes. Then Abram said, "I have to get back there. I must see her."

"Not tonight. They are going to be searching for us. We'll go, but we have to give it a little time. Right now, they're probably hot on our heels. I am just hoping they don't send their dogs looking for us."

"What if she is? I mean, what if she is . . ."

"Abram, stop it. There is nothing we can do. It's in God's hands. We have to trust God."

"How can I trust God? With everything I've seen, with everything I've been through. You expect me to trust God?"

Moishe put his hand on Abram's shoulder. "You have nothing else. You must turn to God."

There were a few moments of silence. An owl hooted in the distance.

Then Abram said, "What do you think was wrong with her? There was all that blood on the skirt of her dress. And she said she was pregnant. With his child? It must be with his child."

"I don't know," Moishe said, not wanting to say much more about it. "I do know this much. She is married to the oberstrumführer, and if she is pregnant with his baby, especially if she is pregnant with his baby, he will see to it she gets the best medical care possible. And let's face it, for her safety and for Karl's too, the last thing she needs right now is a Jew hanging around."

Abram sighed. "Did you hear what she told Karl? She told him I was his father."

"I heard. That was not good. It wasn't good because they all heard it. I'm hoping that they will think she was delirious because of the loss of blood. It would be best for her and Karl if the guards don't suspect the truth. And . . . it would be best for you too, Abram. The oberstrumführer wouldn't take something like this lightly," Moishe said.

"Yes, I know," Abram said. "I wonder if that girl was her sister. They look a lot alike, don't you think?" Abram speculated. "She was always close to her sister."

"They do look a lot alike. You never met her sister?"

"No, I couldn't because her sister was married to a Nazi. Everything between Kara and I had to be kept secret, even Karl. Kara ran away from home when she found out she was pregnant. She moved in with me and my mother. I loved her so much. I still do, but we couldn't get married legally because of the laws. So, we were married in our hearts and before God. For a couple of years while we lived together, I was the happiest man in the world." He sighed. "Then I was arrested. I don't know what happened to my family after that. But somehow, Kara ended up married to that bastard. I think it might have something do to with her sister's husband. But I am only guessing."

Moishe nodded. "It doesn't matter." Then he looked over at Abram, who was his best friend. They'd been through so much together that they were bonded like brothers. He squeezed Abram's shoulder. "Listen to me. It's not an ideal situation. I know that, but at least we know that Kara is safe. Your son is safe. That's what matters."

"That is if she survives this illness. Dear God, please let her survive. I would rather give my own life than see anything happen to her. I tried to stay away from her. I would have, but when I saw the blood . . ."

"I know."

"But if she does survive, and I pray with all my heart that she does, I am worried about them hearing that I am Karl's father. What if they believe her?" He shook his head. "I just don't know what she was thinking."

Moishe shook his head. "We can sit here and contemplate this all day. But in the end, we won't know anything until you can speak to her again."

Abram nodded. "I have no idea how I am going to do this. I don't know how I am going to get back to her."

"Well, first we have to let all of this settle. Then once things calm down, we'll go back to the house. I saw that the backyard of the house backs on to some trees and bushes. We'll wait there and watch until we can find her alone."

"Moishe, you don't have to do this with me. You're a free man now. If you keep running, you have a good chance of getting away without them catching you."

"I wouldn't leave you alone to go back there. You're all I have left in the world. My family is gone; my life is gone. You're like a brother to me. I'll go with you," Moishe said. "I want to go with you."

Abram nodded. Then he said, "And when this is over . . . and when this is over . . ." Tears came rushing down his cheeks. "If it ever ends, you will come and live with me and Kara and our son. You will be my brother. We will always be together."

"Yes. And I'll bake my mother's famous challah for the whole family," Moishe said.

"Rich egg bread," Abram said. "With real butter."

"Of course, with real butter," Moishe said, "but for now, we should keep moving just in case they come looking for us. The more distance we can put between us and them, the better."

CHAPTER FORTY

As soon as Bertram lay Kara on her bed, he ran to call the doctor. She was still bleeding and the deep-red blood against the white bedspread sent his heart thumping in panic. Then when the doctor said she must be admitted to the hospital, he was consumed with worry. Oskar had not left any information as to where he could be reached. And Bertram knew he would be frantic when he found out that Kara might be miscarrying their baby. Not only that, but he would be raging, looking for someone to blame. And that blame would probably fall on Bertram.

The guard and the driver were terrified about how the ober-strumführer would respond when he heard about the prisoners who escaped, but they, too, were more concerned about how he would react when he heard about Kara. This was serious. If she died, the oberstrumführer would be inconsolable, and the three of them—Bertram, the guard, and the truck driver—were sure to pay a hefty price.

Anka sat beside her sister's bed weeping, holding Gretel in her arms, who was fussy and crying as well. Karl's face was red and stained with tears. His eyes were wide with fear. "Auntie Anka, where is my father? I need my father."

Anka knew Karl was talking about Oskar. But when she heard him mention his father, she thought about what Kara had said about the Jew in that prisoner uniform who had come rushing over to them. A chill ran up her spine. But she decided that Kara was confused from the loss of blood. "You mean Oskar, of course?"

"Yes, Auntie Anka. Where is he? I need him. My mutti needs him."

"He's away on business. No one knows where to call or how to reach him."

There was silence for a few minutes. Then Karl asked in a small voice, "What did Mutti mean when she said that strange, dirty man, who looked like a skeleton, was my father?"

"Nothing, Karl. Nothing at all. She was just very sick, and sometimes when someone is sick like that, they start hallucinating."

"What does that mean?"

"Hallucinating means they see things that aren't there."

"Mutti told me that Oskar is my new father. She said he adopted me because he loved us both so much. But she said that I had another father before him. Do you think that dirty man I saw was my other father?"

"No, I don't. In fact, I am quite sure he wasn't your father," Anka said. But the more she thought about it, the more it seemed possible. And yet she didn't want to believe it. Still, her mind was haunted by memories of Kara standing up for Jews. She shivered. *If it were true . . . if it were actually true, where does that leave my beloved nephew? Where does that leave Kara?*

"Did you know my other father, the man who was my father before Vati adopted me?"

"No, I never met him, I am afraid," she said. Her lips quivered as she tried to smile. *It can't be possible. It just must not be true. It must not,* she thought. *Karl's father was a married SS officer. A pure Aryan man. That's what Kara told me. Not a Jew.* Anka shook her head at how impossible, yet at the same time how possible this idea actually was. There was ring of truth to it that terrified her.

Karl sat beside his aunt quietly staring at his shoes for several moments. Anka did not speak; she looked out into space, seeing nothing. Then in a small voice, Karl said, "Auntie Anka . . ."

"Yes." She turned toward him.

"Is Mutti going to die?"

"Oh, Karl. She must not die."

"You love her, don't you, Auntie?"

"Yes, I love my sister more than anything," she said, her voice cracking. Then she reached out and took his hand. Anka had never been a strong person, but she knew Kara would want her to take care of Karl right now. Kara would want her sister to comfort her son. So Anka sucked in a deep breath and said, "When we were little girls, when your mother and I were scared, your mother would tell me stories to help comfort me. Since we are both scared right now, you and I, Would you like to hear a story? I could tell you one the way Kara used to tell them to me."

He nodded.

"All right." She patted his hand. "All right, I'll tell you a story," she said, and then her mind drifted back to the nights when their father and mother were fighting, and Kara pulled her into her bed and told her the story of *The Ugly Duckling.* She hadn't prayed or even believed in God since she had married Ludwig and become active in the Nazi Party. The Nazis believed that Hitler was their god, and she'd accepted it. But right now, she needed the real God. She needed him more than she ever had, and so she began to pray silently. *Please, God. Please don't let my sister die. I'll do anything, anything. I know I haven't prayed to you in a long time, but I am begging you now.*

A few moments of silence passed. Anka felt a calm come over her. She took a deep breath and sighed. Then she turned to Karl, and as a single tear rolled down her cheek, she squeezed his hand and said, "Once upon a time there was a family of ducks . . ."

CHAPTER FORTY-ONE

WHAT HE WAS ABOUT to do was nasty but necessary business, Oskar thought as he washed his face and quickly shaved the shadow of a beard that had grown since his last shave early that morning. Slowly, he ran the razor across his handsome, strong chin and thought, *When I was Erich I would never have had the courage to eliminate a German woman. But as Oskar, I have enough courage to do whatever needs to be done to secure my marriage and continue my comfortable life.* Oskar smiled at his reflection in the mirror. He was proud of the powerful man he'd become.

Quickly, he dressed in a clean, pressed uniform, and then before he left, he picked up the phone to call his wife. He wanted to hear her voice. He needed to hear her say, "I love you." That would give him all the incentive he needed to carry out this abhorrent task.

He waited while the operator connected him. But the phone rang and rang. No one answered. He sighed. *She must be out with her sister and the children. Well, since I can't reach her, I must do this on my own. I want to be done with it as soon as possible so I can return home.*

"I'm sorry, there's no answer," the operator said as she returned to the line.

"Yes, I know. Thank you," Oskar said, hanging up the receiver. Tucking his gun into his pocket, he left the hotel room.

CHAPTER FORTY-TWO

AFTER SHE AGREED to have dinner with Oskar, Aloisa couldn't concentrate on her work. She was on edge, nervous, unsure of what to do. Shuffling through the papers on her desk, she tried desperately to convince herself that Oskar would never go so far as to actually hurt her. He might threaten her, but he wouldn't actually hurt her, would he? For a second, she wondered if she had put Ludwig in danger by telling him what Oskar had done.

She felt her heart sink. That was the last thing she wanted to do. Ludwig had always been kind to her. Kinder than any of the other men she'd become involved with. Most of them just wanted sex. But Ludwig always wanted more; he wanted to make her happy. He wasn't handsome, or even charming, but he was honest and always so generous with her. He'd helped her financially more than once when she'd gotten herself into a bind during this past year. And she was grateful to him for it.

Reichsführer Himmler was coming next week. He came once a year to give names to each of the children at Steinhöring who had reached a year old. They must be named before they could be adopted. And because there were so many, Aloisa was supposed to be working on preparing all of the paperwork. But she couldn't seem to concentrate. *Could it be that Oskar found out that Ludwig and I are lovers, and like a typical man, he wants to see if he can't seduce me too? Perhaps that's all it is. A man wanting to outdo another man. Maybe I am just on edge and worried for no reason at all. Men are competitive. And a man like Oskar would never let himself be outdone by a man like Ludwig. Ludwig isn't like the rest. But Oskar would not want to be outdone. He would want to be sure he'd slept with Ludwig's mistress.*

As she shuffled through the enormous pile of papers in front of her, her mind drifted back to the first time she'd met Ludwig. He arrived at Steinhöring with his wife early one morning. Oskar had telephoned the weekend before to tell her that his brother-in-law and sister-in-law were coming to adopt a child. According to Oskar's wishes, Aloisa was to send the paperwork through as quicky as possible. Her first thoughts were about money. She knew Oskar always paid well for any favors he asked of her. So if she cooperated with his request and got the paperwork approved quickly for his relatives, she could expect a nice comfortable number of reichsmarks as a fee for her troubles.

The first thing she noticed about Ludwig and Anka was how Anka treated Ludwig. No one could mistake it. Anka talked down to her husband. He didn't fight back, not at all. Another man would have slapped her in the face for how she was talking to her. And there were a few times during that first meeting when Anka humiliated Ludwig so badly, that Aloisa felt genuinely sorry for him. She couldn't remember the exact words, but she remembered the look on Ludwig's face, and it had torn her apart.

There was something about him that she liked. She knew what it was. Ludwig reminded her of her father. Aloisa could never forget how her mother had shamed her father publicly all the time when Aloisa was growing up. But she understood her father better than anyone. He was a quiet man, not a fighter. And Aloisa had been his favorite child. Until his death, a year ago, she made sure to go and see him at least once every six months. She knew he loved her. And she believed wholeheartedly that he was the only person who did. That was until she met Ludwig. They both had a way of making her feel special. Aloisa could see their eyes light up when she walked into the room, and it made her feel important.

As Ludwig and Anka were going through testing on that first day they'd come to Steinhöring, something happened that caused Anka to become annoyed with Ludwig. In a voice loud enough for everyone to hear, she told Ludwig to shut his mouth because everything he said made him look foolish. Aloisa didn't know what Ludwig said to evoke such anger in his wife, but as she watched Anka and Ludwig interact with each other, she felt her heart break. Anka treated him like he was nothing, and in turn, Ludwig hung his head in shame.

It was then that she decided to discreetly hand him her telephone number. She'd never done anything like this before with any man who'd come to the home for the Lebensborn with his wife to adopt a child. And even though she wasn't sure he would ever call—he was so timid and afraid of his wife—she felt fairly certain that he would never tell anyone she'd given him the number.

After the intense testing was complete, Anka went to the ladies' room, leaving Aloisa and Ludwig alone. Quickly, Aloisa said, "I know this is highly inappropriate, and I don't even know why I am doing it, but please . . . take this."

He looked at her puzzled. Then she handed him a piece of paper with her name and telephone number written on it.

"What's this?"

She said in a small voice, "I was thinking that maybe you might want to telephone me if you are ever in town." Then seeing the surprise on his face, she was suddenly ashamed. "Oh dear, I don't know what's gotten into me. I'm sorry. I mean . . . never mind." She reached for the paper, trying to take it back, but Anka returned.

Ludwig slid the paper into his pocket. Then he and Anka thanked Aloisa and left to return home and wait for their papers to be approved.

Aloisa was embarrassed. Her face as red as a ripe strawberry, she went quickly into the ladies' bathroom to hide. It took several moments and several forbidden cigarettes for her to calm down enough to return to her desk.

She had never expected Ludwig to call. He seemed so totally devoted to his wife regardless of the way she treated him. A week passed, then another, and the memory of her embarrassment faded, and she forgot about him. Then one evening, just as she returned home from work to the woman's hotel where she lived, someone knocked on the door to her room. "You have a call on the telephone," the girl at her door said.

It must by my mother. "All right. I'm coming," Aloisa answered, then she walked into the hall and picked up the phone receiver.

"Aloisa?" a male voice asked.

"Yes, this is she."

"This is Ludwig. I don't know if you remember me or not." He cleared his throat, and she thought he sounded nervous and awkward as he added, "You gave me your number a couple of weeks ago."

"Of course, I remember." Her palms were sweaty. Her face felt hot.

"Well, I was just calling to see what you wanted," he said.

"What I wanted?" she asked. She wasn't sure what he meant.

"I mean, I wasn't sure why you gave me your number."

She laughed a short, nervous laugh. "Do you ever come to Munich . . . alone?"

"Oh," he said, "I think I know what you are after."

Neither spoke for a moment.

Then in an apologetic voice, Ludwig said, "I can't do this. I'm married."

"I know you're married. Do what, exactly?" she asked, feeling uncomfortable.

"This . . . well . . . you know."

"Then I guess we don't have anything more to say," she said, wishing he'd never called. Wishing she'd never given him her number.

There was an awkward split-second of silence. Then Ludwig coughed, cleared his throat, and said, "Well, I suppose I could arrange a trip to Munich on my day off."

"Really?" She was immediately ashamed of how eager she

sounded. But she couldn't control her joy at not being rejected. "That would be wonderful. I'd love to see you."

"I'll speak to my superior in the morning and call you tomorrow evening to make plans."

"All right," she said. "I look forward to hearing from you."

"Yes, I look forward to seeing you."

Aloisa shook her head. *That was a strange and uncomfortable conversation.* She hung up the receiver and went back to her room thinking, *He doesn't have much experience with women. But at least he didn't reject me. And I have a feeling things are going to be good between us.*

When he didn't call the next day, she thought he had probably decided it wasn't worth the aggravation of having an affair. He wasn't willing to take the risk. She was terribly disappointed, again. She decided that when he and his wife came to pick up their baby, she would have someone else work with them. She never wanted to speak to him again.

But the following evening he called.

"Allo," she said.

"Hello," he said breathlessly as if he'd been running for miles.

"Allo" she said. She forgot her promise to herself never to speak to him again. Instead, trying to sound cold, she said, "I didn't think you were going to call."

"I was nervous," he admitted. "I still am. But I would love to see you."

She felt a surge of joy run through her. *He likes me. He's just afraid.* "Were you able to make any arrangements with your job to take some time off?"

"Yes." She heard him take a deep breath. "I can come to Munich next week for two days. I hope you will have some time to see me. We could have dinner, or lunch, or whatever you want."

"Yes, we'll have dinner, but I don't have my own flat. I live in a women's hotel."

There was a second of silence. "Shall I get a room?" he asked, sounding embarrassed.

"Yes."

157

CHAPTER FORTY-THREE

THE FOLLOWING WEEK, Ludwig telephoned Aloisa again. "I'm here in Munich," he said. "Can I pick you up after work and take you for dinner tonight?"

"Yes, that would be very nice."

"Where shall I pick you up, at your hotel or at your job?"

"The hotel. I'd like to go home after work and freshen up. I'll give you the address. Take this down." She gave him the name and address of the hotel where she was living.

"Do you like to go dancing?" he asked.

"Yes, I love to dance."

"That's great! I'm not a very good dancer, I'm afraid, but I know women love to dance," he said clumsily. "So wear your prettiest dress, and we'll go somewhere nice, somewhere we can dance. What time would be good for you?"

"Eight?"

"I'll be early," he said.

She laughed and hung up the phone. *He does like me. He likes me a lot.*

Ludwig was ten minutes early, so he waited in the lobby until she came downstairs.

"You look beautiful," he stammered, handing her a bouquet of flowers.

No one has ever brought me flowers before, she thought. "This is so sweet of you."

He smiled shyly. "I thought you might like them," he said.

They went to an expensive steak house that Ludwig and Anka had been to with Oskar and Kara when they were married in Munich. This was an exclusive restaurant for SS officers. It was a beautiful place with crystal chandeliers, white tablecloths, and waiters wearing white gloves. Aloisa looked around; her lips trembled when she smiled at Ludwig. "I've never been to a restaurant like this before."

"Do you like it?"

"I feel a little bit out of place."

"Why would you feel that way?"

"Everything is just so lovely."

The maître d' led them to their table. Ludwig pulled out Aloisa's chair. Then he sat down across from her. "Nothing here is as lovely as you."

He saw that her hands were trembling as she studied the menu. "I can't believe it; they have real beef and chicken. And . . . coffee. But everything is so expensive. I don't know what to do. I have no idea what to order."

"What would you like?"

She shook her head. "Anything."

"All right. I'll order for both of us," he said, and he did, sparing no expense.

The other men Aloisa had dated in the past had taken her to biergartens or the movies. No one had spent so much money on her. She gazed down at her dress and compared it to the dresses the other women wore. It was shabby in comparison, yet it was the best dress she owned. She imagined the eyes of the other women in the room scrutinizing her dress, her stockings with the small run, her shoes, her handbag. *They know I don't belong here. But I'll bet that if I was Ludwig's mistress, I would have nice things like theirs. I would be accustomed to dining at places like this. I could get used to it.*

After they finished dinner and were sipping steaming cups of real coffee loaded with real sugar, she reached across the table and took his hand. Then in a quiet voice, she suggested they go to his hotel room. He agreed. But she could see he was nervous. After he paid the check, they left, and neither of them spoke on the way to Ludwig's hotel.

She followed him upstairs to his room where Ludwig had a bottle of wine. After he poured two glasses and handed one to Aloisa, with trembling hands, he said, "I've never done this before."

"I know. I can tell."

"Is it really that obvious?" he said, raising his eyebrows.

She smiled. "It's charming."

He walked over to her and went to take her into his arms, but he knocked the wine bottle onto the floor. It didn't break, but the red wine spilled everywhere. "I'm so sorry," he said quickly, picking the bottle up and placing it back on the table. "I am so clumsy. And . . . quite honestly, I am so embarrassed."

"It's all right," she assured him, touching his brow gently.

"No one has ever been so nice to me," Ludwig said, "especially, not a woman."

He was taller than her, but she got up on her tiptoes and then gently kissed him. Ludwig responded by putting his arms around her. Then she took his hand and led him to the bed. Aloisa could feel him shaking as he lay down beside her. "It's all right," she repeated. "It will be all right." She began to unbutton his shirt.

And so, their affair began. He traveled to Munich as often as he could, always bringing gifts for her. She had been right. He did give her lovely well-made dresses, expensive shoes, real silk stockings, and fancy handbags. They dined at fine restaurants, and he had a way of making her feel like a lady. Then one day he told her that he would like to pay to rent an apartment for her, a nice place over-looking the park, where she could enjoy a cup of ersatz coffee while gazing out her living room window. It would be nicer to stay with her in her own place when he came to town rather than staying in a hotel. When he told Aloisa of his plan, she wrapped her arms around his neck and squealed. "Oh, Ludwig, you are so generous. So good to me."

"You deserve it. You deserve to be treated like a princess." He touched her cheek.

And from then on, he stayed with her whenever he went to visit in Munich.

CHAPTER FORTY-FOUR

LUDWIG WISHED he could have spent the night with Aloisa. But he knew he had to get back to work, or he was going to lose his job. He was tired, but he drove from Munich directly to the fortress called the Wolf's Lair where he worked. He had helped build this compound for the protection of his beloved führer. It was located deep in the Polish forest, but it offered every luxury that an SS officer might desire. The compound was complete with a casino and a movie theater. It had plenty of comfortable bunkers. And because it was hidden deep in woods, it offered safety from enemies.

The only problem thus far had been with the air quality. Many of the men, including Ludwig, had been experiencing trouble breathing and had developed nagging coughs. But the führer was not at the lair long enough or often enough to have trouble with his respiratory system, and so far, nothing had been changed.

As he drove, Ludwig felt uneasy. He tried to tell himself that Oskar would never hurt an Aryan woman. But he just wasn't totally convinced. It was still so hard for him to believe that Oskar would have arranged to have Karl kidnapped. Oskar seemed like such a decent fellow. But it made sense, and he believed Aloisa wholeheartedly. She had never lied to him. At least not that he knew of. He shook his head remembering how Kara had not been interested in Oskar when they'd first met. But after the ordeal with the kidnapping, and his role in helping her to find her son, she'd fallen in love with him, and then she'd married him, even though Ludwig thought it was despicable to have arranged to have Karl kidnapped just to win Kara's heart.

In a way, Ludwig envied Oskar. Oskar took what he wanted. And Ludwig wished with all of his heart that he could have found a way to make Anka love him. He'd tried, oh how he'd tried. But she had never shown him the least bit of affection or respect. If she had, he would never have become involved with anyone else. And even now, Anka still owned his heart. He cared deeply for Aloisa. She was a sweet girl, who made him feel like he was worthy of love. But as hard as he tried to get over Anka, he couldn't. His heart still belonged to his wife.

Ludwig let out a long sigh. *How did things ever go so wrong?* he thought, shaking his head. *I wish that somehow Anka would call me and ask me to try again. I know it would hurt Aloisa, and I would never want to do that. But I would leave her for Anka. Ohhh . . . if only Anka could love me the way Aloisa does, I would be the happiest man alive.*

He had a feeling in the pit of his gut that told him that he should not have left Aloisa alone in Munich. *I probably should have insisted she come with me back to Poland. But if she had come with me, there would be no chance at all that Anka and I could ever reconcile. And I am just not ready to accept that yet. Besides, I can't imagine that Oskar would actually kill Aloisa. I refuse to believe he is really capable of such a thing. Kidnapping a child is one thing; killing a woman is another. Besides, even if he did have Karl taken, Karl was returned unharmed, so clearly he isn't that bad.*

I think perhaps Aloisa is just nervous and afraid. Oskar's behavior was devious, no doubt, but no one got hurt. Murder is another thing altogether. I don't believe he would kill an innocent girl. He isn't that ruthless. Ludwig tried to convince himself. And he made a good argument. But that nagging feeling in the pit of his stomach didn't go away.

CHAPTER FORTY-FIVE

"YOU LOOK LOVELY," Oskar said to Aloisa as she got into the automobile he'd borrowed at Nazi headquarters. "I haven't seen you in quite a while. Love looks good on you."

She tried to smile but her lips were trembling. *He knows. He said love looks good on me. That means he knows. I don't want to ask him any questions. I dare not say, "What do you mean love looks good on me?"*

"Are you hungry?" Oskar asked.

"Yes," she lied. She wanted to get to a public place so she could get out of his car.

"Well, good. So am I."

They were silent for a few moments.

"Do you know where the restaurant is located? The one you suggested with the yellow umbrellas?"

"Of course," he said.

Then neither of them spoke. Aloisa bit her nail.

When they arrived at the restaurant and got out of the car, Aloisa felt herself relax a little. She was certain that if had planned to kill her he would have done so already. He would never have taken her to this place. He would have driven right to some secluded area, and that would have been the end. So she breathed a sigh of relief.

They were seated outside at a table with a large yellow umbrella where they could watch people walking by on the street. He ordered a pitcher of dark bitter beer and two mugs.

"So, how is your work going?" he asked in a pleasant voice.

"Very good," she said. "I am being considered for a promotion."

"I'm pleased to hear it. The last time we spoke you said you were being considered for a promotion."

"Yes, but I didn't get that one. I am being considered again. I hope to get this one."

"Perhaps I could use my influence." He smiled.

She suddenly felt foolish thinking he had any intentions of hurting her. He'd come to see her. He might want to sleep with her. And he probably wanted her to reassure him that she would not tell Ludwig about what he'd done. *I'm not going to tell him that Ludwig knows. If I call Ludwig when I get back to my apartment and tell him there was nothing to worry about, he will keep quiet.* "Would you really do that for me?" Aloisa asked.

"But of course. You have been careful with my secret, haven't you? So I would be happy to help you."

"You mean the secret about the little boy and the kidnapping?"

He nodded gravely.

"Yes, of course I have kept your secret. I would never tell anyone."

For a moment he studied her, and it felt as if his eyes were boring into her own eyes. She shuddered. But then his mood changed back, and he gave a cheery easy laugh. "I'll do what I can to help you get that promotion," he said, then his face became serious. "By the way, so, do tell me, what is going on between you and my brother-in-law?"

"O-Oh," she stammered, "you know about us?"

"My wife's sister, who as you know is Anka, Ludwig's wife, came to stay with us. She told my wife everything. Anka is devastated."

"Do you want me to break it off with Ludwig?" She hoped he

would say no. But if it meant her safety, she would do it if she had to.

"I don't care who you sleep with. It's the pillow talk that concerns me. Have you told Ludwig anything about my secret?"

"No, never," she swallowed the lie. Oskar looked at her as if he could see through her and knew she was lying. "Never," she repeated firmly.

"Good. Make sure you don't," Oskar said, his voice was a deep, threatening whisper, and she felt a tingle of terror shoot up her spine.

"I would never tell him. I have no reason to tell him. It has nothing to do with him, or with us. What happened with the boy and your wife is your personal business," Aloisa said, but she knew she was talking too fast.

"Good. Well, that's all I ask," he said and then his demeanor changed again. He seemed to believe her. Everything seemed to be fine. "I knew you were a smart girl from the first time we met. Now, why don't we order some dinner."

Oskar asked Aloisa about her work during dinner, and she told him that things were going well. She mentioned that the reichs-führer was coming the following week to name a large group of babies. "So, we are working extra hard to make sure everything is in order. You know how Reichsführer Himmler is. He expects perfection."

"Yes, I know." Oskar smiled. "He does. But that's why he's so good at his job."

"That's true," Aloisa said.

The waitress walked over. "Can I get the two of you anything else?"

"Let's have some strudel and coffee," he said.

She nodded in agreement. "Sure, if you'd like." Her lips trembled as she smiled; her heart was hammering in her chest.

"We have cherry or apple. Which would you like?" the waitress asked.

"You decide," Oskar said to Aloisa.

"Apple," she said.

"Then apple it is."

After the strudel and coffee arrived, Oskar smiled at Aloisa and said, "I'm so glad we had dinner together and worked all of this out. Now I am quite certain I can trust you."

"Of course you can trust me," she said with a smile. Then she patted his hand.

Oskar hummed a tune under his breath as he pulled the automobile up in front of the apartment building where Aloisa lived. Then he turned to her and said, "Thank you for a lovely evening."

"Thank you for dinner."

"Of course, it was my pleasure." He smiled his most charming smile, then added, "and, you will remember not to tell anyone any of my secrets, yes?"

"Yes. Of course," she said, smiling. Then feeling bold because he'd seemed so friendly and not at all frightening, she said, "I was hoping maybe you might want to come upstairs?" He was a heartbreakingly handsome man. And she wouldn't have minded a night with him.

He smiled. "Perhaps another time."

She nodded. Then she thought why not get a little extra money. He could always be counted on to pay for favors. "I was hoping, maybe you might be able to spare a few reichsmarks."

He tilted his head and looked directly into her eyes. A dark flash of anger came over his face. "Are you blackmailing me?"

"No, not at all. But I could use a little extra money."

"Of course," he said, smiling. The anger disappeared as quicky as it had come. Then he handed her a few reichsmarks. "You very well could blackmail me for all that you know, now, couldn't you?"

"I suppose, but I wouldn't. Your secrets are always safe with me," she said.

"Good. I knew I could count on you." Oskar winked at her as she climbed out of the car.

He watched her walk inside the building, then he pulled away slowly.

CHAPTER FORTY-SIX

KARA LAY IN BED. Loss of blood had left her weak, but she was young and strong, and the doctor said she would recover, physically at least.

"She's just lost the baby, so don't be surprised when she shows signs of depression. Just be kind and patient with her," the doctor told Anka. "I asked her if she wanted to go to the hospital to recover, but she said she wanted to be at home with her family." The old doctor patted Anka's arm, then continued. "She's strong. I think she will do better at home. I'll come by each day to see how she's doing"

"Thank you, Doctor," Anka said. She was worried sick about her sister, but she also knew Kara needed her to handle things right now. In her entire life Anka had never been the strong one. She'd never been in charge. Someone else had always taken care of her. First it was Kara, and then it was Ludwig. But now Ludwig was gone, and Kara needed to lean on her. Tears burned the backs of her eyelids. She thought of Ludwig. She never realized how much she would miss him, but she did. Anka wished she could lay her head on his teddy bear-like body and depend on him the way she'd always done. But he was gone. *I drove him away. I drove him into that woman's arms.*

It was only two days since Kara had fallen ill, but it seemed like years already. The responsibilities of preparing food and caring for the children were overwhelming to her. Anka had to get up early to feed the children. Then she had to make sure not to let them out of her sight, so that they didn't get into any trouble and hurt themselves. They left toys and clothes all over the floor, and she picked them up only to find them scattered again an hour later. They seemed to move so fast and to get into everything. Their clothes were always dirty and needed to be changed more than twice a day. *Soon, I am going to have to wash their clothes,* Anka thought as she looked at the pile of dirty clothes in the hamper.

The children were fussy at lunchtime. Karl refused to eat. He was worried about his mother, and he wanted to know when she was going to be well.

"She's feeling better, Karl. But she needs her rest. The best thing you can do right now is to be a good boy. I need your help. You are older and more grown-up than Gretel. She admires you. She'll listen to you," Anka said, "I need you to help me to get Gretel to take a nap. Can you do that for me?"

Karl straightened his back. He seemed to like the idea of being older and in charge of helping with Gretel. "I'll help you," he said.

He told Gretel stories and rubbed her back, with Patches sitting beside them until Gretel drifted off to sleep.

"Aren't you tired?" Anka asked Karl.

"No. I'm fine."

"Why don't you try to take a nap. Just lie down for a few minutes. If you can't sleep, just come back into the living room and let me know."

"All right. I'll try," he said.

A half hour passed. Anka looked in on Karl. He was fast asleep. She smiled. Relieved to have some time to herself, she boiled some water and prepared a cup of tea. Once it was done, she went outside and sat in the backyard. She was tired, emotionally and physically. She couldn't do all of this on her own for much longer.

Anka was thinking about calling Ludwig, considering begging him to come and help her, when she heard a sound coming from the trees. Her heart skipped a beat. *There's some kind of wild animal in those trees. Should I run? I don't remember if Ludwig said to run or stay still when approached by a wild beast. Ludwig, I wish you were here.*

But it wasn't a beast. It was a man. It was the same scruffy, dirty man she remembered from the day Kara had fainted on the pavement. She remembered how her sister had looked directly at him and said, "He's your father, Karl." A shiver traveled down the back of Anka's neck. *I can't believe he's here. I can't believe he's come back. This is the last thing we need.*

There was a yellow star on his striped uniform. *A Jew*, she thought. *He's a Jew. He's also a prisoner, a criminal against the Reich.* She was confused and terrified. "Who are you and what do you want?" she said, standing up and trying to look and sound brave.

His voice was soft, kind, and gentle. "You must be Anka," he said. "I've heard a lot about you. And you look so much like your sister."

He knows my name. *He knows Kara and I are sisters.* Anka stared at him in disbelief. *Maybe Kara wasn't delusional after all. Maybe he really is Karl's father.*

"I am Abram. I am here to see Kara."

"But . . ."

"Is the oberstrumführer here?" he asked carefully.

She shook her head, not sure if she should tell him the truth that Oskar was out of town. She was still afraid of him.

"Please, I beg you, Anka; tell me, is she all right? I was there that day that she passed out."

"I know. I remember."

"And . . . do you remember what she said?"

Anka swallowed hard. "About Karl?"

"Yes, I am his father. Kara and I were very much in love."

"But you're a Jew."

He nodded.

"I never knew," Anka said. "I never knew the truth about you."

"She wanted to tell you. We both did. But we didn't know how."

Anka was shocked. But all of this rang true. It rang so true that she turned to him and said, "You'd better come inside right away before anyone sees you. If the people in this neighborhood see you in that uniform, they'll call the police. There is no one here but Kara and me, and the children."

Abram followed her into the house. They walked through the kitchen where he saw a loaf of bread. It had been days since he'd eaten. He would have liked to take the bread and share it with Moishe, who was waiting in the bushes behind the house. But he would not steal from Kara. He would never steal from her.

"She's in here," Anka said, pointing to the door of Kara and Oskar's bedroom.

Abram opened the door and walked into the room. Kara lay on her back with her head turned toward the window. She'd drifted off into a light sleep.

"Kara," he whispered.

At the sound of his voice, her eyes opened slowly. "Abram?"

"Yes, it's me, it's Abram."

Anka's mouth fell open. It was all true.

Kara took his hands in hers and began kissing them. Tears spilled down her face, but she was laughing as well as crying at the same time. Abram took her into his arms and held her close to him. "Kara. I never thought I would see you again." He held her so tightly that she could hardly breathe, but Kara didn't care, and she didn't seem to care at all that he was filthy. "I love you. I love you," he whispered as he planted soft kisses in her hair and on her face.

"I love you," she whispered.

"Are you all right? I saw all the blood, and I've been worried sick."

"I had a miscarriage. But I am all right."

He didn't ask her any questions. He didn't want to know if the baby belonged to Lerch. He didn't care. Instead, he held her in his arms.

"You risked death coming here," Anka said.

He nodded. "Yes."

"Weren't you afraid?"

"I am still afraid. But when you love someone the way I love Kara, you will do whatever you must to be with that person. Even if it's only for a few moments."

"I don't know what to do. I am married to Oskar Lerch. He's out of town, but he will be home any day now," Kara said. "It won't be safe for you to be here when he returns."

"You're married to the oberstrumführer. I am surprised. He's such a sadistic man. But he must have offered you and Karl protection."

"Sadistic? You have the wrong man. You can't be talking about Oskar. In fact, I must admit, I feel so torn because I love you, but he has been so kind to Karl and I, so very kind."

"He's not kind if you're a Jew. He's the oberstrumführer at the camp I ran away from. He beat Jewish men to death all the time. I saw it with my own eyes."

Kara sat up in bed. "You must be mistaken."

"I am not mistaken, Kara. And, you know me. I would never lie to you."

"Oskar? I can't imagine him doing such a barbaric thing. He would never do that. Never, Abram. You must have him confused with someone else."

"I am telling you I have seen him do it. It was him. He's known throughout the camp for being cruel and heartless."

She shook her head. Kara was confused.

"I can see the confusion in your eyes. But I promise you, this is the truth."

"Anka, can you please leave us for a few minutes."

"Yes, but you must hurry. I don't know when Oskar will be home," she said, "or when the children will wake up. I am afraid that if Karl sees this man in the house, he will tell Oskar as soon as Oskar returns. Karl wouldn't be meaning to cause trouble, but you know how children are. They talk without really under-standing the meaning of what they have done." Anka was wringing her hands.

"I know. We'll only be a moment."

Anka nodded and left the room.

Once they were alone, Abram pulled Kara to him, and they kissed long and passionately. "I can't believe you're here," she said.

"I know for your sake and the sake of our son that I must go soon. It's imperative that I am not here when the oberstrumführer arrives. But I want you to know that no matter what happens to me, I will treasure these moments with you until the day I die."

She held him tightly. "My dear God, you are so thin. You feel like skin and bones." Then she added in a desperate voice, "I can't let you go. I can't. I might never have another chance to hold you like this . . ."

"Believe me, I don't want to leave you. I want to be with you more than anything in the world. But if I stay here, you and Karl could be in danger. The oberstrumführer must never find out that Karl is half Jewish. And although it is less important to me than the safety of the two of you, if Lerch finds me here, he will shoot me on the spot. If I leave and run, I can try like hell to stay alive until we can find a way to be together again."

"You mean, like an end to all of this? That is the only way we can be together?"

"Yes."

She was quiet for a moment, then she said, "Take me with you. I'll leave Karl here with Anka. He'll be safe. Take me with you. I don't care what happens to me as long as you are by my side."

"No. I can't. You would be in danger, and I won't do that. I refuse to do that."

She began to cry softly.

"Do you remember that morning I was arrested?"

"Of course. You never returned to us. Your mother and I were beside ourselves. We didn't know what to do. We didn't know why you'd been taken."

"The Gestapo beat me until I was half alive. Then they threw me into a truck that took me to a ghetto."

"The one in Warsaw?"

"No, it was in Lodz."

"Why did they arrest you? What did you do?"

"Kara, you still don't understand. All you have to do to be

173

arrested or murdered is just be a Jew. They've built camps where they are putting us. Sometimes they are killing us in these places."

"Killing?"

"Yes, killing. There are gas chambers where they gas many people at once. Old people and children don't have a chance at all."

"I can't believe this."

"It's true. And if you were with me, you might as well be a Jew. They would kill you and ask questions later. I refuse to let that happen. I'd rather die than put you or our son at risk."

"I'm shocked. I can't imagine a camp where they are killing people."

"You know the ashes that fall from the sky around here every day?"

"Yes, Oskar says they are from the chemical plants."

"They are not. They're ashes from the crematoriums. The Nazis are burning bodies."

"Dear God. Those poor Jewish people. My heart hurts," Kara said.

"Not only Jews, political prisoners, Gypsies, Jehovah's Witnesses, children and old people who can't work, and anyone else they think is not fit to live. They think we are subhumans."

"I can't believe they would murder people outright."

"They are. I would never lie to you," he said gravely.

"I know that."

"And that's why you must stay here and pretend you don't know anything. You must keep yourself and Karl safe under the protection of the oberstrumführer. This nightmare can't last forever. God has to be watching. This must come to an end."

She began to cry. "You guessed right; I've been hiding Karl's identity. I don't know what came over me when I said that you were his father in front of Bertram and that other man. Who was that other man?"

"A guard. He was a guard from the camp where I was transferred. It wasn't the camp with a crematorium. It was another camp; one where they had two coal mines. Horribly dangerous."

"Dear God," Kara said, "Being half Jewish could cost our son his life."

"It could and it would if they found out the truth. They would not think twice about killing him. And you as well. This is very crucial. You must tell them that you were hallucinating when you said I was his father. You must pretend that you saw someone else. A gentile. You must never tell them that Karl has a drop of Jewish blood. Can you trust Anka to keep this secret?"

"Yes, I think so. After all, she's my sister. She would never put Karl or me in danger."

"That's good. I didn't think she would. I know how close the two of you were. Now I have to get going."

"No, a few more minutes. Please, Abram."

He kissed her again. Then he put his face into her hair and inhaled her essence. "Remember today. Remember my arms around you and know that with every breath I draw, I will be trying to survive so that I can return to you someday when it's safe for you and Karl."

"Don't go. Please don't go," she said. Then she tugged at the shirt of his uniform. "I'll leave Karl here with Anka, and I'll come with you. I don't care what happens to me as long as I am with you."

"I told you before you must stay here. If not for your sake, then for Karl's. I don't want to be apart from you, but Kara, it's dangerous. It's so dangerous. They'll kill us if they catch us."

"I'd rather die with you than live without you."

"No. You must live, and Karl must live."

"Without you?"

"I don't know. But what I will promise you is that I'll do everything I can to get back to you. But in the meantime, you must protect Karl. You must live the lie until it's safe to no longer do so."

"But what if this never ends?"

"It will. It must," Abram said, not sure if he was telling the truth.

"And then . . . once it ends?"

He squeezed her tighter. "I'll come back, if I am alive. And if not . . . you must find a good man. A truly good man. Not a Nazi. A man who will be good to you and Karl. No one should live their lives alone."

"I don't want you to leave here without me. Please, Abram . . ."

Abram wiped the tears from his face with the back of his hand. "I must leave now. Not so much for my own sake but for yours and Karl's. I don't dare stay a minute longer. You must do as I ask. You two are the most important people in the world to me. No matter what happens, it will comfort me to know you two are safe."

She stared into his eyes.

"Promise me you'll do as I ask. Promise me you won't tell the oberstrumführer that you know the truth about him. You don't want to anger him anyway. Believe me. I know."

"How can I live this lie?"

"Because you have to. You must in order to keep Karl safe. Please, do this until you can get away safely."

She nodded.

He touched her face gently. "You're so beautiful. Every night before I fell asleep, I would picture your face. I thought I remembered you exactly, but you're even more beautiful than I remembered."

"I love you so much," she said.

"I know. I love you too."

"Do you need food? You look so thin?"

"Yes, my friend and I have escaped from the camp. We are on our own, and we have nothing to eat. Can I take the loaf of bread in the kitchen?"

"Of course. Take the bread, and there might be some cheese or potatoes too."

"Are you sure?"

"I am sure."

"I love you. I love you with all my heart," he said, then he gently peeled her hands off of him, bent down, and gently kissed her.

"Wait," she said. "Take some clothes out of Oskar's closet. You won't be as noticeable if you're not wearing that uniform."

"Are you sure? What will he say if he sees his clothes are missing?"

"I don't think he'll notice."

"It's too dangerous, Kara. I won't put you in danger for my sake."

"Please . . . it might help you. I want you to take the clothes."

He shook his head. "No, darling." Then he touched her face, bent to kiss her one more time, turned, and then he left the room.

Anka was standing in the hallway.

"Anka," Abram said, "thank you."

She nodded.

After Abram left the house, Anka went into the bedroom to see Kara.

Kara looked at her sister with sad eyes and a tear-stained face.

"Tell me everything," Anka said, having lost all of her color as she sat down on the edge of the bed.

"All right," Kara said. "But you must promise me you won't tell anyone, because if you do, they will take Karl away, and they might even decide to kill him."

"I promise you," Anka said.

Kara told her sister everything from the day she met Abram until she arrived at Anka's house with Karl. When she finished, Anka stared at Kara, her eyes wide with shock. "I blame myself," she said. "You went out to find forbidden books for me. If you hadn't gone to the Jewish sector of Berlin searching for those books, you would never have met him."

"I don't regret a minute with Abram. Not a single second. He brought love and light into my life, Anka. And . . . he gave me Karl."

"But he's a Jew, and now you and Karl have to be so careful because you have so many secrets. You're living a lie."

Kara nodded, and in a small voice, she said, "Yes." Then she cleared her throat. "I would have left here and gone with Abram if he would have let me." Then she took Anka's hand in hers. "Do you know that the Nazis are murdering people in gas chambers. Lots of people. I don't even know how many. They are murdering them, Anka. Mothers, fathers, sisters, children."

"I don't believe it," Anka said.

"I do. Abram would never lie to me. He said they're killing all the people they don't think are worthy of life. Jews, Gypsies, children, old people . . ."

Anka looked away. "But Jews are dangerous. They aren't human beings like us. They are another species, a lesser species."

Kara shook her head and sucked in her breath. "No Anka. I know we grew up believing this, but I promise you it's not true."

"I am afraid of them."

"No, you mustn't be. Jews are just people; they are just like us. I know. I lived with Abram and his mother. They were wonderful people, kind, loving. You don't really know any Jews; that's why you feel this way. If you did, you would feel differently."

"I have always been afraid of them. In school they told us how dangerous and evil they were. Mutti and Vater were afraid of them. I know our parents weren't the kind of people you could trust or believe, but they were the only parents we had. And I suppose that whatever they believed, I believed."

Neither of them looked at each other. Then Kara turned to Anka and took both her hands into her own. "Do you remember when we were children, and I told you the story of *The Ugly Duckling*?" Kara asked gently.

Anka let out a short soft laugh. "How could I forget. It was my favorite story, and you must have told it to me a hundred times."

"Yes, it was your favorite." Kara smiled at the memory. "Do you remember the story? How sad it was because all the baby ducks hated the ugly duckling because he was different?"

"Of course, but he fooled them when he grew up to be a beautiful swan."

"Yes, exactly right. And that it how it is with the Jews. At least for me, that's how it was. Because we were raised to believe that the Jews were different. I thought they were dangerous, ugly. But when I got to know them, to really know Abram and his mother, I saw their beautiful hearts."

Anka closed her eyes. For a moment she didn't speak, then she said, "So, now I understand why you got so upset when I took you to the ghetto to buy the furs from those Jewish women."

"They are people. When I saw those children starving, and you offered their mothers so little for the only things of value that they had left to sell, it tore my heart out," Kara said.

"I remember," Anka said. "I was so angry with you for spoiling our day together, but I didn't think of it that way. I didn't know about you and Karl. Everyone I knew, all of the other wives of German officers, were going shopping in the ghetto. Some of them took what they wanted and didn't pay at all. I never thought about how my actions were affecting the people who lived there. At the time I thought of them as subhumans. The way we'd been taught. I didn't care about them. I only thought about the furs."

"I know you, Anka. I know you better than anyone else. You can be self-centered and childish. But what I also know is that deep down in your heart, you are not a mean or cruel person. You've made mistakes, but who hasn't, and you have misjudged people based on a lack of information. But your heart is good."

"I still find it hard to trust Jews, and I can't help it, Kara. I am still afraid of them. But I love you and I love Karl. And I don't care if he's half Jewish. He's my nephew."

"So, as a special favor to me, will you just try to see that the Jews are not the monsters we grew up to believe that they were. I know it will take time to get over your old beliefs. I ask only that you try."

"I'll try. For you and for Karl. I'll try."

Kara was silent for a moment. "Now that I have seen Abram again, I have hope. I have hope that someday he and I will be together again."

Anka squeezed Kara's hand. Then in a small voice, she said, "Kara."

"Yes?"

"Am I really self-centered and childish?"

"Yep."

"That's awful," Anka said. "Am I really?"

"Well, sometimes you are. But I love you anyway." Then she

179

added, "Come here." And she pulled Anka into a bear hug. "You're my sister. You'll always be my sister. The same blood runs through both of our veins. We're connected by that blood. And even though Karl is half Jewish, he has the same blood in his veins. He is my son."

"I know."

"We need each other, Anka. We need each other more and more all the time. This war has set us against each other. But the truth is we should be closer now than ever.

"I want that," Anka said. "So can you forgive me for being selfish and childish?"

Kara laughed. "Absolutely. How could I ever feel otherwise?" Then Anka laughed too.

CHAPTER FORTY-SEVEN

LUDWIG WAS in the kitchen of the messy house where he and Anka had lived together. He was washing the dishes from the poorly prepared dinner he'd cooked for himself when the phone rang.

He picked up the receiver, his hands still wet and soapy from the dishwater. "Allo," he said.

"It's Anka. I don't know if you tried to telephone me, but the children must have knocked the receiver off the hook. Oskar hasn't even called, and we have no way of reaching him. So, it must have been off for a while." She hesitated, hoping he would say he'd tried to call. But he said nothing, so she cleared her throat and said, "I'm sorry."

He wiped his hands on his pants and sat down in the chair next to the phone. "Anka." His heart was thumping so hard, he thought it might jump right out of his chest. "Are you all right?"

"I'm all right, but Kara's not. She had a miscarriage."

Ludwig sighed. "I'm sorry. That's terrible news."

"I just called to tell you that I miss you," she said in a small, tearful voice. "I really do miss you."

He let out a sigh. "I never thought I would hear those words from you," Ludwig said.

There was a moment of silence. He thought she'd hung up the phone. "Anka, are you still there?" he asked.

"Do you love her, Ludwig?"

He knew she meant Aloisa. He sucked in a deep breath and said, "You are my one true love; you know that . . . but you never loved me."

There was silence again. Then she said, "I did. I just never knew it. I never knew how to show it."

Ludwig had to steady his trembling hand, or he would have dropped the receiver. "Can I come over there. I need to see you."

"Yes, please come," Anka said.

"I'll leave now. I should be there by tomorrow night."

CHAPTER FORTY-EIGHT

WHEN ANKA SAW Ludwig's car pull up in front of the Lerches' house at a little before six in the evening, she ran out the door to meet him. And just as the door swung shut behind her, the phone began to ring. Kara had drifted off to sleep along with the children. So no one heard the ringing, and no one answered.

In all the years Anka and Ludwig had spent together, Anka had never been happier to see her husband. She'd never realized how much she needed him. Practically flying into his arms, she embraced him.

"It's been so hard," she said, "It's been so hard. With Kara stuck in bed recovering, everything is my responsibility now, and I can't manage it."

"Shhh, I know. Don't you worry. It will all be fine now. I'm here. I will take care of everything."

Anka began to cry. "Is it over between you and her?"

"If you want it to be," he said.

"I do. I want to try again. I love you."

"Then it's over. I am yours," he said, holding her tightly. "I've always been yours."

CHAPTER FORTY-NINE

LUDWIG KNEW Aloisa would be arriving home from work at seven. So, at exactly seven o'clock, he picked up the phone to call her. He had to tell her that he and Anka were going to try again. It was only right. His heart was beating fast in his chest as he listened to the phone ringing. He didn't relish the idea of hurting her. But he wanted things to work out between himself and Anka so badly that he felt he must end it with Aloisa as soon as possible.

"Allo," Aloisa said.

The sound of her voice sent a wave of guilt coursing through him. "It's me."

"Ludwig. I'm so glad you called. I just walked in from work not five minutes ago," she giggled. "I'm glad I didn't miss your call."

"I-I . . ." he stammered. "I have to tell you something."

"Yes? Is everything all right? It doesn't have anything to do with Oskar, does it?"

"No. It doesn't have anything to do with Oskar." His voice was soft and riddled with guilt. "I don't know how to say this. But I saw Anka, and we talked things over. We have decided to try again."

There was silence for a moment. He could hear her breathing.

"What does that mean?" she asked in a small voice.

He didn't answer. "I'll send you rent money for the next three months. I hope that will help you to get on your feet."

She didn't answer.

"Aloisa?"

"I don't know what to say." Then she asked, "So, it's over with us?"

"I'm sorry, but yes. I'm afraid it is."

"And so, what happens to me? You just leave me?"

"I'm sorry. I have a wife and child. You knew that."

"But you left them. She was horrible to you. Did you forget? How could you forget? She treated you worse than a Jew. And you want to take her back after all of that? I don't understand you."

"I know. It doesn't make sense. But I love her. I am sorry."

She didn't say anything for a long time, then she said, "Well, there's nothing else to say, is there?"

"I'm sorry," he said again. He couldn't think of anything else to say.

"Goodbye, Ludwig."

"Goodbye, Aloisa," he said and hung up the receiver, glad to be done with that call.

CHAPTER FIFTY

ALOISA ROLLED herself into a fetal position and lay down on her bed. She was devastated by the breakup. She had become attached to Ludwig, and she didn't know how she was going to survive without him. He was her best friend and her anchor. And now he was gone. *I can't understand how he could leave me for that mean and wretched wife of his.*

She pounded her fists into her pillow. *Damn it. I don't know what he is thinking. But lying in bed and feeling sorry for myself isn't not going to solve anything. Ludwig doesn't love me enough, so he is gone. There is nothing more to say or do about it. I can be miserable, or I can go out and get drunk.*

She stood up and looked in the mirror. Then she picked up a comb and ran it through her hair, applied a fresh coat of lipstick, grabbed her handbag and keys and walked out the door. *He's a good-for-nothing bastard. A stupid fool too,* she thought as she climbed down the stairs. *And now I am going to have to move back into that hotel. I hate to give up my apartment. But I can't afford it without Ludwig's help. Damn that wife of his. She doesn't love him. She just misses the comfortable life he provided for her. I am sure of it.* It had been raining all day. *Of course, today is one of those dismal, rainy days that always leave me feeling so depressed. It's just the perfect day for something like this to happen,* she thought.

When she got to the bottom of the stairs, she slid on some rain-water that someone had tracked into the lobby, and dropped her handbag. The contents of her purse spilled on the floor. "Shit," she said. She was feeling miserable, but she told herself that life must go on. *I'll go out and get drunk. Maybe I'll even meet someone and spend the night with a stranger. Sometimes that's just what you need to get over a breakup. Alcohol and sex. She* reached down to pick her things up so she could put her handbag back together, when she felt someone grab her from behind. She tried to turn to see what was happening, but whoever had her was very strong, and she was unable to move.

Her heart pounded so hard that it felt like it was going to burst. She tried to fight, to kick, to scream, but the assailant's hand covered her mouth, and she wasn't strong enough to pull away. Tears fell from her eyes. *Take my handbag, take whatever you want,* she thought. But she was unable to speak.

Then she found herself under the stairwell. If she could escape that menacing hand, she could scream. She bit at the palm. He let out a cry of pain. For a moment, she was free. She began to run and let out a scream. But he pulled her back by her legs. "I'm warning you. Be quiet if you want to live. If you scream again, I'll kill you." The voice was deep and unrecognizable. She didn't let out another scream, nor did she try to kick him again.

"Please, let me go. Take what you want. I am begging you." He still held her from behind. She flung her handbag backward toward him. Aloisa turned her head to the side, and then she saw him. A tall, dark-haired soldier with a mustache and thick glasses. He held her close to his chest for a moment. Then he let out a short laugh. Terror shot through her. She thought he might rape her. But then he put his hand over her lips again, though this time, he inserted the side of his hand deep into her mouth so that he was choking her. She couldn't bite or scream.

"Pretty good disguise, eh?" he said. This time, his voice was different. He held her like that, her heart fluttering like a captive animal. "It's me, your old friend, Oskar."

Aloisa tried to answer, but she choked on the words.

"I'm sorry it had to come to this. I truly am." His voice was soft

187

but terrifying. "You see, my dear, you just know too much. I couldn't let you live. How could I?"

She began to struggle. Now tears flooded her face. She whipped her head from side to side.

"I do so much enjoy feeling a woman helpless in my arms. However, someone might come downstairs at any time, so, I must end our little tryst," he said.

Aloisa desperately tried to say no. But all she was able to get past the hand that was choking her were pathetic grunts.

Then with a single twist of his arm, Oskar broke her neck. She went limp in his arms. He checked her for a pulse. Once he was certain she was dead, he let her body fall to the floor. Then he ripped off her underclothes, spread her legs and raped her. The power of her fear had excited him, and he was spent quickly. Next, he ran to the lobby, and gathered all of the things that had fallen on the floor when she'd dropped her purse. He took all the money she had and threw the handbag and the remainder of its contents down beside her. Then tucking the money into his uniform, he made sure the lobby was empty. It was. Leaving her naked and exposed, he walked out of the building. *When the police find her, they will think she was robbed and raped. They will probably assume it was a stranger. After all, no one saw me anywhere near this place. Instead of a blond SS officer, what they saw was a dark-haired soldier with thick glasses. My mission has been accomplished. My secret is safe; she will be silent forever*, he thought as he left the building.

CHAPTER FIFTY-ONE

THE RAIN HAD TURNED to a light drizzle. Oskar turned up the collar of his jacket as he walked to the corner. Then he sat down on a bench and waited. It had been easy to walk the streets unnoticed. There were so many other soldiers all around that no one paid him any attention. *How very different people are toward SS officers. They are afraid when they see the uniform, but they aren't intimidated by ordinary soldiers.* A few minutes later, the bus arrived. He boarded it and paid his fare. No one on the bus even looked up when he entered.

It was all over. He was on his way back to the cheap hotel where he was staying under the name of Franz Muller. He'd checked in three days ago after he'd purchased the costume he now wore. It was a seedy hotel where no one knew him. And that was just the way he wanted it. *Everything is going according to plan. Soon I'll be back home with Kara, and this nightmare will be over.* When Oskar entered the hotel, he shook the rain off his coat. It smelled of sauerkraut and spices. Oskar walked past the front desk. As he did, a tired old woman who was the desk clerk looked up from her magazine.

"Good evening," the handsome dark-haired soldier with the thick glasses, said.

"Good evening, Herr Muller," she answered, clearly charmed by his attention.

She remembered my name. That's good. If the police come by here for some unknown reason, she will say that Franz Muller, a dark-haired, studious-looking soldier was staying here. If they ask her about a blond-haired SS officer, she will say she never saw him.

A half smile was on Oskar's face as he walked up the rickety wooden stairs to his room. He was glad that he had already fulfilled his obligation to spread his Aryan seed at Steinhöring, home for the Lebensborn. He'd registered there as Oberstrumführer Oskar Lerch and had then spent the entire afternoon and evening there during which time he had lain with two women. They were both young, pretty, and blonde. Both of the girls had been hopeful that he would leave them with child. It had been a tedious and boring experience for him. The girls were far too willing, which left him unchallenged. He'd had to close his eyes and think of Kara in order to perform. But he knew it was clever of him to use Steinhöring as an alibi for why he'd come to Munich. Plenty of SS officers came to Munich for just this very reason, to lay with young women under the guise of fulfilling their obligation to the fatherland. So the alibi was as good and solid as he could have hoped for.

And while he'd been at Steinhöring, he'd been careful not to encounter Aloisa again. It was not difficult to avoid her. She was in the adoption section, while he was on the other side with the women who waited for the SS officers to come and impregnate them. Oskar knew that after their dinner together, Aloisa thought he'd returned home. It was best that she believed she was safe, and so she had let down her guard. That was what he wanted. Because she would not have been alarmed, and therefore she would not have contacted Ludwig. He would wait a day or two to drop off the car he'd borrowed so he didn't look suspicious in any way, although he couldn't imagine why he would. Before he returned the car, he planned to rid himself of any evidence. He would throw his black wig, the glasses, and the soldier's uniform into the river. Then he would board a train and return home.

CHAPTER FIFTY-TWO

FOR THE FIRST time since they were married, Ludwig and Anka made love like lovers. There was a mutual caring and warmth between them that seemed like a dream to Ludwig. Once they'd finished, they lay side by side, breathless and spent. It was almost nine o'clock that evening when the phone rang.

"Lie here," Anka said gently. "I'll get it."

He overhead her in the other room. "Oskar. I'm so glad you called. I didn't know where to reach you. There's been an emergency. Kara miscarried the baby."

A few moments passed. Then Anka said, "Yes, she is all right. I'll see you in a day or two."

When Anka returned to the bedroom, Ludwig was sitting up in bed. She got in beside him. "It was Oskar; he's on his way home."

"Where was he; do you know?"

"I think Kara said he was going to Munich."

Ludwig felt a chill run down his spine. He considered telling Anka everything Aloisa had told him about Oskar. He was afraid for Aloisa. But he had never had a night like this with Anka. He'd dreamed of it often, but this was the first time it had happened, and he didn't want to bring up Aloisa and possibly spoil the mood. So although there was a nagging worry in his gut that Oskar had done something to Aloisa, Ludwig ignored it. Instead, he took Anka into his arms and made love to her again.

CHAPTER FIFTY-THREE

AFTER OSKAR HEARD about Kara losing the baby, he changed his plans. He wouldn't return the car that he'd borrowed. He decided to drive rather than wait for a train, so as to get home as soon as possible. Kara needed him, and his love for her was so strong, it was almost painful. He telephoned the Nazi headquarters and explained that he had to drive the car to Poland because his wife had miscarried. He promised to return to Munich and bring it back the following month.

Then he forced himself to take a serious inventory of the room to make sure he'd not been careless and left anything behind that could link him to the murder. It was hard to be meticulous in the cleaning, because he wanted to get on the road. He was sick with worry and longed to be at Kara's side. But he forced himself to be thorough. Once he was sure he'd left no trace of Oskar Lerch, he rolled the costume, the wig, and the clothing he'd worn during the murder, into a ball, put them into a bag, and slipped out the back door of the hotel. He looked around to make sure no one had seen him. Then he climbed into the auto and began to drive.

He drove through the night. His hands trembled on the wheel. *Kara needs me. I must get to her.*

At the crack of dawn, he saw a body of water. It was barely sunrise, so no one was around. Quickly, he pulled the car over and took the bag with the clothing and wig and tossed it into the water. Then he got back into the car and drove as fast as he could toward home.

Oskar arrived the following evening. He didn't stop to say hello to Anka, Ludwig, or Karl. He ran up the stairs to his bedroom where he knew Kara lay. His heart pounded in his chest. Without knocking, he went straight into the room he shared with Kara. Kara was on her side on the bed. She turned when she heard the door open. "Oskar," she said.

"Yes, I'm here. I came as soon as I heard." He knelt at her bedside, his stomach in knots. With trembling hands, he took both her hands in his and began kissing her palms. "My darling, I am so sorry," he said. "Anka told me what happened."

She nodded. "I know. I'm sorry too." Then she tried to force herself to give him at least some sort of a smile. But instead her lower lip jutted out, and she began to cry again, her face already a tear-stained mess.

"Kara, my darling, my love," he said as he took her into her arms and rocked her gently like a baby. "Please don't cry. At least you are all right. We'll have more children. We'll have as many as you want. Just please don't cry. You need your strength to get well."

Now, as he sat beside her, and she was looking at him, she found it so hard to believe what Abram had told her about what he'd done to the Jewish prisoners. *He is so gentle and loving toward me. Could Abram be mistaken?* Kara longed to ask Oskar if it was true. But she knew deep in her heart that it was. Abram would never lie to her. And although she was certain that Oskar loved her, she also felt that there was a line she dare not cross. Somehow, she believed that if she did cross that line, she might get a glimpse of the man Abram had told her about.

The very thought was terrifying. Oskar would be angry if she asked him about his work. He would want to know how she'd found out. Kara looked into his eyes and decided it would be a mistake to open that Pandora's box, because once it was open, there would be no going back. Besides, she'd promised Abram that she would never let Oskar know that she knew who he really was. And the last thing she needed was for Oskar to ask her any questions. Until now he'd never asked about Karl's father. She had to keep it that way. Right now, Karl was safe. She was safe too. She must live this lie as Abram had instructed her to do, until she could find a way to free herself and her son.

"I am here with you now. I'll take care of you," Oskar said, touching her face.

"I feel so bad about the baby, Oskar." It was true. She did feel bad about losing the baby. She'd felt life in her womb, and now that life was gone. Her womb was empty, and although the child was Oskar's, it was hers too, and she missed it.

HE NODDED and took her into his arms. She wept. She wept for the child who had been a part of her if only for a short time. The child whose small kicks had made her smile, who's knee, or elbow had rested on her bladder keeping her awake and urinating at night. She wept for Karl who did not, and might never, know the wonderful man who was his real father. And she also wept for herself. Somehow, each night, she must lie beneath this man who was her husband and make believe that she didn't know who he really was.

CHAPTER FIFTY-FOUR

ANKA AND LUDWIG took Gretel and returned home three days later. They would have stayed longer, but Ludwig had to return to work.

The following day, after Ludwig left for work, there was a knock on Anka's door. It was the new neighbor, Erna Hoffenberg. She and her husband Werner had moved in while Anka was away. She brought a plate of cookies and introduced herself. Anka put on a pot of tea. She was glad to make a female friend. As they sat sipping tea and eating cookies, Erna told Anka that her husband, Werner, was older than she was. "But he's a wonderful husband. A war hero too. He was in the Great War. And now he works at the lair with your husband. You husband works at the lair too, doesn't he?" she said.

Anka smiled. "Yes, actually he does. And you must be very proud to be married to a war hero."

"Oh, I am," Erna said. Erna was Anka's age, and they got along well. For the time being, Erna served as a surrogate sister to Anka, who missed Kara terribly. Of course, she could never take Kara's place in Anka's heart, but she was cheerful, and at least she took up Anka's time while Ludwig was at work. The couples became close friends in a short period of time. Erna had no children, but she adored Gretel, and because she'd helped her mother raise her younger brother, she proved to be a great help to Anka. One afternoon, Erna took Gretel to her house for a few hours so Anka could get some peace and quiet. It gave Anka great comfort to know she had someone she could rely on, the way she'd always relied on Kara.

When Anka called Kara to see how she was feeling, Kara told her that Oskar hired a nurse to come in each day to help Kara with Karl and with anything else she needed until she regained her strength. Kara whispered to Anka on the phone that it was hard for her to see Oskar, a man who was so totally devoted to her, as the brute Abram had described.

"He is so kind to me," Kara said into the receiver. "He brings me flowers each day when he comes home from work. And he tries very hard to prepare meals he thinks will appeal to me. His kindness to Karl and the dog is unsurpassed. And yet, try as I might to push the words Abram said about Oskar to the back of my mind in order to make living with him easier, I can't. When I close my eyes, I can still see Abram's face when he told me that Oskar was a sadist, that he beat Jewish men to death."

"You must put all of that out of your mind, Kara. Oskar is good to you. That's what matters," Anka said. "Whatever you had with that other man is over now. You must forget it. He is a Jew. That is dangerous, not only for you but for Karl. Remember that," Anka said.

"Yes, I know you're right, but although Oskar is a wonderful husband and father, there is a dark cloud that hangs over him, now that I know what I know."

"You must put it out of your mind. I am warning you," Anka said.

"I will try. I promise," Kara said. "Good night now."

"Good night."

Each evening, Anka called to ask Kara how she was feeling and to tell her how happy she and Ludwig were. She told her about the Hoffenbergs next door, and how helpful Erna was with Gretel. "But Ludwig thinks Erna will get tired of me asking her for help with the child," Anka said. "He is afraid it will put a damper on the friend-ship. I can't help it though. You know how hard it is for me to care for Gretel on my own. I am just so glad to have Erna living next door."

"Yes, but perhaps Ludwig is right. Maybe you shouldn't put so much pressure on the friendship so soon. You've only known her for a week or so. How often do you ask her for help?"

"Every day," Anka admitted.

"I have to agree with Ludwig. I think it's too much too soon to ask of a new friend."

Anka groaned with disappointment. Then she said, "Well, I must go now. I have to get Gretel off to bed."

Kara knew she'd upset her sister. But she wanted to see Anka happy and comfortable in her life, so she'd told her the truth.

A few nights later, when Anka called, she told Kara, "Ludwig hired a nanny for Gretel. He knew I couldn't manage without help. So now I have someone to help me. He understands me. Kara, you are the only other person who has ever understood me fully. So, you understand that I am just not capable of handling all of this. Ludwig knows it too. He knows that I can't do it alone."

"I'm so happy to hear that the two of you are doing better."

"We are. I am so glad that we worked everything out between us. I had to come very close to losing him before I realized how much he meant to me," Anka said.

"Well, at least you finally realized."

"Yes, I'm glad I found out in time. I could have lost him to that woman forever." Anka sighed. "Are you alone?"

"Oskar is in the bedroom and Karl is in bed. So, yes, I am alone in the living room. Why?"

"Did Karl ever mention Abram again?" Anka asked.

"No. I hope he doesn't. Why, did he ever ask you about my telling him that Abram was his father?"

"Yes, but I told him you were hallucinating because you lost a lot of blood during the miscarriage," Anka said.

"Good. That was good thinking."

"I just wanted to be sure that he didn't say anything in front of

Oskar," Anka said. "And, of course, you know that your secret is safe with me."

"I know. You're my sister, and you will always be my best friend."

"Always, Kara. Through thick and thin," Anka said, her voice so emotional that it caught in her throat.

"Yes. Through thick and thin. Like always," Kara said.

CHAPTER FIFTY-FIVE

THE FOLLOWING MORNING, at almost dawn, a pale hint of light flickered through the kitchen window where Kara was busy preparing Oskar's breakfast. Karl was still asleep. But Oskar would be ready for work soon. Her heart was still heavy from the loss of the child, but she was physically well enough to get out of bed and do a few things around the house. And she wanted to stay busy. It made life easier when she had less time to think. Kara was slicing a piece of bread when the phone rang. Kara jumped. It was too early for a call. She ran to the phone and answered on the first ring.

"Allo."

"Kara, it's Anka. Something terrible has happened." Anka was hysterical. "Ludwig has been arrested. The police came an hour ago and took him into the station for questioning."

"What do you mean Ludwig has been arrested, taken in for questioning? Questioning about what?" Kara asked frantically. She smelled the eggs in the kitchen burning but she didn't ask Anka to hold on. *Let the eggs burn; my sister needs me.*

"I find it all so hard to believe. But apparently that girl Aloisa, the one who was Ludwig's mistress, was murdered. I know he called her and broke things off the other night because he told me he did.

It was part of our new start. But now she's dead. They are blaming him. How can that be? He was here with me. I told them that, but they took him anyway. I'm beside myself."

"Murdered? I can't believe it."

"Yes, the police said she was murdered, robbed, and raped. The police found her naked body under the stairwell in her apartment building. All of her valuables were gone. How horrible. They kept insisting that Ludwig was involved. But I know it's impossible. I know because he was here with me. I told them that. They still took him in. They said they had to question him. I am so worried, Kara."

"All right, all right. Calm down. Now, we know that he couldn't have done it. So, you have to believe that they'll be able to see the truth once he explains everything. They'll see that he was here with you, so he couldn't have been involved."

"I hope so," Anka said. "Oskar has so much influence. can you please ask him to help? He has friends he could call, important men who could intervene on Ludwig's behalf."

"Of course I'll ask him. I know he'll help."

"Thank you, Kara," Anka said. "I really wish you were here. I am shaking. I can't take care of the baby, and the nanny won't be here for two hours. I don't know what to do. I need you."

"I know. But I can't get there fast enough to help you. Even if I left right now, the nanny would be there long before I would."

"You're right," Anka said.

"So, I'll stay close to the phone. Call me as soon as you hear anything, will you?" Kara said.

"Of course, you know I will."

Kara hung up the receiver just as Oskar walked into the kitchen. He was tall and handsome in his uniform. Leaning over, he kissed her. "Good morning, my love," he said. "How are you feeling today? You know you don't have to get up and prepare my breakfast. I'd rather you got your rest."

Kara didn't address anything he said. She turned and looked directly into his eyes. "Oskar, that was Anka on the phone."

"I didn't even hear it ring," he said casually as he sat down at the table. Then he looked closer at her face and saw the worried look. "What is it? Is something wrong?"

"Ludwig has been arrested for murder. The girl from the Lebensborn that he was having an affair with was found dead. But she had to have been killed when Ludwig was here with Anka. He couldn't have done it. Is there some way you might call one of your influential friends and ask them to help, Ludwig? I am worried."

Oskar turned away from her. He didn't want her to see that the blood had drained from his face. "Certainly," he said in the most casual voice he could muster. "I'll do what I can."

"I knew you would," Kara said. "Let me get your breakfast. I'm afraid I will have to remake the eggs. I burned them."

He'd lost his appetite. "Oh, please don't trouble yourself. I'm sorry. I failed to tell you that I had to be in to work early this morning. No time to eat, I'm afraid."

"It's all right," she said, "Do you want me to pack you something to take with you?"

"No, it's not necessary." Oskar managed a smile. Then he stood up from the table and kissed her again. "I'll see you tonight," he said and walked out the door.

Bertram was standing outside beside the automobile waiting for Oskar. "Good morning, Oberstrumführer," he said as he opened the back door for Oskar.

Oskar didn't answer. He had too much on his mind to be bothered. He climbed in and then nodded for Bertram to close the door.

Bertram had come to know when his boss was not in the mood to talk, so he didn't try to initiate a conversation. He started the car and began the drive to work.

Oskar watched the scenery out the window without really seeing it. His mind was occupied. He drummed his fingers on the door handle as he thought, *I am so glad I am rid of Aloisa. At least I got her out of the way before she had a chance to tell Ludwig anything. I am sure that if she had told him what I did with Karl, he would already have told Anka. And there is no doubt that Anka would have gone to Kara right away. So, I am sure he knows nothing. So he can't squeal like a pig to the police, now that he's been arrested. Not only would Kara learn the truth, but I might be arrested and sentenced, who knows. But all signs point to Ludwig. And that's just the way I want it. Ludwig has always been a weakling. But he is caught in his own trap right now. Even if he gets off, he has no evidence against me, and with Aloisa gone, he will never know my secret.*

CHAPTER FIFTY-SIX

THE POLICE ROUGHED UP LUDWIG, and they questioned him several times that day trying to force him to admit his guilt. He insisted he was innocent. He told them the truth, that he was with Anka. He wanted to tell them what Aloisa had said about Oskar kidnapping the child, but he was too afraid. Oskar had friends with high positions in the party. It was a dangerous thing to bring suspicion onto a man like Oskar. Ludwig was certain that Oskar could easily arrange for him to quietly disappear without ever leaving this police station. It was best, Ludwig decided, to stick with his alibi and pretend he had no idea who killed Aloisa. Let them think it was a random rape and murder.

Finally at nine o'clock in the evening, after a full day of relentless questioning, Ludwig was released and allowed to return home.

Gretel had just fallen asleep, but Anka was still awake when Ludwig opened the door. "Are you all right? Did they hurt you?"

"No, they hit me a few times. But I'm fine," he said wearily. "I'm tired and hungry, but at least I'm home."

"Let me call Kara and tell her that you are home. She's been waiting for my call."

He nodded. He was glad that Anka was at home and not at Kara's house with Oskar. He didn't trust him.

Anka told Kara that Ludwig was home safe but that he was hungry and tired. "I'll call you in the morning," she said.

"I'm so glad he's all right," Kara said.

After Anka hung up the phone, she took a slice of bread and some butter and placed them on the table. She scrambled two eggs and put them on a plate in front of Ludwig. Then she sat down across from Ludwig and touched his hand. "I'm so glad to see you," she said. "I've been worried."

"I must be mad. Even with all that is going on right now, it still feels so wonderful just to hear you say that you care," he said, smiling. And she noticed the police had split his lip.

"I do care. I am so glad we have finally worked things out between us," she said.

"I love you, Anka. I've always loved you. And even though I went through a terrible, frightening day, I am so happy to know you cared enough to worry about me."

"Ludwig," she said, "I am glad you still love me after everything we've been through."

"Love doesn't disappear. In fact, the truth is, no matter what I did, I never stopped loving you. Not even when I thought you wanted me to let you go."

She smiled at him. "Eat something. Then you'll take a nice hot bath. Yes?"

He nodded.

For a few minutes, he ate, and she sat beside him silently. Then she said, "I called Kara as soon as you were arrested. I am so thankful that Oskar has so much influence. She asked him to help. Maybe he did. Maybe he is the reason you're home safe with me right now."

Ludwig put the slice of buttered bread down on his plate. He looked directly into Anka's eyes. Holding her gaze, he said, "I doubt that." He couldn't lie to her now that they'd worked things out. He'd always hated lying to her. Taking her hands in his, he said, "I have something I think I should tell you."

"Please, Ludwig, tell me you had nothing to do with that girl's murder. I know you couldn't have killed her because you were here with me. But what is it that you have to tell me?"

"I didn't want to bring this up because we were doing so well, and we were both so happy. I didn't want to think about it. In fact, I was ridiculously hoping it could all just disappear, but secrets and lies never do. And now, I feel that if I don't tell you, I'll be holding something back that will be a wedge between us."

"Did you do something terrible, Ludwig? Something I don't know about? You didn't kill that woman or have her killed, did you?"

"No." He shook his head. "I didn't. And it wasn't me who did something despicable this time. It was Oskar."

"Oskar?" Anka cocked her head, and her eyes flew open wide. "How does Oskar enter into all of this?"

"It's all a long story."

"I think you should tell me. I think you should tell me everything. Don't you?"

"I am going to tell you now," he said. Then he stood up and poured himself a glass of whiskey. "Do you want one?"

She shook her head.

"You might need it."

"All right, then."

He poured her a glass of whiskey, too, and handed it to her. Then he sat down beside her and began. "Of course, you remember when Karl went missing."

"Of course," she said.

"Well, you must also remember how Oskar acted like he was some kind of a hero to Kara. He did everything for her. Do you remember?"

"Yes, he was very helpful, always right there by her side the entire time until they finally found Karl."

"Do you know why?"

"Because he loves her?"

"Yes, but his love is a warped, sick, manipulative love. You see, he arranged the entire thing."

"What exactly do you mean? What are you saying?"

"I'm saying that Oskar planned for Karl to be kidnapped. He arranged for Karl to be stolen and then to be taken to the home for the Lebensborn. It was all Oskar. He made sure that Karl was kept in the home until Oskar was ready to bring him back to his mother."

"Why?" Anka said. "Why would he do that?"

"So he could make Kara dependent on him. He wanted to be Kara's hero. Oskar is a smart man. He knew if he rescued Karl, it would make her fall in love with him. And she did. Didn't she?"

Anka thought of Abram, but she said nothing. She wanted to unburden herself, to tell Ludwig about Kara and Abram. But she'd made a promise to her sister to keep silent and she would. "Are you sure of this?"

"I am. Aloisa told me everything. She was involved."

"Your mistress?" she said with just a hint of irritation in her voice. "The one is who is dead now? She was involved?" Anka shook her head.

"Yes, and I am sorry for what I did as far as cheating on you. But that's not why I have to mention Aloisa. I think that perhaps because Aloisa was involved in the kidnapping, and she helped Oskar to carry out the plan, he might have silenced her. Last week, before you and I were back together, Aloisa called me and told me that she had to see me. She was frantic. She said she had to tell me something. I went to Munich to see her, and this was what she told me. She was afraid of Oskar. Terrified that he would kill her because of everything she knew. She thought he was afraid that she might tell me. And now . . . she's been found dead." Ludwig started coughing. Since he'd started working at the lair, he'd developed a cough that was even worse whenever he was nervous. "Excuse me," he said weakly.

"You're not smoking again, are you?" Anka asked.

"No, it's the air in the bunkers. All the men who work at the lair have developed breathing problems."

She shook her head. "You should see a doctor."

"I know. I will. I promise you."

"I knew that Karl's kidnapping couldn't have been my fault. And to think I have been blaming myself for it this entire time." Then she looked at Ludwig, bit her lower lip, and said, "What should we do about this information about Karl?"

"I don't know."

"I'm worried about Kara. And about Karl," Anka said. "If Oskar could do a thing like that, what else is he capable of?"

"My thoughts exactly. It's one thing to kill Jews. We all have to do that. And they are subhuman after all, but Oskar murdered an innocent girl," Ludwig said.

Again, Anka thought of Abram. In her mind she saw the gentle love in his eyes when he looked at Kara. "You know, it's not right to murder Jews either," she blurted out.

"You're getting soft like your sister?"

"Perhaps I am," Anka said.

"They're not really human, you know. And for the sake of the future, for our children's sake, we must rid the world of them. It's the only way we are going to build a better world for our children."

"I can't talk about this now," Anka said. The subject was confusing to her. She didn't know how she felt about it. "I am worried sick about Kara. Do you think I should tell her?"

"I don't know."

"I think I have to do something. She is my sister. I am going to go and see her. I'll be leaving tomorrow. I'll take Gretel with me."

"I want to come with you too. I'll call work in the morning."

CHAPTER FIFTY-SEVEN

ANKA DIDN'T SLEEP a wink that night. She lay in bed tossing and turning. *To think, for years I have been so jealous of Kara for finding a man like Oskar. I thought he was the perfect man, handsome, ambitious, rising in the party in a way Ludwig never could. Now I know better. The reason Oskar has done so well is because he is ruthless. If he could have had Karl kidnapped, then I have no doubt in my mind that he is capable of hurting my sister if she ever defies him in any way. Not only that, but if he ever finds out about her and Abram, he will be repulsed by her, and he might even kill her. It makes me shiver to think of what he would do if he found out that Karl is half Jewish. He would be horrified, and then who knows what would happen.*

I wish I could go back to when I didn't know all of this. I am not fond of Jews, but I wouldn't hurt my nephew for the world. Even though his father was a Jew, he is still my sister's son. His blood is my blood. I wish I could talk to Ludwig and tell him about Kara and Karl, and Kara's affair with a Jew. I know Ludwig, and I know he would never hurt Karl because of Kara and because of his love for me. But I am sure he would never feel the same way about Karl if he knew the truth. He would always look at Karl as a Jew and not as his nephew. So, for Kara and Karl's sake, I can't tell him.

She glanced over at Ludwig, who was sleeping deeply. *He's been through hell today. I'm sure it was worse for him at the police station, than he is telling me. I know how they are; they wanted to be sure he was telling the truth. My poor Ludwig. And tomorrow is going to be tough too, because we have to tell Kara the truth. I don't know how she will react.*

Anka fell asleep just as the sun peeked through the night clouds. Ludwig awoke to Gretel's lusty cry for her morning bottle. He got out of bed still exhausted, but he did the best he could to quiet Gretel and change her diaper. Then he gave her a warm bottle. Sitting with her in a rocking chair, he fed her until she drifted off to sleep. Once she was sleeping soundly, he got up, put her in her crib and prepared breakfast for Anka and himself. Ludwig didn't care that this was women's work. He knew his wife was delicate and spoiled, but he adored her and was so grateful to have Anka's love that he would have scrubbed the floors if she asked him to.

When the coffee and breakfast were ready, Ludwig went into the bedroom and gently kissed Anka's cheek until she awakened.

"I'm sorry to wake you, but I know you wanted to get on the road early," he said.

"It's all right. I do want to get going."

"You just take your time waking up. I'm going to call my superior at work and ask him for a couple of days off. He won't be pleased. I've been taking off far too much time."

"I can go alone," she suggested.

"I wouldn't let you. Not under any circumstances." Ludwig gently ran his fingers across Anka's cheek. "I love you. I can't let anything happen to you."

"Do you really believe that Oskar would harm me, or Kara?"

"I don't know what to believe anymore," he said, "but you just lie here and take a few minutes to wake up. I'm going to make that call."

She nodded.

Anka forced herself to get out of bed. She headed to the bathroom where she relieved her full bladder. Then she splashed her face with cold water. Looking into the mirror over the sink, she was startled. The face staring back at her from the mirror was not the face of the carefree girl that she was used to seeing. No, this was the face of a woman burdened by worry. Closing her eyes, she found herself saying a silent prayer.

It had been years since she'd prayed. In fact, as her ambition in the Nazi Party grew, she'd forgotten God. Hitler, his rules and his doctrine, had become like her god and religion. But now as she felt fear rising within her, and she worried that she might lose her sister, the most important person in her life, she realized Hitler and his entire regime were just men. Often cruel and very demanding men.

And right now, she desperately needed the real God. The only God who could save Kara, if Oskar learned the truth. *Jesus, I realize that there were many years when I didn't talk to you. It had been years since I prayed when Kara and I were young, and my mother took us to church. And lately I have been bothering you a lot. I know I begged you to help me when I was afraid Kara was dying. And you did. You saved her. I was afraid you would ignore me because you might be mad at me for not praying for all those years, but you helped me. You saved my sister. And now, here I am in desperate need of your help again. I hate to keep bothering you, but I am so scared, and I really need you now. I remember that the pastor said you were forgiving. I am hoping you will forgive me for everything I've done. And please watch over my sister; don't let anything happen to her or Karl. I know I have been a selfish person.*

I even remember something in the Bible about you being Jewish. If you were, I am sorry. I am confused. I don't really know what is right and what is wrong anymore. All I know is that I'm scared of Oskar and what he could do if he finds out the truth about Karl. I don't know what he knows or what he will do. But I promise you, if you help us, I'll start reading the Bible again in secret. I still have a copy that no one knows about. Remember the one my grandmother on my mother's side gave me when I was eight? I still have it. I haven't opened it in a long time. But I promise I will. Please, I am begging you to help us.

She felt a little relieved as she slipped on the champagne-colored satin robe that Ludwig had given her as a gift for her birthday last year and went into the kitchen.

Ludwig was sitting at the table drumming his fingers. His face was gray. He'd taken the plates down from the shelf, but he had left them stacked on top of each other instead of setting the table as he usually did. Still dressed in his underwear and white sleeveless T-shirt, he stared out the window blankly. His mouth was slack.

"Are you all right?" Anka asked, putting her hand on his head to see if he had a fever.

He looked up at her. Then he nodded and tried to smile.

"You don't look all right. What is it?"

"My superior officer at work gave me an ultimatum. Either I come in to work or I will lose my job."

"How can that be?"

He shrugged. "He said I've been taking too much time off." Ludwig reached up and caressed her hand on his shoulder, then he shook his head. "Oh, Anka, I've made so many mistakes. I should never have become involved with Aloisa."

Hearing him say that felt both good and bad at the same time. She was glad he regretted the affair. But she also knew he was not entirely to blame. A lot of what went wrong in their marriage was her fault, and she had come to realize it. Anka took a moment to pour herself a cup of coffee before sitting down beside Ludwig. "We've both made a lot of mistakes," she said.

For a few moments, they didn't speak. Then he said, "I am going to forfeit the job to go with you."

"I don't know what to do. I don't want you to lose your job. We need the money. But I can't stay here now with all that I know. I must go to my sister and tell her the truth. It might save her life."

She set the plates, forks, knives, and napkins in front of each of them. Then she served eggs onto each plate. But neither of them ate.

He didn't say anything for a moment while he played with his fork and stared down at his plate. Then he finally spoke, "I don't believe she is in danger, do you? I mean as long as she doesn't know the truth, I think she will be safe."

Anka shrugged. "I don't know. I don't know if she would be safer not knowing or if it's better that she knows what he is capable of." A chill ran up her spine. She thought of Abram and Karl. "It's too big of a risk, Ludwig. I don't dare ignore this. If I lost my sister, it would kill me."

"So, then we'll go."

"And what will you do for work?"

"I don't know. We'll have to go home to Berlin for a while and live with my parents until I can figure out what to do. My father might be able to find work for me," he said, "but I'll find something. I promise you." Then he swallowed, and his Adam's apple jumped up and down. Offering her a reassuring smile, he reached over and squeezed her hand. Then in an overly cheery voice he said, "Now, I don't want you to worry. I'll find a way to take care of you. I won't let you down." He reached up and gently pinched her chin. "Come on, eat your breakfast, so we can be on our way."

"You must eat too," Anka said.

Ludwig nodded and began to shovel the food into his mouth.

Anka forced herself to eat a forkful of scrambled eggs, which had grown cold over the last few minutes. She could hardly swallow. But she ate until she absolutely couldn't bear to take another bite without vomiting. She glanced over at Ludwig. His plate was empty. "I'm ready when you are," she said.

"I'll go and get Gretel," he said.

Ludwig fed and dressed the baby. Then he put her in Anka's arms, and they walked to the car. But when he tried to start the engine, the car was dead, and he remembered that he'd meant to put gas in the tank before he was arrested. Anka looked at her husband anxiously. "What are we going to do?" Then she hesitated, but her voice indicated that she was getting nervous. "I suppose I could leave the baby with Erna and take the train. But it will take much longer to get there than driving would. I don't know what to do."

"Shhh, love. It's all right. I'll go next door and ask Werner if I can borrow his car. He can get a ride to work from one of the other fellows at least for a couple of days."

Anka sat in the automobile holding the baby in her arms as Ludwig got out. He smiled at her, then he went to the house next door and knocked on the door.

"Ludwig," Erna said, "Come in. Werner is getting dressed for work."

Ludwig sat down on the sofa. "I need to speak to him," he said. "It's an emergency."

213

Werner came out of the bedroom wearing his uniform. "Ludwig. Good morning. Is everything all right?"

"No, actually it's not. I need help. It's an emergency."

"Tell me how I can help you," Werner said.

Ludwig explained everything. He told Werner all about the murder and how he must get to Poland to speak to his sister-in-law as soon as possible. Werner nodded as he listened. When Ludwig finished, Werner said, "I was planning to go to Auschwitz next week. I have some papers that I need to deliver to one of doctors who works there. I will just call into work and tell them that I've decided to go today instead. That way, I can drive you."

"You are a good friend. This is very kind of you."

"Of course, don't mention it. Why don't you have a cup of tea while I give them a call at the lair."

CHAPTER FIFTY-EIGHT

W<small>HEN</small> <small>THEY</small> <small>ARRIVED</small> at Kara's home, it was midafternoon. When Werner turned off the car, Gretel woke up and began fussing."

"She's hungry," Ludwig said.

"Yes, I know. And we can feed her inside. Oskar should still be at work," Anka said. "Don't you think so?"

"I would hope so. I think it's best that we're here now, when he's not at home."

"I don't know if Kara is fully recovered from her miscarriage yet, or not. When I telephone her, she says she is, but you know Kara. She never wants to worry me. We might get in there and find out she's still bedridden and has a nurse helping her out," Anka said.

"Well, I don't see the auto anywhere, so that's a good sign. Oskar must be at work," Ludwig said, "You didn't tell Kara we were coming, did you?"

"No, I didn't. I didn't want her to tell Oskar. I think we should have some time alone with her to tell her what we know and then decide what to do."

He nodded. "All right." Then taking Gretel from Anka's arms

and lifting the bag they brought with them, the three of them all headed up to the door.

Anka knocked and Kara answered. "What a wonderful surprise," she said.

"This is Werner Hoffenberg. He's a very good friend of ours," Ludwig said. "My auto wouldn't start, and he offered to drive us all the way here."

"That was very kind of you," Kara said to Werner.

Anka grabbed Kara and hugged her tightly. "You look good. I'm so glad to see you're back to yourself."

"I'm doing fine," Kara said, "A little emotional still, but I feel better."

Anka just nodded and then hugged Kara even tighter.

"Come in, all of you. What brings you here?" Kara said, taking the baby from Ludwig's arms.

"We need to talk to you," Anka said, her voice grave.

"Are you both all right?"

Gretel began fussing again.

"I'll feed her," Ludwig said, taking a bottle out of the bag he'd packed. Sitting down on the sofa, he gently put the nipple into Gretel's mouth, then rubbed her cheek until she began to suckle.

"Where is Karl?" Anka asked.

"Visiting a friend. They walk home from school together each day, then they either go to his home or come here," Kara said. "I'm glad that he's made friends with this nice little boy who lives a few houses down the street."

"Is Oskar here?" Anka asked nervously.

"No, Oskar's not here, why? Anka, what is it? What's wrong?"

"I don't know how to tell you this. All I know is that you must be told."

Kara shook her head. "I don't understand. Please be clearer."

Anka nodded her head, then she bit her lower lip. She glanced over at Werner. "Perhaps we should go into the kitchen and talk," she said.

"No, why don't I go outside and have a cigarette so you two ladies can speak to each other," Werner offered.

"Are you sure?"

"Of course. I am dying for a smoke." Werner smiled and walked outside.

"Gretel finished her bottle, so I'm going to put her in her crib to take a nap." Ludwig said as he carefully took her into another room, then came back into the living room.

Once they were alone, Anka took Kara's hands and said, "Kara, when Karl was kidnapped, it was not a random kidnapping. He was not taken accidentally. The people who took him, knew exactly who he was, and they took him for a reason."

"What? What are you talking about?"

Ludwig looked up at Kara. "Oskar had Karl kidnapped."

"That's insane. Why would you say that?"

"Because I know it's true." Ludwig coughed nervously, then he cleared his throat. "Aloisa, the girl who was murdered, she told me. She was involved in the kidnapping. That's why she was killed. It wasn't random."

"Then I'll ask you, did you kill Aloisa, Ludwig?" Kara asked Ludwig, her eyes wide with disbelief. She was confused.

"No, not me," he said. "Oskar. Oskar killed her?"

"Oskar?"

"Yes."

"I don't understand. Why would Oskar have Karl kidnapped? And why would he kill a girl?"

"Because you didn't want him. Remember? When you first met him, you didn't like him. He had to find a way to win you. So, he thought of a way to make you depend on him. He found a way to be your hero. When Karl was taken, you were devastated and totally dependent on him for help. Then when he found Karl and brought him back to you, he won your heart, didn't he?"

She stared at him in disbelief. But she couldn't speak. She was thinking about Abram's words.

Ludwig coughed, then he continued, "Oskar is a smart man. He was in love with you, and he knew that you didn't return his love. But he also knew that if he could find some way to be your savior, he could make you love him."

ROBERTA KAGAN

"That's madness."

"It worked, didn't it?" Ludwig said. "Last week, Aloisa called me. She asked me to come to Munich so she could talk to me. She told me all about what Oskar did. How he had Karl brought to the home for the Lebensborn and how Oskar had Karl kept there for months until he was ready to pick him up. Aloisa was terrified when she told me. She was so afraid that Oskar was going to kill her to silence her forever. I didn't think he was capable of it. But now . . . she's dead."

"My mind is whirling. How could he do that to me? I suffered for so many terrible months. I was so afraid that Karl was gone forever. And now you say he knew where Karl was all along?"

"Yes, that's exactly what I am saying. I'm sorry, Kara. But he did it."

Kara looked into Anka's eyes, which were filling up with tears. "Ludwig and I want you to take Karl and come and live with us," Anka said.

"I need time to think. I am shaking."

"There are so many secrets. It feels like we're caught in a web of secrets," Anka said, looking directly into Kara's eyes, and Kara was certain she was referring to Abram being Karl's father.

"Do you think I should talk to Oskar and see what he has to say?" Kara asked.

"No. I think you should just leave with us," Ludwig said. "Look what happened to Aloisa."

"Are you sure he killed her?" Kara was still not believing that Oskar was capable of such violence. But then in the back of her mind, she heard Abram say, "You don't know him. You don't know the cruelty he is capable of."

"I'd bet my life on it," Ludwig said.

Just then Oskar's automobile pulled up in front of the house. Bertram climbed out and opened the door. Oskar, carrying a bouquet of flowers, glanced over at Werner suspiciously, then continued to walk up the walkway.

Kara, Ludwig, and Anka all stared out the window.

"He's home," Kara said anxiously.

218

Oskar and Bertram exchanged words, but Kara could not hear them. She saw Bertram nod. Then he got back into the automobile and drove away. *Oskar must have sent him somewhere.* She thought.

Oskar came inside. "Ludwig, Anka," he said, trying to sound cheerful, but Kara could hear a touch of nervousness in his voice, which he immediately covered up. Then handing the bouquet to Kara, he kissed her quickly. "It's so good to see you both, and I see you have a new car and a driver? But to what do we owe this honor?" Oskar said.

Ludwig was staring at Oskar.

"We came to see how Kara was feeling," Anka said quickly.

"Well, my wife is doing very well. Aren't you, love?" Oskar said.

Kara nodded.

Then Oskar looked directly into Ludwig's eyes as if he were trying to get into his mind. "But I think there is more to it than that," Oskar said. "Isn't there, Ludwig?"

Ludwig shivered and began coughing. His face turned bright red as he tried to catch his breath. He was clearly unnerved.

Oskar let out a short laugh. "So, Kara told me that you'd been arrested," Oskar said shaking his head.

Kara thought, *Oskar is trying to sound confident. But I can tell he isn't; his hands are shaking; his eyes are darting around the room. I think he is pressing Ludwig to see if Aloisa told him anything about the kidnapping.*

"I was arrested because Aloisa was murdered."

"How terrible," Oskar said. "You and Aloisa knew each other?"

Ludwig was coughing harder now. He handed the baby to Kara and ran to the kitchen to get a glass of water. When he returned, his face was the color of fresh blood, but he was more composed. "Yes, we knew each other, Oskar. We were lovers. I regret it. But it's true. And then she was murdered. The police thought I was responsible. I love my wife, and I am grateful that Anka and I are back together, but I would never hurt Aloisa. I saw pictures of the murder; it was terrible. Very terrible."

A half smile came over Oskar's face. It was a smile of malice rather than joy. Then in a deep, menacing voice, he said, "You still haven't told me why you came here."

Ludwig began coughing again. Kara was fed up. She'd had enough of this cat-and-mouse game. She needed to know the truth. "Oskar," she said, and suddenly all heads turned to look her way. "What happened between you and Aloisa?"

"Me and Aloisa?" he said innocently. "I never touched that girl. Do you think I had an affair?"

"No, that's not what I think at all. What happened with you and Aloisa . . . and Karl? Did you have Karl kidnapped? And was Aloisa involved?"

"That's ridiculous," he said, but quickly he turned away from her. And Kara could see it was true. He couldn't meet her gaze. There was no doubt that he was hiding something.

"Is it true?" she demanded.

"Of course not," he said, immediately catching himself and sounding confident again.

"Don't lie to me, Oskar. I know everything. I know you had Karl kidnapped, so that I would need you and then fall in love with you," Kara said.

She knew, as soon as he turned on his heel and glared at her, that he was as angry as a wild animal caught in a trap. It seemed as if his face had changed. He no longer looked like Oskar. And she knew this face was the face of the man Abram was talking about. Oskar's eyes were like glass, devoid of emotion as he stared at Kara. Then he said, "It's not always good to know things. Sometimes, it's best to let secrets lie. You should know that, Kara. So . . . you've decided that you must know the truth?" He nodded. "Then here it is. Yes, I did it. I had Karl kidnapped, so you would fall in love with me. And you did. He was never in danger. Not for a single second."

"That was despicable," Kara said. "You put me through hell. You lied to me. You kept secrets from me. I could never trust you again."

He let out a cruel laugh that sounded like the bark of a hyena. Then he said, "Do you want to talk about liars and despicable behavior? You, my love, are not innocent. I wasn't going to mention your secret. I was going to let it go unnoticed. But now, since you've brought all this to light, I should let you know that we caught two

Jews running away. You know the ones, don't you, Kara? The same two Jews who were here at the house building your garden. I personally shot them both on sight."

"What does that have to do with her and what you did with Karl?" Ludwig said, and he began coughing again.

"She knows what it has to do with her and her bastard half-Jew son. Don't you Kara? You're a Jew lover. You let a Jew touch your body, but I didn't say anything. You know why? Because I love you. That's why. But it sickens me. It makes me want to puke. And that bastard kid of yours, I'm raising him for you, but the truth is he's nothing but a Jew."

Karl came running through the door. Kara's face turned porcelain-white when she saw him. "Mutti, can Artur come over and play tomorrow after school?" Then before Kara had a chance to say a word, Karl turned to Oskar. "Hello, Vater. I'm so glad you're home. Artur had to go on an errand with his mutti, so we can't play any more today. But, Vater, can you please play ball with me?"

"Go to your room," Kara said to Karl, her eyes still glued to Oskar's face.

"But Mutti . . ."

"Go to your room right now. I said go," Kara said to Karl in a strong voice. She had never spoken to her son in anything but gentle tones, but today her voice was harsh.

Karl looked at his mother with wide eyes. His lower lip jutted out, and she knew he was crying. But she couldn't go to him. Karl ran to his room.

"He's a half Jew," Oskar said. "You've made me a fool. You lied to me. I took your bastard son into my home, fed him, and clothed him like he was my own son. All the while he was nothing but a filthy Jew rat. That Jew that I shot who was building the garden? He was Karl's father, wasn't he?"

Kara was stunned silent for a moment. In her mind's eye she saw Abram lying dead in a field, and she wanted to scream. The room went black. She didn't care about her own safety. Wild with rage, Kara ran toward Oskar and threw herself at him beating him with her fists. "You bastard, you killed Abram," she repeated over and over. "You killed Abram." Tears ran like rivers down her face.

"I did it for you, Kara. To hide your dirty secret. To keep your son from suffering the fate every Jew deserves."

"You liar. You filthy liar," she said. "I hate you."

"You don't hate me. You love me. I made you love me," he said.

She glared at him, her eyes red with crying. Then in a low growl, she said, "I never loved you. There was a time I might have cared for you because I thought you were a different man. But now, I only pity you."

Oskar was shaking. He grabbed Kara. She let out a loud scream.

Werner came rushing through the door as Oskar put his hands around Kara's neck. He pushed her against the wall. Anka screamed, "Please, Oskar, let her go. Please, I'm begging you."

Oskar ignored Anka. His eyes were fixed on Kara's. "I should choke the life out of you. I should kill you, right here, right now. Put an end to this mad obsession I have with you." He pulled his gun from its holster and pointed it at Kara.

"Come on. Let the woman go," Werner said as he started walking toward Oskar. "Give me the gun."

"Go to hell," Oskar said, turning toward Werner. Their eyes met. Werner saw Oskar's face for the first time that afternoon. He went pale.

"I know you." Werner paused for a second. Oskar's face turned white, then red with rage. Werner continued, "You're not Oskar. You're Oskar's twin brother, Erich. Your brother saved my life. I will never forget his face. His eyes. Give me the gun, Erich. I don't know what kind of a lie you have been living. But your brother would be ashamed of you and the dishonor you've brought to his name."

"How dare you. How dare you mention my brother. How dare you come into my home and disrupt my life," Oskar said, then he turned his gun at Werner and pulled the trigger. In an instant, Werner's face disappeared. He fell to the ground his face a mass of blood. Kara knew he was dead. Anka screamed, and Ludwig gasped. But Oskar still held Kara by the neck against the wall with one hand.

"This is insane," Ludwig said, trying to sound reasonable, but he was trembling. "Oskar, come on. I am begging you, please, just let her go."

"Shut up, Ludwig. I've had enough of you," Oskar said. "One more word, and I'll shoot you too." Then he turned back to Kara and, still holding her against the wall, he said, "Did you think Bertram wouldn't tell me what happened when you had the miscarriage? Did you think he wouldn't tell me what you said? Bertram works for *me*, Kara. There is nothing that goes on in this house that I don't know about. Including the disgusting fact that the filthy Jew went into your bedroom when I was out of town. What happened between you? I can only imagine." He spit in her face. She trembled, but he still would not release her. "Kara . . . Kara . . ." Oskar said, shaking his head. "How could you? In my home? In my bed. And still, if you had not brought up the kidnapping, I would have forgiven you. I would have let it go. I would never have mentioned it. I loved you that much. I wanted our lives to go on as before. But you couldn't let it lie; you had to dig deep, didn't you? It had to come to this."

Kara was crying. The pressure he was putting on her neck was making it hard to breathe. But even so, the words rang in her ears like the loud whistle of a train. *Abram is dead. I just found him again, and now my Abram is gone forever. Oskar killed him. And now, what about Karl? Oskar has turned on me and on him. What will he do to my little boy now that he knows his secret?* She shivered.

"I'm sure there is some mistake about Karl being half Jewish. Kara would never let a Jew touch her like that," Ludwig said, but his voice was filled with fear. He was trying desperately to calm Oskar.

"Shut up, I already told you to shut your mouth, didn't I, you half-wit?" Oskar said, and Ludwig began coughing. "You should have left well enough alone. But you had to get involved with Aloisa and find out everything, didn't you? Well, now you know. And you know what? I'm tired of you. I'm tired of your stupidity, and your self-righteousness. You have no right to poke your nose into my business," Oskar said to Ludwig, then he shook his head. "So, all right. I did it. I had the child kidnapped. But he came back unharmed, didn't he? You stupid-ass fool, you should have minded your own business. If Kara had never found out the truth about the kidnapping, I would never have had to mention that dead Jew. So, Ludwig, this is all your fault. How do you feel?"

"I feel like you have taken way too many liberties, Oskar. I feel like I must go to the authorities and tell them what you have done. It would be the right thing to do." Ludwig said as boldly as he could manage, but his entire body was trembling.

"And then you would put Kara and her son at risk?" Oskar said, a wicked smile coming over his face. "You are even dumber than I thought."

"I don't believe a word about that Jew situation. I refuse to believe it."

"I don't care what you believe. I'm sick and tired of you," Oskar said, then holding Kara against the wall with one arm, he fixed the pistol on Ludwig's face.

Anka held her head in her hands, weeping hysterically.

Ludwig was coughing hard now. He couldn't catch his breath. "You stupid bastard. You brought all of this here, didn't you? You brought that man," Oskar said, indicating to Werner's lifeless body. "And you had to tell Kara all about the kidnapping. You destroyed my life, Ludwig. I owe you this," he said and shot Ludwig in the face, which turned to a bloody mass of tissue as he fell to the floor. Kara's body shook hard. Anka gasped in horror.

"What have you done, Oskar," Kara said. "You've killed them both."

"Yes, and now I must kill you too. Don't you see, Kara? It's the only way I will ever be free of you."

Hearing the gunshots, Karl came running into the living room. "Mutti!" he screamed when he saw the two men on the floor and the blood pooling all around them.

"Let go of Mutti. You're hurting her, Vater," Karl said.

Oskar whirled around and turned the gun on Karl.

Kara saw Oskar turn toward Karl and aim his gun directly at Karl's face. She tried to scream, but she couldn't; his arm was blocking her windpipe.

"He's just a child," Anka said.

Oskar ignored her. Then in a voice that was too calm, he said to Kara, "Even after all you've done to me, I am still in love with you. I'm a fool, Kara. I'm pathetic. It's true. I am no war hero. I am only Oskar's weak brother. And you? You're the only woman I've ever loved. My heart aches. I love you so much. But now, I must rid myself of you and this hold you have over me. You know too much now. So, as hard as it is for me to kill you, I must, and at the same time, I'll get rid of the boy."

Kara tried to shake her head. Her eyes were wide with fear. He was pointing the gun at Karl who stood looking at him in disbelief. She reached up and pulled at his arm, trying to take the gun. But she was no match for his strength. "I don't care who you are, Oskar. I'll accept anything you want me to accept. I'll do anything you want me to do. Just please, I'm begging you. Don't hurt Karl. Please, we can go back to the way it was before. I'll pretend I don't know anything, just let him be." She was crying hysterically.

"I'm sorry, my love. I can't do that. I—" Oskar said.

Then the sound of a single gunshot filled the small room and Oskar fell. Kara turned to see Anka standing behind Oskar with a gun in her hand. "You shot him?" she said in disbelief.

Anka was shaking, but she nodded. "He was going to kill Karl. He was going to kill you. He killed my Ludwig." Anka dropped the gun. She put her face in her hands and started to cry.

"Kara," Oskar said, choking on his own blood, "don't you know I was only bluffing. I wouldn't have hurt him. And I couldn't have hurt you. How could I when you are my heart and soul, my everything?" Blood was bubbling from his lips. Kara kicked his gun away from his body. But he wasn't looking for the gun. He was trying to talk. Then in a whisper, Oskar said, "From the day I met you, you became my reason for living. And now, my love for you is the reason I am dying. But even with my last breath, I want to tell you that I have loved you so deeply, and although you betrayed me, I still have to thank you for the moments of joy you gave me . . ." He stopped speaking. His head fell to the side. Kara looked away. She felt bile rise in her throat.

"He's dead," she said.

Anka rushed over to Kara and took her into her arms while Karl watched them wide eyed. "It's going to be all right," Kara said. Her body was shaking so hard she couldn't hold still. "It's going to be all right."

"I killed him," Anka said, her voice filled with shock.

"It's all right," Kara repeated as if she were in shock.

"And Ludwig is dead. What am I going to do without him?"

"I'll take care of you and Gretel, the way I always have, Anka."

Karl ran over to his mother and aunt, and they both held him tightly. The three of them embracing. For a few moments, they were frozen in each other's arms. Kara wept; she wept for the loss of the man who she had once believed Oskar to be. She wept for her sister and her sister's husband. But she wept hardest for Abram. Now she knew for certain that he was gone forever. *I must pull myself together. I have to cover up this crime. Anka and I must not be accused of murdering an SS officer.* Then Kara steadied herself. She cleared her throat. "All right, now both of you listen closely to me. We are going to tell the authorities that the men all got into a fight and shot each other. We'll put a gun in Ludwig's hand. And the other gun in Oskar's."

"Mutti, I don't know what happened. Vater looked at me like a monster. Auntie Anka saved my life," Karl said. He was shaking. "I don't know what I did wrong. I don't know why Vater was so mad that he would want to kill me. I thought he loved me."

"I know, Karl. I know. I'll explain everything as soon as we get through this. At least I'll try." Then she ran to the window. Patches was outside, barking. But she couldn't let him in. Her eyes were searching frantically for the automobile. "Thank God. The automobile is gone. That means Bertram wasn't here when we shot Oskar. He can't be a witness to what happened." *At least we won't have to kill him too.*

Then they realized that Gretel was in her crib, crying. "The gunshots woke her up. I'll go and get her," Kara said.

She returned moments later cradling the baby in her arms. Gretel began to quiet down.

"Karl, you must never tell anyone what you saw here tonight. Do you understand me?"

He nodded. His eyes were wide with fear.

"And you must never tell anyone what Mutti said about that man with the striped uniform. Do you remember that man?" Anka asked.

"Yes, I remember him. He was dirty and looked like a skeleton. Mutti was sick when she said he was my father. I was scared, so I asked the doctor what you meant when you said that man was my father. But the doctor told me that you were seeing things that weren't there because you'd lost so much blood."

"Well, that's right," Kara said. "If anyone asks you, you must tell them what the doctor said."

"Is it true? Were you really seeing things that weren't there?"

"It's what you must say. You must not ask me any more questions right now. Just do what I tell you. Please, Karl."

Karl looked up at Kara. She could see in his eyes that he was hurt by her curt answers. "Mutti, why are you acting like this? Why are you being so mean to me? Are you angry with me?"

"No, I am not angry with you. Right now I just need you to do as I say. Will you please? Will you be my big, strong man and do what I ask?" she said, gently touching his cheek.

He nodded. "I will, Mutti."

"Good. You're such a good boy."

"What should I say if anyone asks what happened here when Uncle Ludwig and Vater got shot?'

He still calls Oskar, vater. Of course he does. How could I expect anything else? He doesn't understand. Oskar is the only father he has ever known. She steeled herself, knowing full well she was asking him to lie, and she'd taught him never to lie. "You must tell them that Uncle Ludwig and Vater where having an argument, and they shot each other. "

"But that's lying. Auntie Anka had to shoot Vater to save my life. He was going crazy."

"I know that. But you want to protect Auntie Anka, don't you?"

"Of course."

"Then you must say what I told you to say. Will you do that?"

"I will," he said, then with a sad look in his eyes, he asked, "What did I do wrong that made Vater stop loving me? I still don't understand why he wanted to kill me."

"Please, Karl, don't ask any more questions now. Bring Patches inside. He's barking like mad. Don't let him into this room though. Take him and put him right into your room. I am going to call the police, and I don't want him outside barking at them. I am afraid they will shoot him if they think he is mean. Make sure to close the door good so he can't get out of your room. And why don't you stay in your room with him. Take Gretel with you, until the police come and then, I can get this all cleaned up."

"Yes, Mutti."

"You're such a good boy," Kara said, and she hugged him. *Poor Karl, he's only a little boy. No child of that age should witness such horror. And yet he saw everything. What am I going to tell him about Oskar? How am I ever going to explain how the man he thought was his father, the man he trusted and loved, could have wanted to kill him?* She sucked in a breath, then said, "Go and get Patches now. Hurry. The neighbors are probably annoyed with his loud barking."

CHAPTER FIFTY-NINE

NEITHER KARA nor Anka found it difficult to cry when the police arrived. Anka wept in Kara's arms as they carried Ludwig's body away. And Kara knew her sister wept out of sadness for her loss but also out of horror. Anka had killed for her sister and for her nephew. This was hard for Anka as she had never been one to look directly at the ugly side of life. But when it had come down to the wire, Anka's love for Kara and Karl had won out. She found strength she never knew she had. Kara hugged her sister. Tears flowed down Kara's cheeks for Anka's loss of innocence that day.

But Kara couldn't bear to look at Oskar. She had tried to avoid seeing the glimpses of the other Oskar, the one Abram told her about. But now as she thought about it, she remembered that there had been the occasional outbursts. She had turned her face away ignoring them, so she could go on living this lie for as long as she had to. But now she'd seen the real Oskar, and it had not only left her angry but also confused. He'd been such a good liar, and for so long she'd allowed herself to believe everything he told her.

And now as they dragged his dead body out of the house, Kara wondered what other lies he had kept from her. When he'd held the gun on Karl and choked her so hard she thought he was going to break her windpipe, she'd finally seen the face of the man who Abram spoke of, the man who was capable of murder and torture. She shivered when she thought about how she had allowed him into her bed, allowed him to touch her, and to join his body with hers. The thought of him inside her made her pelvic muscles tighten as if to expel anything left of him.

She watched them through the window as they loaded Oskar's dead body into a truck. *This man killed Abram, and he would have killed Karl. How could I have been so stupid? How could he have fooled me so easily? The man I thought I knew never existed. He was a person Oskar carefully invented and then played like an actor to win my love.* The idea of it made her feel sick to her stomach. She felt vomit rise in her throat and ran to the bathroom.

Kara scrubbed the blood off the floor, and then she sat down on the sofa and tried to take deep breaths.

After she calmed down, Kara took a hot bath and wept as she scrubbed her body until it was almost raw. She could hear Gretel crying and Anka whimpering softly in the living room. Karl was speaking to Gretel in quiet tones, and it broke her heart to think of how much he'd seen at such a young age. *I should get out of this tub and help Anka. I need to comfort Karl. But I can't move. I feel like the life has been drained out of me.*

CHAPTER SIXTY

1944

After a full investigation, it was decided that Ludwig and Oskar had shot each other during an argument. Their wives were rendered blameless, and Kara and Anka were granted permission by the Nazi Party to stay in the house where Kara and Oskar had lived. They would be allowed to raise their children there because as far as the party knew, both children were pure Aryans. And both Oskar and Ludwig had been such loyal and devoted servants of the Reich. Kara was relieved they were not put out of the house and onto the street, because if they had been, she would not have known where to go. With Germany at war, she'd heard about the bombings, and she was afraid to return home to Berlin.

But although she didn't discuss her feelings with Anka, things had changed for Kara. She felt differently about the neighborhood now that she knew the truth about where the ashes came from that fell on her shoulders every time she went outside. It made her cringe to know that they were the remains of families, people who were just like her: Abram, Hoda, and Yitzar. They were ordinary people just trying to live in peace and love each other when their lives were brutally stolen from them without reason.

When she went outside walking or looked out the window at the garden, with its roses in bloom, she thought of Abram. He'd grown that garden for her with his own hands. His hands, Kara remembered his hands as he would pat her back soothingly when she was sad. And so, because Abram had created it, she made an effort to keep the garden up. At first, she'd found it taxing, because all she really wanted to do was watch the clock and wait for another day to end. But as she tended the earth, with the sun caressing her shoulders, she found her depression lifting. It was almost like making love to Abram in a strange way. With loving hands, she cared for the shrubs and flowers that he'd planted, and as they grew in response to her love, she felt that she was closer to Abram. The neighbors, when she saw them, always made mention of how beautiful the garden was. Kara would smile and thank them. And deep in her heart she felt that each flower that bloomed was a tiny living symbol of the love she and Abram shared.

Although Kara and Anka were raising the two children together, Kara took on the brunt of it. And Anka slipped back into her role as Kara's protected younger sister. But Kara didn't mind. She was glad to be the mother to all of them. It gave her something to do, occupying her mind so she didn't spend too much time living in the past. Kara had no desire to marry again. As long as the four of them were safe, and had food, she would be content. But now food was becoming a problem, even for Hitler's Aryan followers. The führer was taking everything for the war effort.

One morning, Anka put on her nicest dress and went into town where she tried to get a job, but she was not qualified to do anything. And it seemed that the Reich had more pressing problems right now than helping German women who had come to settle in the East on behalf of Hitler. The Nazis were losing the war.

Anka made friends with other women who lived in the neighborhood. They were women living alone with their children because their husbands were off fighting for Germany. They invited Anka to card games at their homes where they spoke in secret, but they all agreed that Hitler's invasion of the Soviet Union in 1941 had turned out to be a big mistake. They'd heard how brutal the Russian winters were, and they'd heard rumors that the German soldiers had been caught in Russia during the winter unprepared. Frightened not only for their husbands, but also for themselves, they were losing faith in the führer. It was becoming clear that Hitler's promise of a thousand-year Reich was not going to happen. Germany was going to lose the war.

The women were heartsick over it, but Kara was not sorry to see Germany lose. She would be glad to see the world rid of Hitler and his horrible regime. But she was terribly afraid of the Russians. She'd heard so many frightening things about them, and it horrified her to think of what would happen when they came through Poland. The women discussed this among themselves. They were afraid of being raped and murdered.

Kara listened. She thought about what the Nazis had done to the Jews and the others they didn't think were fit to live. *And even though I am one of them, I am a German, I still believe that we deserve whatever happens to us. I am so afraid for my family, but I can't say that we are all innocent,* she thought, but she didn't say a word.

CHAPTER SIXTY-ONE

1945

January hit Poland with a gust of ice and snow. Each day there was less and less food, and the children were constantly complaining of hunger. Not only that, but lately the smoke from the nearby camp had increased. Now there was so much smoke in the air, Kara and Anka began to worry about the children's lungs.

"There are fires burning somewhere in the distance. The smoke is killing my eyes. The children are having trouble breathing. They cough at night," Kara said.

"Do you think it's the chemical plant that's caught fire?" Anka asked.

"I don't know. It's been burning for days now. I can't imagine that it's that horrible thing that Abram told me about."

"What are you talking about?"

"I told you. Don't you remember? Abram said that the Nazis were killing people in that camp and then burning their bodies in a large crematorium."

"Oh, Kara. No wonder I forgot. That's horrible. Just horrible. I can't imagine that something like that is true," Anka said, shaking her head. "I refuse to believe it."

"It's true. I believe Abram."

"But why would there be so much more smoke now than before?"

"I don't know," Kara said.

"I'm going to walk over to some of the other houses in the area and ask the other wives in the community if they know what is going on. I think I'll go and see Ingrid first. She's so nosy; she always knows everything that is going on. I don't know how she does it. But she might know what is on fire," Anka said.

"All right. Just be careful. It's very icy out there."

Anka dressed in her heaviest clothes and left the house. As she walked to Ingrid's home, a frozen wind whipped at her hair and stung her face. Her lips were already chapping, and her hand was red from the cold as she knocked on the door.

Ingrid answered. She had three children at her feet. "Come in, Anka. Is everything all right?"

Anka walked inside. She rubbed her hands together, then she said, "Do you have any idea what is burning? The smoke is so thick, the children are having trouble breathing."

"Of course. It's Auschwitz."

Anka glanced around the inside the house. It was lovely, not as ornate as Kara's, but lovely nonetheless. "Please, sit down."

Anka sat down.

"Can I get you some tea?"

"That would be lovely."

Ingrid put a kettle of water on for tea, then she sat down beside Anka. "Auschwitz is burning."

"Are the Russians here?" Anka asked fearfully.

"No, not yet anyway. It's our own men. They are burning Auschwitz."

"But why? Why would they burn that place? They built it."

"Do you know what it is? Do you know what happened there?" Ingrid asked. The women had never openly discussed Auschwitz at their meetings. It was a subject that was off limits.

"No, I don't. I know it's a prison," Anka said, but she had an idea from everything Kara had told her.

"You're right. It is a prison for Jews and other subhumans, homosexuals, Gypsies, Jehovah's Witnesses, sordid people of all kinds. Germany had the unsavory job of eliminating them."

"Eliminating?" Anka felt a shiver run up the back of her neck. *Could what Abram told Kara really be true? Could it really be true that a country as civilized as Germany would do such a thing?*

"Yes, eliminating them in mass quantities. The men tried very hard, but there were so many of them, you understand. They did what they could, but they were unable to rid us of all of them before the war ended. So now they must destroy the evidence, so the enemy doesn't know what went on there."

"I don't understand." Anka didn't want to understand.

"Of course, it's an ugly business and, well, rather complicated. My husband returned last week, and soon he and I will be taking our children and leaving here. It's too dangerous for us to stay with those barbaric Russians marching toward us. I suggest you and your sister get out as soon as you can."

"And where will you go?"

"I don't know. My husband has a plan, but he won't tell me anything more. I must put my trust in him, follow him, and do as he asks."

"The other women in the neighborhood? Are they leaving too?"

"I can't say for certain, but they would be wise to get out of here. All Germans would be wise to get out of here."

Anka watched the children on the floor without really seeing them. She was stunned and terrified. "I don't know where we would go. And the weather . . ."

"I don't know what to tell you. All I know is that we are leaving as soon as we can. The Russians are brutal, vicious people. They are not like Germans who are refined and civilized. They are completely barbaric," Ingrid said.

The kettle that Ingrid had put on the stove for tea let out a loud whistle. Anka jumped.

"It seems our water is ready."

"Oh, thank you anyway, but I think I should go home and tell my sister what you just told me," Anka said.

"Very well, then. I wish you luck."

"I wish you luck too," Anka said.

Anka left just as a heavy snow began to fall. She trudged back to Kara's house. She stomped the snow off her boots, then walked inside the house, her face beet-red from the cold. As she took off her coat and hat, she glanced at the sofa where Kara was waiting for her.

"You look frozen," Kara said. Then she stood up and took Anka's coat and hung it on a hook by the door. Next, she wrapped a blanket around her sister's shoulders. "Come, sit down. I'll put another blanket over your legs."

Anka told Kara everything that Ingrid had said. Kara listened, then she looked away. "Abram was right. He told me all of this. It's good that they are burning it down," she said.

"Yes, good," Anka said, "But what about us? We must get out of here before the Russians come. They're barbarians. They killed our soldiers without a thought. And I have heard plenty of rumors that they don't respect women. They will rape them without blinking an eye. They're not like us Germans, Kara. I'm so afraid of them."

"And tell me this: Do you really think the Germans are any better? Look what they did to those poor, innocent people in that camp. Abram said they were gassing people by the hundreds and burning their bodies. How can you say that the Russians are more barbaric than that?"

"They'll rape us. They might kill us and the children too. All I know is we are in danger."

"So where do you propose we go?"

"I don't have any idea. But we have to get away from here. Maybe we should go back home to Germany."

"I'm not leaving. I don't know where to go, and so I am not going anywhere," Kara said. "I'll take my chances."

"And if they come?"

"If they come, I'll tell them the truth. I'll tell them that I didn't know anything. At least not until Abram told me. And even if I had known, what could I have done? One woman against the German

Army? I was powerless. I am still powerless. I was at their mercy; now I will be at the mercy of the Russians."

"As if they will really care what you tell them. We'd better hope that the British or the Americans come before the Russians. I don't think they're nearly as bad," Anka said.

"I don't know, Anka. I don't know what's going to happen. I don't know who is bad or worse. Right now, all I can say is I am staying here. But you're free to take Gretel and go home if you want to. I'm just never going back to Germany. I don't want to go there."

"Then I'll stay with you."

CHAPTER SIXTY-TWO

THE FOOD RAN OUT. Kara was forced to leave the house and go into town to purchase whatever supplies she could find. As she walked past the empty shops, she saw several SS officers herding a large group of prisoners through town. The prisoners did not have coats. They wore the same thin threadbare uniforms that Abram had worn. Many of them were barefoot, and their feet were bleeding onto the snow. They were all painfully thin, with dark, empty eyes. Kara gasped and stared with her mouth hanging open as one of the SS Officers pushed a man until he fell. Then the officer pulled a gun and shot the prisoner, leaving his bleeding body on the street. She looked away.

A half hour before she saw the men, Kara had been fortunate enough to purchase a few soft and nearly spoiled potatoes. She had been on her way home. But now as she saw these men walking, her heart broke. As she looked into their faces, in her mind's eye, she saw Abram's face. With a trembling hand, she reached into her bag and pulled out one of the potatoes. It was a great sacrifice to spare a potato, as food was not easy to come by. But when the officers were not looking, she threw the potato to a prisoner. He caught it and looked at her with such gratitude that she wished she could give him all that she had.

But she couldn't. There were hungry children at home, and they needed to eat. So she stood there watching and thinking of Abram. If he had survived, he would be marching alongside these men, starving, bleeding, and dying. Her heart hurt as she thought that perhaps it was better that he was dead. At least he was not suffering. Kara stood, unable to move, her feet freezing, the icy wind whipping her hair as she watched, not even aware of the tears that spilled from her eyes and froze on her eyelashes.

CHAPTER SIXTY-THREE

THE POLISH WINTER, with its ice and snow, seemed endless. The emptiness in Kara's heart was filled with the chill of each passing day. But even though she'd lost Abram forever, she forced herself to remember that she still had blessings to be thankful for. Karl and Anka were alive, and they were all together. She added some newly cut potatoes to the soup she'd been boiling all morning. They would be fully cooked in a half hour when everyone would eat.

Patches had been playing quietly with Karl on the kitchen floor. But then the dog stood up and began barking. He ran in circles as if he were chasing his own tail. "What is the matter with that dog?" Kara said, not really expecting an answer.

"He's probably hungry like the rest of us," Anka said.

"He's barking at the door, Mutti. I think he has to go outside to do his business," Karl said. "I'll take him for a walk."

"Not too far," Kara said, "It's bitter cold out there."

"I promise. I'll just take him in the front yard."

"Make sure you avoid the garden," Kara said. "You know how I feel about him doing his business near the garden."

"Yes, Mutti. He is never to do his business near the garden."

"That's right. Now, hurry because lunch is almost ready," Kara said as she wrapped Karl's scarf around his neck and put his hat on his head.

"Gretel is napping, so I'm going to lie down until lunchtime," Anka said. "When do you think the soup will be ready?"

Kara nodded. "About a half hour or so."

After Karl and Patches closed the door behind them, Kara began to stir the thin potato soup. She glanced out the window just as a light snow had begun to fall. Then she noticed Karl and Patches were in the garden. A moment of rage came over her. She grabbed her coat and put it on, then went outside to yell at Karl for not following her directions. She ran toward her son. "Karl, didn't I tell you—" Kara stopped short. She looked down at the ground. Could it be? Were her eyes deceiving her. "Abram?" she choked out. "Abram, is it really you?" She fell to her knees beside him and put her head on his chest. Tears ran like a river down her cheeks, and her eyelashes froze.

"Kara, I'm here. I came back to you."

"Praise God," she said.

"Is it all right for me to be here?"

"It's safe. Oskar is dead. How did you get here?"

"The war is over. The Nazis abandoned the camp."

"Come, let's get inside where it's warm. You're home now."

CHAPTER SIXTY-FOUR

ABRAM'S BODY felt like a bag of bones as he leaned on Kara. They walked into the house. She helped him into a chair in the kitchen, then ran to get blankets to cover him with. When she returned, he was trembling from the cold. She wrapped him gently with the blankets until he stopped shivering. Then in a soft voice, she whispered, "Thank God, you're alive. I thought you were dead."

He managed a smile.

"Oskar told us he'd shot you. He found out all about you and me and Karl from Bertram, his driver."

"You said Oskar was dead. What happened?"

"He got into a fight with Anka's husband. They shot each other. I'll tell you the whole story while you have some soup. I'm afraid that some of the potatoes are still hard because I just added them. But the carrots and celery should be soft. And at least it's hot." She ladled him a bowl of steaming soup.

"I have to remember to eat very slowly. I can't remember the last time I ate, and I want to keep it down," Abram said.

She nodded. "Do you want me to tell you what happened with Oskar?"

"Yes, please . . . tell me," he said.

Kara proceeded to tell him everything. She told him about the kidnapping, and what Werner said about Oskar stealing his brother's identity. She told him all about Aloisa, and Ludwig. She left nothing out. She even told him the truth, that it was Anka who killed Oskar, because she knew she could trust Abram. Once she'd finished, she looked into his eyes. "I guess I was a fool. I couldn't see who Oskar really was."

"You are no fool, Kara. You did what you had to do to protect our son, and I will always be grateful to you for it." He had finished his soup and put down the spoon. Leaning toward her, he took her face in his hands. "I love you so much."

"How did you escape? How did you ever get back to us?" she asked.

"Now it's my turn to tell a story, yes?"

She nodded. "Yes, please tell me."

Anka walked into the kitchen. "Abram? We thought you were dead," she said, shocked.

"I know. Kara told me."

"How did you get away?" Anka asked.

"I am going to tell you now," Abram said. Then he thought he heard his father's voice come through his own as he remembered how his father had told him so many stories of his life.

Anka poured herself a cup of tea from the kettle on the stove and sat down. Karl and Patches remained at Kara's feet. Everyone listened as Abram began to tell his story.

Abram turned to Kara and said, "After I left you that day when you were recovering from your miscarriage, my friend Moishe and I were hiding in the forests. I can't tell you how many days had passed since I saw you, because every day began to blend into the next. We ate the food you gave us right away. We knew we should try to ration it, but we were so hungry and so tired. The only thing that kept me from laying down and dying was knowing that you were alive, and no matter what, I must find a way to return to you and my son." He glanced down at Karl, who looked away embarrassed and confused. Then Abram continued.

"We stole whatever food and blankets we could get our hands on from barns along the edge of the forest, and the entire time we kept hidden. But then the oberstrumführer, Oskar as you call him, sent out a pack of dogs to find us. We heard them barking and began to run. I ran even though I knew it was useless. I knew the dogs would be faster, and they were hot on our scent. Soon we were surrounded. The armed Nazis followed. The oberstrumführer was heading the search party. When he saw me, he was seething with anger. He told me that he knew about you and I, and about Karl being my son.

"When I heard that, I didn't know what to do. I no longer cared about my own well-being. I was terrified of what he might do to the two of you. And I felt so helpless. I wanted to beg him to kill me and let you two be, but I had learned over the years that to beg a Nazi never worked. They enjoyed seeing Jews in pain, and the oberstrum-führer was no exception. So I sat quietly as he paced back and forth. I was certain that he was going to shoot me. But at that point it didn't matter. All that mattered was what he might do to you and Karl.

"He didn't shoot me. Instead, he did something far worse—he pulled his revolver on Moishe and shot him in the head. His head exploded, so I know that Moishe died instantly. I was heartsick. I wanted to throw myself in the snow and weep." Abram sucked in a ragged breath. Kara reached over and took his hand.

"You don't have to go on, Abram. It's all right."

"No, I must tell you everything," he said. "After the oberstrum-führer murdered Moishe, he turned to look at me, and said, 'I suppose you'll miss your friend. Well, you only have yourself to blame for his death. If you had stayed away from my wife, none of this would have happened.' And Kara, I do blame myself. I know I will never be able to forgive myself for what happened to Moishe. He was my best friend. We met in Auschwitz, the most horrible place on earth. Moishe was like a brother to me. He was smart and kind.

"And when I thought I was ready to surrender, he always lifted me up and reminded me of why I had to go on. And that reason was you. Oh, Kara, how you would have loved him." Abram sighed as tears began to course down his cheeks. For a moment, he stared at the ground as if he were reliving a memory, then he continued.

"The oberstrumführer was not mollified. He wanted more. He shook with rage as he told me that death was too good for me. He promised that I would suffer. He said he was going to take me back to the camp, and each day he would torture me until I longed for death. He thought he had frightened me. But at that point I was so distraught with grief over Moishe and my fear for my family that I didn't care what he did with me. Needless to say, the oberstrum-führer kept his promise. He was brutal, that's for certain. But his methods of torture only lasted a couple of days, but then he stopped sending for me. And it was a good thing that it didn't continue, because my body was so broken, and I didn't know if I would survive another beating. I didn't see him anywhere in the camp. I thought it was a cruel trick at first. I thought that he was trying to pretend to give me hope."

"Yes, that's probably when he died," Anka said quietly.

"Then it became apparent that something was happening in the camp," Abram continued. "There had been rumors that the Nazis were losing the war, so I deduced that this was what was taking place. The guards and SS officers became nervous. They paid less and less attention to us prisoners, yet they began to run the gas chambers and crematoriums all day and all night. I overheard two guards talking; they said they wanted to liquidate the camp before the enemy arrived, and that meant they wanted to kill as many prisoners as they could.

"Early one morning, when the guards began to gather the prisoners into a line, I knew that something bad was going to happen, so I hid under a pile of dead bodies and watched as they began to march the prisoners out of the camp. I stayed there under the bodies of those dead men until the next day. I was afraid the guards might return. But once I was sure they were gone, I came out. I quickly took clothes from the dead prisoners and layered them over my own uniform so that I might bear the cold better. I tried to find shoes, but every one of the dead bodies were barefooted. Then I looked up at the watchtower."

"Watchtower?" Kara asked.

"Yes, there was a watchtower in the camp that was always manned by an armed guard. The tops of the walls were covered in barbed wire. So that if a prisoner tried to escape, they would either get cut up on the barbed wire or shot to death."

Kara gasped. For a moment she'd been so distressed by Abram's story that she'd forgotten about Karl. But now she glanced over at him. Karl's eyes were wide, but he did not say a word. He lay his head on Patches, his mouth hung open with shock and fear.

"Karl, I think you should take Patches and go to your room." Kara said

"No, let him stay. He should know what happened. He should understand. After all Kara, he's half Jewish. He's our son."

She nodded. Then she swallowed hard and looked into Abram's eyes. "Please, go on."

"Once I saw that no one was in the watchtower, I ran to the entrance of the camp. I still couldn't believe that a guard wasn't watching from somewhere, and that I hadn't been shot already. But there was no one there. I walked out of the camp. Then I ran as fast as I could until I couldn't run anymore."

Kara looked down at his feet; they were covered in dried blood. Tears came to her eyes. "Oh, Abram," she said.

"It was a perilous journey. I was hungry, so hungry, and thirsty. I sucked on snow. I thought I wasn't going to make it. And just as I got to the garden, the garden that I made for you, I fell. I tried to get up, but I couldn't. I was too weak. I laughed a little at the irony of it. I had come all this way, and you were only a few feet away from me. Yet I was going to die alone, right here in this garden. Then like a miracle, I saw the dog. At first, I was afraid he was a Nazi dog that had been sent by a search party to find me. But when he started licking my face, and then I saw Karl, I was sure I had died and that I was in heaven. And then, Kara, and then I saw you . . . and all I could think of was . . . God is good. I am with my family again. God is so good."

CHAPTER SIXTY-FIVE

ON A SPRING MORNING, about a year after the war ended, Anka got dressed and went into town to the market, leaving Gretel at home with Kara and Abram. It began to rain. She cursed because she'd set her hair in pin curls the night before, and now her hair was wet, and all the curls were gone. She hated to be seen when she was not at her best. And if they hadn't needed the food, she would have gone home and tried again the following day. But she knew if she did, Kara would be angry with her. She was thinking about this, instead of paying attention to where she was walking, when she slipped on a stone and fell. A handsome American soldier saw her trip and immediately came to her aid, helping her to her feet.

"Are you all right, miss?" he said. He spoke perfect German.

"Yes, I'm fine. Just a little embarrassed. But thank you," Anka said, wishing her hair was still dry and curly.

"It's quite all right," he said. "I'm Private Herman Fischer. What's your name?"

"Anka Hausser," Anka said, smiling as she tried to pat her hair down with her palm.

"It's nice to meet you," Herman said. "May I buy you a drink or a coffee perhaps?"

"That would be nice. You'll have to excuse my appearance. I got caught in the rain."

"It's all right. You're really quite lovely," he said.

They spent the afternoon together sitting in a café and talking. When it started getting late, Anka told the young soldier that she had to go and see if she could find any food to purchase. He gave her a smile and a wink and said, "Don't you worry. I'll get you some food. You wait right here."

When she arrived back at home with a sackful of potatoes, carrots, flour, and some eggs, she told Kara about the man she'd met.

"His father was of German descent, but his family has been living in the city of Milwaukee in a state called Wisconsin, that is somewhere in America."

"Oh? Kara said. "And he gave you all of this food?"

"Yes, he did. And he admitted to me that he had trouble at first when he'd joined the American army because his family was German. He said it was hard to fight against his own country of origin. In a way, I guess his loyalties were divided. But after he liberated one of those camps, like the one at Auschwitz, he changed his mind about fighting against Germany. He said it wasn't Germany he felt he must defeat; it was the Nazis."

"I must say that I agree with him," Kara said.

That Saturday night, Anka invited Herman to dinner. Herman was polite, and he got along well with Kara. But Abram was quiet, distant, unreachable. The Abram who had once been a man of dreams longing for adventure was no more. The war had not killed him, but it had left him deeply scarred. No one knew the demons that haunted him except Kara. And he didn't tell her everything; she only knew bits and pieces of what had happened to him at the camp.

What she did know was that he didn't sleep well. Sometimes at night he would awaken crying and calling out for Moishe. Sometimes he would awaken screaming and sweating profusely. The sound of Abram screaming in the dark of night sent Karl running into his mother's room. When Abram saw his son, he would hug

Karl so tightly that Karl would have to push away to breathe. Abram's face would be covered in tears. And because Karl didn't understand Abram, he'd often told Kara that Abram scared him. She tried to tell Karl that Abram was his father, and that he loved him. She tried to explain that Abram had been through a lot of terrible things, but Karl had his own demons that haunted him, and he was too young to comprehend all of them.

Kara and Abram searched relentlessly for his mother. Going from displaced-persons' camps to hospitals, and to the Red Cross, they begged for any information. Abram gave them both of her names, the surnames of both of her husbands, Abram's father, and Yitzar. "Can you tell me anything about a woman by the name Hoda Ehrlich, or she might be going by Hoda Stein?"

He asked everyone the same questions.

They all shook their heads sympathetically. No one had any information.

"I'm so sorry," one young soldier at a DP camp said, "but there are so many who are just people missing, and unaccounted for."

It was as if Hoda had never existed.

"Do you have any information about a Yitzar Stein?" Abram asked.

And again, there was nothing.

But people were checking in and registering constantly, so Abram continued to return to all of the places that displaced persons might go, to see if perhaps his mother had registered. And each time he left disappointed.

Meanwhile the relationship between Herman and Anka was growing. He was generous and loving to Anka and always kind to Gretel. He told Kara that she reminded him of his niece. For an entire year they saw each other twice a week. Then when he was about to be discharged, he proposed to her. She agreed to marry him and move to America.

"Come with us. I want our children to grow up together. They are so close," Anka said to Kara. "I spoke to Herman; he said he will help Abram find work."

"I would love to, but I don't think Abram is ready to leave here yet. He is still searching for his mother."

"Maybe you will come in a year or so?"

"We'll see. Abram is too proud to go to another country where he would be living off Herman until he could find work. His English isn't as good as he would like, and that would make working in America very difficult for him."

"But he has no work here. What would be the difference?"

"He is constantly looking for work here. He speaks German and Polish fluently, so he feels he might have a chance. But in America, he would be dependent on your husband for everything. I know Abram. He couldn't do that."

"We will see each other again, won't we?" Anka said.

"Of course," Kara said, smiling, but tears began to form in her eyes. "We'll find a way."

"Yes, we will, won't we?"

Kara nodded. "We're sisters, aren't we?"

"Yes, we've been through thick and thin together."

CHAPTER SIXTY-SIX

KARL WAS HAVING a difficult time adjusting to the changes in his life. Kara told Abram about Karl's kidnapping and all he'd been through. She told him how Karl had grown to trust Oskar and then how Oskar had almost killed him. Abram didn't say a word as she explained. But when she finished, she saw that he was crying. It was hard for Abram to manage his own pain and horrible memories, but he knew he must if he was going to help his son. And so he made every effort to win Karl's trust. He tried to play ball with him, to read to him, to talk to him. But nothing seemed to win the boy over. At night when they were alone, Kara and Abram discussed the fact that Karl refused to see Abram as his father.

"He's built a wall around his heart, so no one can hurt him again. I blame myself," Kara said. "I let Oskar act as a father to him and he trusted Oskar. I can't blame him for being afraid to trust again."

"It's not your fault. You did what you had to do to survive. We all did. But no matter what he says or does, I'll keep trying to reach him. I will never give up on him."

And then one afternoon, God intervened, and something happened that opened the gateway to Karl's heart. No one knew how it happened, but Patches broke his leg. He couldn't move. He lay outside in the grass whimpering.

"You'll have to shoot him," one of the men who lived in the neighborhood told Kara.

"Shoot him?" she said.

"No!" Karl screamed.

"Yes, it's what you're going to have to do to put him out of his misery."

"I'll go and get Abram," Kara said.

Karl lay beside his beloved dog weeping when Kara and Abram came out of the house.

"Let me take a look at him," Abram said as he sat down beside Karl.

"Are you going to shoot him," Karl asked, his eyes filled with terror and sadness.

"No, Son, I'm not."

Karl moved out of the way, and Abram got down on his knees. "Well," he said as he looked at the dog's leg, "it's broken."

"Please don't shoot him. I love him," Karl said. He was clearly panicked.

"Don't you worry. I'm not going to shoot him. I'm going to set his leg. He'll be all right. He might walk with a limp like I do sometimes, but he'll be just fine," Abram said reassuringly.

"You know how to do that?" Kara said.

"Actually, I do," Abram answered. "One of the many gifts I received from reading so many books over the years. All right now, let's get started."

Karl sat beside his father quietly while Abram set the dog's leg. Then Abram carried Patches into the house and laid him down on a blanket on the floor. "He's going to need some time to heal. But he'll be all right," Abram said to Karl.

"Thank you, Vater," Karl said. This was the first time Karl had called Abram, vater. Kara and Abram exchanged a glance. Kara felt her heart swell.

"Of course, Son. I'll always help you if I can," Abram said.

There was silence for a moment. Then Karl blurted out, "Why

did you leave me? If you're my real father, why did you leave me? Why did you leave Mutti? Didn't you love us?"

Abram knelt so that he was the same height as Karl and put his hands on his son's shoulders. Then he looked directly into Karl's eyes. "I never left you. I would never leave you if it had been my choice. I was arrested by the Nazis. They took me away and put me into a camp."

"Why, what did you do? What kind of a camp?" Karl asked.

"I didn't do anything. I was born Jewish. That's all that I did. It was a crime to be a Jew in Nazi Germany. They put me in a prison camp."

"I don't understand why they would arrest you if you didn't do anything wrong."

"I know. It doesn't make sense. But it's true. And not one single day went by when I was in that prison that I didn't think of you and your mother. I never stopped loving either of you. The two of you kept me alive until I could escape and come back to you." Abram felt the tears roll down his cheeks. Then he saw Karl start to cry too.

"You are my son. You are my blood. I love you. I promise you. I swear to God above that I will never hurt you or your mother. I will protect you both as best I can for the rest of my life."

Karl put his arms around Abram's neck, and Abram hugged him tightly.

CHAPTER SIXTY-SEVEN

1949

Following the Arab-Israeli War, the Jewish state of Israel was born. Patches passed peacefully during the night as he slept on Karl's bed. He was an old dog, and Abram and Kara had prepared Karl for the loss. Still, when it happened, the boy was heartbroken. But Abram was glad that Karl not only turned to his mother for comfort but to him as well. And Abram saw that, little by little, the wall Karl had built around himself was breaking down, and he was accepting Abram as his father. Over the past few years, Abram had come to love the dog. He took care of Patches when the dog was sick. He took him outside to walk beside him each day. And so he, too, felt the loss. Karl and Kara stood beside Abram as he dug a grave and then carved a gravestone into a tree trunk. Then together, the small family had a funeral for Patches.

The search for Abram's mother was beginning to feel futile, and Abram was losing heart. German reichsmarks were worthless. Kara sold the jewelry Oskar had given her, but she received a lot less than it was worth and money was running out quickly. Although Abram searched for work each day, he still had not found steady employment. He did odd jobs at the DP camps and for local shops. But money was hard to come by.

So when Abram and Kara were offered an opportunity by a friend they'd made at a DP camp, who worked for one of the Jewish organizations, to take their son and to move to Israel, they talked it over that evening.

"I'm ready to start over in a land where my son can be proud to be a Jew."

"I know. I think it might be good for us," Kara said. "The only thing is, I will be even farther from Anka."

"Yes, I realize this. But we'll find a way to visit her. I promise you."

THEY KNEW little about life in Israel. Only that they had been offered the opportunity to live on something called a kibbutz. From what Abram had been told, a kibbutz was a sort of communal living where they would not need money to live. Everyone on the kibbutz had a job that they must do to keep it running. And regardless of their job, everyone was treated equally. He told Kara, "It will be a new beginning for us."

She agreed to go, hoping that somehow they would find a way to visit Anka in the years to come.

Arrangements were made, and fifteen months later the family boarded a ship bound for the promised land. It was a boat filled with people who had survived the horrors of the war. The ship was overcrowded and not comfortable by any means. They slept on deck. But as the waves heaved the vessel forward, the very air itself aboard that ship was filled with hope. No one had much to speak of. But Karl found other children to play with. And Kara and Abram were so deeply in love that all they needed was each other.

In early October, Abram, Kara, and Karl stepped onto the soil of Israel for the first time. The temperature was a warm eighty degrees Fahrenheit, and above them the sky was a brilliant turquoise blue. Kara took Karl's hand, and they boarded a bus that bumped and shook as it made its way through a rough terrain to what looked like a small village in the middle of the desert. Abram helped his son off the bus, then he extended his hand to Kara. She climbed down the stairs and looked around her. They followed the rest of the passengers into the entrance of the kibbutz, where they were greeted by a dark-haired woman with a deep tan and a big smile.

"Welcome home! Welcome to Israel!" she said to the group of newcomers. "We are so glad to have you!"

Some of the people who had been on the ship bent down to kiss the ground. Others were crying. Kara and Abram were holding hands and looking around them.

The woman explained the workings of the kibbutz. "We don't get paid here. Everyone has their job, and we all work together to build a good life for ourselves and our families. Every child here is loved and looked after, not only by their own parents but by everyone who lives on this kibbutz because they are all our children. The future of our Jewish state."

"People have come to live here with us from every walk of life. You will meet Sabras; they are our Jewish cousins who were born here in Israel. And, of course, you will meet plenty of survivors from Hitler's hell. Among us, we have teachers, doctors, nurses, and artists of all kinds. We have musicians . . . well, I could go on and on. But you'll see for yourself . . . what we truly have here is a Utopia!"

A young man with a full head of wild, dark curls sat on the ground playing guitar. He was surrounded by a group of preteens who were singing a song in a language Kara didn't understand. But the music was calming, and welcoming.

"I like it here, Mutti," Karl said. Then he pointed across the field. "What are those people doing?"

"I don't know," Kara said as she glanced at a group of people who were gathering tree branches and flowers. Turning to Abram, she said, "Do you know what they are doing?"

He let out a laugh. But he was not laughing at her question. He was laughing with joy. "They are building a sukkah. Do you know how long it's been since I've seen anyone build a sukkah? My family wasn't religious, but I saw plenty of the people in our neighborhood build them in the autumn."

"A sukkah? What is it?" Kara asked.

"It's an outside enclosure made of branches, decorated with items that reflect the harvest season. There will be a party for a holiday called Sukkot when everyone will eat inside the sukkah."

"A party?" Karl asked.

"Yes. A party!" Abram answered.

"Can we help them build the sukkah?" Karl asked.

"I'm sure we can," Abram said, then he turned to the woman who was welcoming them all and asked, "Can we help with the sukkah?"

"Of course. Everyone here is family."

Karl ran ahead, followed by Kara and Abram. There were so many children Karl's age working on the sukkah. Several boys and a girl walked up to Karl and introduced themselves.

"I'm Ari."

"I'm Shanna."

"I'm Eli"

"I'm David."

"I'm Paul."

"I'm Karl," Karl said. Kara watched him, and she felt her eyes fill with tears. Her son would be all right here.

Abram saw his son making friends. He looked over at Kara and smiled. "I think we made a good choice by coming here," he said.

"Yes. I think so too."

Then an old man who had been sitting in the shade of an olive tree, with leaves that looked silver in the sunlight, called to them, "Aren't you Abram Ehrlich?"

"Yes. I am. But I'm sorry, I don't recognize you." Kara and Abram walked closer to the old man.

The old man's wrinkled face broke into a smile. "I know you. Dear God be praised. I can't believe I have found you. And I know you too," he said to Kara. "I see you have a son."

Abram cocked his head. Then he said, "I don't mean to be rude, but may I ask who you are."

"I'm Dr. Klugmann. You came to see me many years ago about having an abortion. I'm glad you decided against it."

"So are we," Kara said, then in unison she and Abram said, "So are we."

"I'm glad I found you. I never thought I would," Dr. Klugmann said. "As you know, after the war, everyone was scattered. But I promised your mother if I ever found you, I would give you something that she gave me to give to you."

"My mother? You knew my mother?"

"Yes, I knew your mother very well. I know she had been married to Yitzar. But he died before I had a chance to meet him. Your mother and I fell in love in the ghetto; it was during the last year of her life. May her memory be a blessing."

"She's gone?"

Dr. Klugmann nodded. "I'm sorry. She got sick. That was how we found each other. She came to see me. I tried to treat her. It was typhoid. And, of course, I had no medicine. Still, I tried, Abram. I tried, but I couldn't save her."

Kara put her arm around Abram to steady him.

"Let me go back to my room. Wait here, please. I have something for you from your mother."

Dr. Klugmann walked away slowly. Once he'd gone, Abram said, "My mother's dead."

Kara didn't speak. She just nodded somberly, holding him tightly.

"I knew it. I felt it. But having this man confirm it . . ."

"I know."

They stood in the sunshine. She held him close as he crumpled in her arms.

Several minutes later, Dr. Klugmann returned and handed Abram a gold and diamond ring. "This was your mother's. I tried to convince her to trade it for food, but she refused. She said someday she was going to give it to you, so you could open a bookstore in memory of her and your father. When she was dying, she gave it to me and said that if I ever found you, I must make sure to give it to you and tell you of her wishes." He handed Abram the ring.

259

"I could never sell it," Abram said.

"But it was her dying wish," Dr. Klugmann insisted.

Abram looked at Kara. Then he said, "Thank you, Dr. Klugmann. Thank you for making my mother's last year on earth a little bit brighter."

"She made my life a lot better too. I loved her."

There was a loud bell that sounded. "What is that?" Kara asked.

"Dinner is served," Dr. Klugmann answered.

Kara and Abram joined the entire kibbutz family for dinner in the large dining hall that evening. They sat at a table with lots of other adults. But Kara made sure she could see Karl who was sitting with a group of children eating, talking, and laughing. The food was different. There was nothing they were used to eating, but it was truly delicious and very fresh.

EPILOGUE

1951

Kara and Abram were married in a small ceremony by a rabbi on the kibbutz before they left. It was hard to leave their kibbutz family behind, but they decided to fulfill Hoda's wish for them. So now they stood side by side, with the sun on their shoulders on a street in Tel Aviv. Karl was busy playing with the new kitten Abram had gotten for him.

Kara and Abram squeezed each other's hands as they looked up at the sign that had just been hung over the small but immaculate and brightly lit bookstore. There was a large gold star of David, and beneath the star it said . . .

"Read it aloud," Abram told Kara.

Kara smiled at him and read.

"The Ugly Duckling Bookshop, proprietors, Kara and Abram Ehrlich."

Her voice choked up as she continued to read. "For Hoda and Kaniel Ehrlich. May their memories always be a blessing."

MORE BOOKS BY ROBERTA KAGAN

AVAILABLE ON AMAZON

Jews, The Third Reich, and a Web of Secrets

My Son's Secret

The Stolen Child

A Web of Secrets

A Jewish Family Saga

Not In America

They Never Saw It Coming

When The Dust Settled

The Syndrome That Saved Us

A Holocaust Story Series

The Smallest Crack

The Darkest Canyon

Millions Of Pebbles

Sarah and Solomon

All My Love, Detrick Series

All My Love, Detrick

You Are My Sunshine

The Promised Land

To Be An Israeli

Forever My Homeland

Michal's Destiny Series

Michal's Destiny

A Family Shattered

Watch Over My Child

Another Breath, Another Sunrise

Eidel's Story Series

And . . . Who Is The Real Mother?

Secrets Revealed

New Life, New Land

Another Generation

The Wrath of Eden Series

The Wrath Of Eden

The Angels Song

Stand Alone Novels

One Last Hope

A Flicker Of Light

The Heart Of A Gypsy